PRAISE FOR ELAINE MURPHY AND

LOOK WHAT YOU MADE ME DO

"Good versus evil has never been so twisted or deliciously cunning. I stayed up all night to see how it ended."

—Alessandra Torre,
New York Times bestselling author

"Murphy sensitively explores the bonds of sisterhood amid all the murder and mayhem. Those looking for an offbeat serial killer thriller will have fun."

—*Publishers Weekly*

"I found it very hard to put down. This story entertained me from beginning to end and I definitely plan to read future books by this talented author."

—CarolesRandomLife.com

"A fun and unpredictable cat-and-mouse game that will leave you guessing until the very last page. Murphy's writing was captivating, the story often had me on the edge of my seat, and the dialogue between the two sisters was really entertaining. There were also a few twists that completely shocked me!"

"Unique in a deep sea of psychological and serial killer thrillers. It's disturbing and twisted, filled with palpable tension and white-knuckle moments. It's unsettling and unpredictable, especially with the twists that come as you start to near the end. The book takes you in directions you'd never expect, but it makes it well worth the read."

"A gripping tale of lies, murder, and danger! These two sisters may have found the perfect way to keep their deep dark secrets hidden, but while doing it they have also caught the eye of an admirer. One that is just as sinister as they are, and one that is merely one step behind them and waiting for their chance to pounce at any given moment!

"I absolutely loved this spinetingling tale. It had me on the edge of my seat the whole way through! The Lawrence sisters have one heck of a story to tell!"

"A refreshingly unique mystery. The storyline is engrossing with intriguing twists and turns. Elaine Murphy brings this diabolical mystery to a pulse pounding, exciting conclusion."

"An addictive and exciting thriller about a woman caught between not one, but two serial killers. I loved the writing and the way she built the tension from the very beginning, I already know that this will not be my last book by Murphy."

—JessicamapReviews.com

ALSO BY ELAINE MURPHY

Look What You Made Me Do

I TOLD YOU THIS WOULD HAPPEN

ELAINE MURPHY

GRAND CENTRAL
PUBLISHING

NEW YORK   BOSTON

Grand Central Publishing
Hachette Book Group
1290 Avenue of the Americas, New York, NY 10104
grandcentralpublishing.com
twitter.com/grandcentralpub

First Edition: July 2022

Grand Central Publishing is a division of Hachette Book Group, Inc. The Grand Central Publishing name and logo is a trademark of Hachette Book Group, Inc.

The publisher is not responsible for websites (or their content) that are not owned by the publisher.

The Hachette Speakers Bureau provides a wide range of authors for speaking events. To find out more, go to www.hachettespeakersbureau.com or call (866) 376-6591.

Library of Congress Cataloging-in-Publication Data
Names: Murphy, Elaine, 1981- author.
Title: I told you this would happen / Elaine Murphy.
Description: First edition. | New York, NY : Grand Central Publishing, 2022. |
Identifiers: LCCN 2021059688 | ISBN 9781538722060 (trade paperback) | ISBN 9781538722077 (ebook)
Subjects: LCGFT: Novels.
Classification: LCC PR9199.4.M86744 I24 2022 | DDC 813/.6—dc23/eng/20211209
LC record available at https://lccn.loc.gov/2021059688

ISBNs: 978-1-5387-2206-0 (trade); 978-1-5387-2207-7 (ebook)

Printed in the United States of America

LSC-C

Printing 1, 2022

For Joanie, who knows all about sisters

I TOLD YOU THIS WOULD HAPPEN

CHAPTER 1

The Brampton Kill Seekers meet every other Wednesday in the after-school program room of the local library. The walls are bright yellow and plastered with corkboards covered in colorful children's artwork, notices for book sales, and volunteer opportunities. A giant rainbow arcs over a chalkboard with READING IS FUN written in perfect cursive.

The dozen members—"kill seekers"—sit in a circle, a mixed group of men and women, young and old, a variety of ethnicities. I get the impression I'm the only new person, and perhaps the first new person they've had since they formed a year earlier, because everyone keeps darting surreptitious looks my way. Even though they invited me, it feels like they're waiting for me to stand and introduce myself. *Hello, everyone. I'm Carrie Lawrence. My sister is missing and presumed dead and I survived a serial killer. Thanks for having me!*

The whispering reaches an almost feverish height, and it becomes painfully obvious that the circle of chairs has fifteen seats and the only two that aren't occupied are the ones on either side of me, making me the painfully conspicuous guest of honor. I'm doing my best to appear immersed in the contents of my phone, waiting for the meeting to begin and not making eye contact, but that's entirely unsuccessful, and it's a mercy when someone decides to break the tension by announcing, "You're Carrie Lawrence."

The room falls deathly silent, and I slowly raise my eyes, searching for the speaker. He wears a plaid shirt and a knitted cap and stares at me with something uncomfortably akin to awe. For some reason, he's also the only person wearing a name tag: EMMETT.

"Yes," I say, when the silence has gone on uncomfortably long. "I am."

There's more astonished murmuring, as though they hadn't just been discussing me.

"I received your invitation," I add tentatively. "And I read about your investigations. I share your questions, and I...seek the same answers."

This is not exactly true, but the group is nodding sagely, so I think I've struck the right somber tone. Now that I'm making eye contact, I see that, like me, they all seem to have come straight from work for this seven o'clock meeting. There's a woman in purple scrubs, a man in a business suit, and two teens in fast-food uniforms. What they all have in common is that they're staring at me with an equal mix of fear and curiosity. They don't want to be through what I've been through, but they want to know all about it. But that's not what I'm here for. The Kill Seekers invited me because they want to know what really happened to my sister, Becca. I already know what happened; I just need to confirm it. I need to find the body.

"My sister is missing," I say, knowing they'll eat it up. It's been five months since Becca's disappearance and the man who took her died, but I've refused to give any interviews or answer questions. Until now. Sort of. "I don't know…I don't know if it was Footloose"—I do know; he sent me a picture—"but I, um, want to know. There are too many missing people in this city—"

Someone actually says, "Amen."

"—and I want to help find them."

Last fall, police found thirteen bodies buried in our local park, each missing a foot, and the press dubbed the killer "Footloose." It was definitely him that took Becca, but I can't tell anyone how I know this. I just need confirmation that she's really, truly, forever gone.

The words earn me a round of applause that makes me flush with embarrassment. And perhaps shame, too, because I know that Becca was not an innocent victim. As far-fetched and impossible as it sounds, Brampton has been home to two serial killers. My sister was one of them, though her deadly deeds have never been discovered. And because she blackmailed me into helping her bury bodies for a decade, I know where too many of those missing people are. The only body *I* need to find, however, is Becca's. I need proof she's dead. Proof that horrible phase of my life is really over.

"Sorry I'm late."

The Kill Seekers and I turn as a unit to see a man standing in the doorway, framed by a wall of paper flowers and streamers, a handmade sign reading WELCOME SPRING! dangling above. He's tall and astonishingly handsome, with shaggy movie-star chestnut hair and cheekbones to match. It could be that he's the only man I've ever seen who could successfully pull off a fake tan, his perfectly bronzed skin contrasting with his starched white button-up shirt.

Unlike everyone who's in their work attire, it looks like he changed into what he thought "kill seekers" might wear: designer jeans, a camouflage jacket, and black work boots that I'd bet my life savings have never actually seen a day of work. A gold watch with diamonds glints on his wrist, and I know instinctively that he bought it from Becca. It takes a second to place him because I only saw him once before, when my sister introduced him as Nikk with two *k*'s. He manages an overpriced gourmet grocery store and was one of Becca's best clients at the jewelry store, shelling out thousands of dollars on jewelry to apologize to his abused wife.

The Kill Seekers must have been expecting him, or at

least hoping he'd show up, because his arrival changes the energy of the room. Emmett looks delighted and hustles over to greet him.

"You must be Emmett," Nikk says, shaking his hand. "Thanks for the invite."

I frown, wondering why both Nikk and I would have scored an invitation to this strange gathering. Surely he's not that invested in the disappearance of his favorite jewelry salesperson.

"Of course, man. Anytime. Anytime." Emmett pauses. "I mean, not...Like, not..."

But for an alleged wife beater, Nikk is gracious. "It's cool; I get it."

"Hey, everyone," Emmett announces, like we're not all watching. "As you know, this is Nikk Boulter. His wife, Lilly Fiennes, went missing three weeks ago."

People start murmuring excitedly, but I try not to look shocked. Becca told me Nikk hurt his wife but not that he might *kill* her. To be fair, Becca was a psychopath, so she may not have thought that detail mattered.

A couple of people look at me to gauge my reaction, so I furrow my brow in consternation. Brampton, Maine, has one of the highest missing persons rates in the country, and yet I haven't heard anything about a recent disappearance. I whip out my phone and search Lilly's name. All that comes up are two posts on Nikk's infrequently updated Facebook page, nothing more.

Eventually, the chatter dies down, and Emmett remains

standing as Nikk takes one of the empty seats next to
me, shooting me a warm smile as though we're friends.
I flinch.

"We've met, right?" he whispers. "You're Carrie?
Becca's sister?"

I nod. I can't imagine he knows that Becca told me about
his jewelry-buying motivations, but I also can't imagine
bonding with him over our missing loved ones, since I'm
sure he killed his wife and knows exactly where she is.

"I remember Becca introducing us," he adds. "When
Emmett told me you might be here, I decided to come. I
was hoping to talk to you."

I don't want to talk to him at all, so it's a blessing when
the lights abruptly dim and the meeting begins. Emmett
takes his place at the front of the room, beneath the rainbow on the chalkboard. He's turned the lights so low that
all the light in the room is now provided by a Himalayan
salt rock lamp that does very little to actually illuminate
things, making him mostly just a vague shape and not the
eerily lit leader he seems to aspire to. No one laughs so I
don't either, though I want to. I think he's attempting to
make eye contact with each person in the room, which is
impossible because it's too dark, and he appears to come to
the same conclusion because, after a moment, he reaches
for the dimmer switch and turns up the brightness of the
ceiling lights. Next to me, Nikk smothers a laugh.

"Death," Emmett says in a deep, resonant voice.
"Disappearance. *Yearning*."

He says these words with the cadence and conviction of a cult leader, and now I want to laugh, too, biting my lip and scrutinizing my feet so I don't embarrass myself.

"Brampton!" he shouts, making me jump. "Population: two hundred thousand. Missing? One hundred twenty-three. Unsolved deaths? Seventy-two. People who truly care?" He makes a show of pointing at each of us in turn, which takes an uncomfortably long time and breaks up his rhythm. "Fourteen."

Nikk scuffs his fancy boots, and I know he's trying to sit still and not guffaw, even though theoretically we should be grateful that a dozen people besides us truly care.

Emmett's just warming up. "We all have something in common," he continues. "Nikk's wife is missing. Carrie's sister has disappeared. Kellie-Ann's brother was murdered in a gas station robbery. Ravjinder's sister went to the grocery store and was never seen again."

I try not to stare at Ravjinder, a pretty twentysomething woman with shiny black hair tied back in a loose bun and wearing a red suit jacket. A necklace with a silver pendant flashes in the V of her white button-up shirt.

"The rest of us *yearn*!" Emmett bellows. This time I'm not the only one who jumps. Ravjinder clutches her chest like her heart's about to give out. "We yearn for answers. We yearn for justice. We yearn to feel safe."

Heads are nodding, as though these wishes are somehow uncommon and shared only by the people in this room.

"Tonight," Emmett says solemnly, "we are blessed. We have with us Carrie Lawrence, who not only saw Footloose—who *slew* Footloose—"

That same person says, "Amen," again, and now Emmett holds up a tablet with a slideshow of newspaper articles about Footloose, like we may have forgotten him in the past few months.

"—but who knew and loved Becca Lawrence."

He taps the screen, and the article switches to an unflattering picture of Becca he must have grabbed from my Instagram before I deleted the account. She would have killed him for selecting this photo, if she were still alive.

"And…" Emmett drums his fingers on the back of the tablet before tapping the screen to reveal a familiar face. "Fiona McBride."

I gasp. After Footloose had beaten Becca at her own deadly game, he'd turned his attentions to me. While leaving him to burn in his murder cabin, I'd heard screams from under the floorboards and discovered another kidnapped woman in the cellar, Fiona McBride. I'd saved her, and together we'd run for safety. Now she's missing a second time, and I'm the only person who knows why.

Several faces turn to look at me, my gasp validating the dramatic reveal.

"Um…" I say, wondering if that gasp sounded to them like an admission of guilt, the way it did to me.

"You're here," someone whispers.

I close my eyes, waiting for the police to sweep in and triumphantly arrest me.

"The one," another person says reverently. "The signal."

I open my eyes and peer around.

"Yes," Emmett says solemnly. "The signal." He taps the tablet again, and a Venn diagram appears. In one circle is Becca's name; in another, Fiona; in the third, Footloose. At the center of the diagram, the circles overlap with one common, unfortunate theme: me. A twenty-eight-year-old stationery designer with the unenviable ability to attract psychopaths.

The room bursts into applause. Nikk glances at me strangely, but eventually he claps, too. I don't clap. I don't know what's happening, and I'm still convinced I'm about to be arrested.

"Good news, Carrie." Emmett shoots me a warm smile that's probably supposed to be reassuring but is not. "We're here to help you."

I try not to appear as alarmed as I feel. "Oh," I say, because they're waiting for something. "Fantastic."

They're all still staring at me. I peek at Ravjinder like she might offer a clue, but she just smiles.

I clear my throat. "With, uh, what?"

Ravjinder's smile widens, confirming I've somehow asked the right question. And, indeed, I have because Emmett taps the tablet again and a picture of a piece of notebook paper with gold writing wrapped in a large squiggle appears. I squint because the text kind of blends into the background and it's really hard to read.

"Just…" Ravjinder murmurs, leaning in to see the screen.

"Justice?" one of the teenagers guesses.

"Justin?" Nikk offers. "I see an *N*. Who's Justin?"

"No," Emmett snaps. He swipes at the screen to enlarge the image but just knocks it to the side so all we can see is *JU*. "It says…Dammit…It says…For crying out…" He gives up fiddling with the picture. "It says 'Just in case.' Guys, I showed this to you before. You've seen it online. It's the same three words."

"Whatever," mutters a bald man in blue mechanic's overalls, the name TODD embroidered on the chest.

I raise a cautious hand. "What is it? What's that from? Just in case. Just in case what?"

"Fiona," Ravjinder answers, as Todd and Emmett glower at each other. "She left a secret note."

My stomach leaps into my throat. I aim for nonchalant but sound like I'm choking on guilt. "And what, uh, what does it mean?"

She shrugs. "No idea. Her mom found it under her pillow the morning after she disappeared, but no one's figured it out."

Emmett has abandoned the stare down with Todd and adjusted the picture on the tablet, coming closer to me and Nikk so we can see it better. It's a piece of paper torn from a spiral notebook, the edges frayed. Gold marker spells out the message in capital letters, a little star decorating the *I*. There's one word per line, filling the center of the page. Starting at the *J* and looping up and over, a gold line wiggles down the edge of the paper and ends in an arrow pointing back up at the little *x* that ends the message in lieu of a period. JUST IN CASE*x*

"Obviously Fiona knew she was in danger," Todd says, arms crossed over his belly. "So she left a clue."

I'm sweating. "Why do, um…why do you…we… think she was in danger? Didn't she just run away again?"

"Who runs away and leaves a mysterious note?" Todd challenges me to my very own stare down, a challenge I do not accept, opting instead to appear absorbed by the minimal contents of the note. "Who leaves their car at the base of an abandoned hiking trail in the middle of a snowstorm? If she was taking off for greener pastures, she would have taken the car."

"Plus, the window was smashed in," teenager number two pipes up. "So that's not good."

"No," I agree. "It's not."

As though sensing my discomfort, but definitely not knowing the reasons for it, Nikk intervenes. "They didn't find any blood in the car," he says. "No signs of a struggle. Maybe Fiona left the car there and caught a ride with a friend."

"We got nine inches of snow that night," Todd argues, now glaring at Nikk. "Any 'signs of a struggle' would have been buried. Tracker dogs couldn't even find the trail."

A fortuitous turn of events, since that trail would have led straight to me.

"And X marks the spot," Ravjinder says. "So—"

"She hid something," Emmett interjects hastily, realizing he's lost control of the group and his audience. "And we have to find it. That's the mission of the Brampton Kill Seekers."

"Except you don't know she was killed," Nikk adds. A muscle twitches in his neck, like he's trying not to laugh.

"We know Footloose murdered thirteen people and hid their bodies in Kilduff Park," Emmett returns coolly, not knowing that's technically incorrect. Footloose hid twelve bodies in the park. Becca and I added the thirteenth. Which is how Footloose found out about us. "And all of them were considered 'missing' by a police department that had neither the enthusiasm nor the resources to properly investigate. Just because we didn't know they were killed doesn't mean they weren't."

Todd nods his reluctant agreement.

Nikk's nostrils flare as he drags in a breath. Technically his wife is also just "missing." Same as my sister. I feel Todd watching me so I blink rapidly, like I'm trying to stave off tears, not that I'm panicked because I came here hoping to put one mystery to bed and instead discovered another far worse scenario that puts my whole future in jeopardy.

"It's okay," Ravjinder whispers, leaning over to pat my knee. "It will all be okay. We can do this."

"We'll get answers," Emmett says, walking back to the front of the room. "We'll get closure. *We'll* get them. Us. The Brampton Kill Seekers."

More heads bob.

"But first," he continues, tapping the tablet for emphasis but only succeeding in enlarging the image so we can see just the *A*, scowling as he hunts around for the *x*, eventually making it front and center. "First, we find X."

CHAPTER 2

So my first meeting of the Brampton Kill Seekers was not successful. Not only did I get exactly zero insight into where my serial killer sister may be buried, but now there's a group of amateur sleuths trying to solve a puzzle I didn't even know existed and almost certainly implicates me in the one murder I *have* committed.

JUST IN CASEx, Fiona wrote.

What did Fiona know? Emmett had harped on the question for the rest of the meeting, writing the words on the board with a nubbin of chalk that screeched painfully with every down stroke. *What did Fiona know?*

She knew too much. But I didn't tell them how Footloose had recorded an audio file where Becca and I discussed her many murders or that Fiona had found the flash drive and taken it with her when we fled the cabin. I also couldn't tell them how she'd blackmailed me for cash in exchange for the flash drive, and in turn, I'd taken the flash drive, pushed her off a mountain in a panic, and destroyed the evidence. But apparently, she'd made a backup and hidden it. Just in case.

"Hey." Nikk startles me as I hunt for my car keys in the parking lot, desperate to go home and be alone with my careening thoughts.

I whirl around, pointing a key at him defensively, and he holds up his hands.

"Whoa," he says, laughing. "Sorry, I thought you heard me coming. Intense meeting, huh?"

"That's a word for it."

The spring night feels too cold suddenly, the descent of the sun having taken all traces of warmth and life with it. It's just us and the library, half a dozen empty cars, and a single streetlight casting ominous shadows on Nikk's face. Emmett would be jealous.

"They're, like, obsessed with this Fiona thing," Nikk adds, "and hardly even talked about our stuff."

Finally, I remember my purported reason for being in attendance. "Right," I say. "Yeah. I noticed that, too. I guess because they have that 'clue,' they think that's the thing to focus on."

"Yeah."

"Obviously, I disagree," I lie. "I think the search for Becca and Lilly should take precedence."

The truth is, I want nothing to do with Nikk or the Kill Seekers. I'd come here with the far-flung hope that they might be able to help me locate Becca's body so I could put her to rest forever—literally and figuratively—and now I have to deal with a much more pressing issue: Fiona's note. And I really don't need an audience while I figure out how I'm going to do that.

"Of course." Nikk combs his fingers through his perfectly tousled hair. Growing up, Becca was always the pretty one. She was the one who knew how to deal with men like Nikk, who looked like Nikk. She felt like their equal and enjoyed the game. I didn't. I always knew that if they were talking to me, it was because they wanted to know about my sister. Which is just one of the many reasons I sigh inwardly when he asks, "What are you up to now?"

"*Now* now?" I clarify, as though it's the middle of the night and not 8:30 p.m. on a Wednesday.

He smiles. "Yeah. *Now* now."

"I was just, um…" I can't tell him I was going to go home and brainstorm until I deduced what the hell "just in case" meant so I could find the evidence of my crimes and destroy it, too.

"Why don't we grab a drink? A coffee," he amends quickly, when my expression makes it clear that us visiting a bar together is not an option. "We can talk more. I feel like those guys don't get me. Don't get us. They haven't been through what we've been through."

"Maybe Ravjinder," I say, thinking of her missing sister. Most of the times, when we buried a body, it was wrapped in Becca's murder carpet and dumped unceremoniously into a shallow grave. I did my utmost not to look at the faces and, for the most part, have no idea who she killed, but something about Ravjinder felt vaguely familiar.

"I guess we could ask her to come, too."

My mind is racing, torn between wanting to investigate this new information about the existence of Fiona's clue and my obligation to continue to play the grieving sister for anyone watching. I'd rather not keep up the charade any longer than necessary, and Ravjinder is just one more witness. Plus, I might have helped bury her sister, which makes things awkward.

"Let's make it only the two of us this time," I say.

Nikk's smile widens. "Great. You know the diner at the corner of Hastings and Pine? With the neon-pink sign?"

"I'll meet you there."

I spend the five-minute trip to the diner debating whether or not I should try to lose Nikk in traffic, but he sits on my tail the whole way, so I stay the course. All too soon we're seated in a booth next to the window, the pink vinyl seats creaking every time we move.

"So," he says, when we each have a mug of steaming, too-strong coffee in front of us, "what did you think?"

I sip my drink. "That was your first meeting, right?"

"Yeah. I'd spoken with Emmett before—he invited me as soon as I made the posts about Lilly—but that was the first time we met in person."

"They really care," I say, because it's true. "That's rare these days."

Nikk studies his left hand, his wedding band glinting in the overhead light. "What are you going to do now?"

Across the aisle, a table of middle-aged women ogles us, not bothering to be subtle about their ruminations on how movie-star handsome Nikk and average, curly-haired Carrie came to be here together. What they don't know, will never know, is that this is not a date, nor is it two grieving people finding comfort in each other. I've learned the hard way, repeatedly, that Becca's friends are not my friends. They're her minions. And I can't imagine what Nikk thinks he's doing "befriending" me after her death, but there's no real-world scenario in which "grieving" is on the list.

"I mean, I guess I'll have to keep searching on my own," I say. I'd come up with the story on the drive over. When you've buried a dozen people, you learn to come up with cover stories on the fly. "If the police aren't looking and the Kill Seekers"—it's hard to say the name with a straight face—"are investigating something completely unrelated, then I guess it's up to me."

Nikk shakes his head, a strand of hair flopping onto his forehead. "You're remarkable," he says, confirming that we're both lying, though perhaps only one of us knows it. "Becca always said you were the best sister in the world."

"Well, I'm her only sister."

"Modest too. She told me that as well. That you never knew how great you were."

I need to interrupt before he can spew more propaganda because I knew my sister, and she definitely never told him any of those things. "You said you came to the meeting because you wanted to talk to me?"

He falters, like he'd forgotten that line. "Oh. I, um, I guess I mostly just wanted to know how you...do it."

"Do what?"

"Cope. Wake up each day and just move on."

Despite my resistance, the therapist I'd been cajoled into visiting after my escape from Footloose really did provide a lot of good insight and advice, though I've mostly been using it to make sure I play my part right, not because it's helping me deal with my pain. Becca's death was jarring, and her absence left a gaping hole in my life, but it's the hole that's left behind after a festering abscess is removed: a reminder of the infection, but a relief, too.

"Every day gets a little easier," I say, staring in what I hope is a pensive way at my coffee. "At least, that's the idea. That's what I tell myself."

"It's hard." Nikk picks at a hangnail, possibly the only piece of him that isn't perfect. "I mean, when I first heard about Becca's death...She was my friend. I don't know if you know that. I knew her from the jewelry store, and then we became friends."

Misery loves company.

"I miss her," he continues. "She was smart and funny and beautiful. I really liked her."

There's a pause, and I realize he's waiting for me to fill it.

"Me too," I say, because I have to. "I loved her, of course. She was my sister. And life will never be the same."

"But you're moving on."

"It's a work in progress."

"She used to say—"

"Your wife's been missing for three weeks?" I interrupt. I have no idea if Nikk really just wants someone to grieve with, but Becca had a predictable pattern: She'd approach you with a problem or a sob story, make you sympathize with her, and then, when your guard was down, she'd pounce. A lifetime of honing my instincts tells me Nikk wants more than company, though what, I can't guess.

"Yeah," he says, sniffling.

"You've told the police?"

"Of course. They have no leads." He laughs roughly and twists his hands together. "Sounds familiar, right? Do you know Brampton has the highest missing persons rate in the country?"

"I do."

"It's like, if someone goes missing in this town, that's it—they're gone. End of story."

I know that all too well.

"Speaking of endings," I reply, "I'm exhausted. It's been a long day. The lighting in that room—"

"I wasn't the only one with a headache, right?" Nikk rubs his temples and winces. "Oh man. The salt light? What on earth? I was trying to be respectful, but…"

In spite of myself, I laugh. The light was ridiculous.

"So what do you think you'll do first?" Nikk asks.

"What?"

"Searching for Becca. What's your next move?"

"I've been searching all along," I say, which isn't entirely true. I did search, at the start, but then Footloose gave me a picture of her dead body and I found her jacket in his cellar with Fiona. "I put up posters. I've checked everywhere. I don't know what's next. I just know I'll never give up."

Like a true minion, Nikk beams at me for spouting the party line.

"What about you?" I ask. "How will you look for Lilly?"

His smile falters, and again he scrutinizes his wedding ring, twisting it on his finger. The thick band has at least a dozen diamonds that catch the light and wink at me, like we're all in on the same joke.

"I was kind of hoping to follow your lead," he admits. "Like, maybe we could work together?"

"I don't think that's a good idea."

Nikk flinches like he's never been turned down before, which is probably true. "Why not?"

"Because my sister is missing and so is Fiona McBride and now your wife. You being seen with someone with connections to several missing women isn't going to help your case. Or mine."

"What case?"

"Figure of speech."

He looks crestfallen. "Oh."

"Anyway"—I push away my coffee cup and reach for my bag—"I need to get going. It's been a crazy day."

Nikk touches my hand to stop me from opening my purse. "I'll get this. I appreciate your time, Carrie. You've been through a lot, and you didn't have to talk to me at all." He blinks, his eyes shiny. "So, thanks. Becca was right about you."

That's a terrible thing to hear, since Becca thought no more of me than she thought of any of the other people occupying the world she believed was rightfully hers. I was her lackey, her fall guy, her favorite punching bag. And for twenty-eight years, she was right. But she's dead and none of that's true anymore, and it will never be true again.

I stand up. "Goodbye, Nikk. And good luck."

CHAPTER 3

I think I'm dying," I whisper Saturday afternoon. "Or do I just wish I were dead?"

"Shh." My boyfriend, Graham, makes a point of peering around the mostly empty theater as though I might prevent someone else from being bored to death by the film.

"I'm going to get more popcorn." I stand and grab my half-full bag. "Want anything?"

Graham shakes his head, gaze never leaving the screen. With a small smile, I slip down the aisle and out into the quiet concession area. I take my time looking at movie posters, arcade games, and even just the street outside, in no rush to get back to my seat. I'm studying the assortment of snacks in the vending machine when I feel someone at my back.

"Sorry," I say, stepping aside. "I was just looking. You can go."

"That's fine," a familiar voice replies. "I was just looking, too."

I turn slowly to see Detective Marlon Greaves, a full bag of popcorn in his hand. He's tall and broad with dark skin and tired eyes, the kind of man who attracts attention and whose calm, reserved demeanor instills confidence in the people he's helping. Except me. To me, he's the detective who tried and failed to find a serial killer and tried and failed to find Becca after she disappeared. That's his forte. Trying and failing.

And following me around town. We have an unspoken understanding that he doesn't believe my version of events of the showdown with Footloose last fall and that I'd swear on my sister's empty grave that they're true. I see him at the grocery store, parked outside my work, sometimes walking his dog on my block. And now here.

"Are you seeing the same movie?" I ask.

"If you're referring to the one that's so boring I needed a second bag of popcorn, then yes."

"Popcorn was Becca's favorite food."

Greaves wipes butter off his hand. "How are you coping?"

"Not knowing what really happened to her is difficult"—this is a lie, of course—"but it gets easier each day. You?"

He considers that for a moment. "Still searching."

"Hey," Graham says, materializing at my side, "you're missing the movie."

I keep my eye on Greaves. "Detective Greaves agrees the movie is boring."

I don't know if Graham's stricken expression is due to his movie choice being given a thumbs-down or if it's just his reaction to seeing me speaking with Greaves, though he knows I bump into the detective all the time. He thinks it's bad for my recovery to continue seeing a man so closely tied to my trauma, but the only threat Greaves truly poses is to my freedom. I don't know what he thinks I know, but whatever he suspects has been enough to convince him to keep following me around. Now, with the discovery of Fiona's cryptic clue, his presence is more alarming than annoying. Does he know what Fiona left behind, just in case? Is he close?

I don't let the thoughts show on my face.

Graham's cheeks are pink. "It got good reviews."

"Well," I say, "if you can't trust the critics, who can you trust?"

"No one," Greaves says promptly.

"We'll let you get back to the movie, Detective. Enjoy the show."

His smile, like mine, doesn't reach his eyes. "Always."

He strides away, and Graham notices my half-full popcorn bag. "You didn't get a refill?"

"I got distracted. Can we go? I really don't need to know how that movie ends."

"I think it's a safe bet that everybody dies and the moral of the story is that life has no meaning."

"You're right. I looked it up online."

He peers over his shoulder. "It's weird that he's here."

"He's everywhere." I toss my bag in the trash as we head for the door.

"It just seems like he should have more to do."

"Maybe it's good that he doesn't. It means Brampton's a safe place to live."

"Is it, though?"

We step out into the sunshine. "What do you mean? Apart from Footloose, our local serial killer, of course."

"Brampton has one of the highest missing persons rates in the country," Graham points out, nodding at a newspaper abandoned on top of a garbage can outside the theater. The gruesome statistics have been making headlines for weeks. "We have one of the highest murder rates, too."

"Thanks to Footloose." And Becca.

"Maybe." Graham sounds stiff and awkward, like he always does when Footloose comes up. Like I'm a layer of ice covering a frozen pond, and he's not confident enough to put his full weight on it, certain there are still weak spots that will crack if he presses too hard. Plus, he's one of the few people under the age of sixty with a newspaper subscription, so sometimes he just sounds that way, no matter the subject.

I'm about to suggest we head to one of the nearby chain restaurants for an early dinner when the cover of the newspaper catches my eye: SECOND HIT-AND-RUN DEATH IN

APRIL! My mouth opens and closes wordlessly as I read it again. And again. I'd seen something online about an elderly man killed in a hit-and-run accident a couple of weeks ago and brushed it off. Two deaths might be a coincidence. But considering vehicular homicide was Becca's go-to stress reliever, it might be more.

"Carrie?" Graham touches my arm.

I jerk away and shake my head. "S-sorry," I say, when he looks hurt. "I, um... I have a headache."

"Do you want to go home?"

I can't pull my eyes away from the headline. I know Becca is dead. Footloose sent me a picture. Plus, I *know* she's dead because she doesn't have the self-control to remain missing for five months. She lives for the spotlight. She *has* to be dead.

"You have today's paper, right?" I nod at the trash can. "That one?" I'm desperate to snag it and scour the article for details but can't stop the paranoid feeling that Graham will think it's weird, the way you fear casually mentioning your crush's name in conversation will convince everyone you're obsessed with him.

"You're still here," Greaves says over my shoulder.

I jolt and whirl around. The detective eats his popcorn and watches me like I'm the main attraction.

"What about the movie?" I demand, my voice sharper than intended, like he's caught me midcrime.

"It didn't get better." His gaze travels to the newspaper and lingers for a moment. Absolutely no one knows about Becca's deadly hobby, and while there are plenty of people who would have described her as unlikeable and manipulative and vain and wretched, she's never once been accused of murder. At least, not openly accused. But still, I can't help but feel that this headline and Greaves are two points of a triangle, Becca's the third, and I'm the unfortunate thing that connects them all.

Graham laughs uncomfortably. "You can't trust the critics, right?"

Greaves picks up the paper, studying the front page as though he couldn't see it from where he was standing. "We've got a wayward driver out there."

"And yet here you are," I reply. "At the movies."

Graham gives a start. "Carrie."

But Greaves just laughs and holds up a hand, his fingertips shiny with butter, reminding me of the night Becca had come to my home after I'd found Footloose lying in wait in my closet. She'd had movie popcorn in her hand, butter making her lips shine.

"No, no," Greaves says. "That's fair. I'd better get to work. There's always someone out there to find."

"Lots of someones," I correct. "We have one of the highest missing persons rates in the country."

For the first time today, Greaves looks like I've hit a nerve. "That's what they say."

"Don't let us stop you."

He folds the top of his popcorn bag, neat and methodical, and tucks the newspaper under his arm. Then he meets my eye and nods. "Never," he promises, before walking away.

"Carrie," Graham mutters under his breath, "you shouldn't goad him."

"I wasn't."

"You were."

"Well, why shouldn't I? He didn't notice a serial killer in our town—one who nearly killed me—and he hasn't found my sister or, like, a dozen other people. If he's not at work, he shouldn't be rubbing it in my face."

"He wasn't—"

"You know what?" I interrupt. "My headache's getting worse. I need some time to myself."

Graham nods reluctantly. He's got a book on his night-stand about loving someone coping with post-traumatic stress disorder, and I skimmed it one day and saw that he'd underlined a passage that said, "Sufferers need time and space, and only they can decide when they're ready for you." He'd underlined "only they" twice.

"Do you still want to look at houses tomorrow?" he asks. "Or should we reschedule? I can call Misha—"

"I still want to look," I assure him, resisting the urge to wrinkle my nose at the mention of our wholly incompetent real estate agent, a friend of a friend of a coworker of Graham's, which apparently means we can't fire her. "But maybe we can go next week instead?"

When Graham had broached the subject of us moving in together last month, I'd been surprised by how ready I was for the move. I bought my house three years ago, expecting to make wonderful, lasting memories. But then two serial killers made themselves comfortable in my home, and those dreams were dashed. With Becca and Footloose finally out of the picture, I'm ready to move on. Graham's been dropping hints about proposing, and home ownership is a step in the right direction. Some people have skeletons in their closets, but mine are buried all over town, and after the madness of the last five months, the only thing I want now is a safe, quiet, boring life with Graham.

"Okay," he says. "Get some rest. Let me know if you need anything."

I wave and hurry away, squinting against the afternoon sunshine. It's a beautiful day in April, the worst is behind me, and if not for that newspaper headline, I'd almost believe it.

But I have too much terrible experience to chalk things up to coincidence, to dismiss strange happenings, to just ignore the warning signs. The alarm bells in the back of my brain aren't panic; they're instinct. And if someone's truly running down people in Brampton, then that someone is Becca.

And she's back.

—

Okay, Becca's not back. That's ridiculous—I know. I've been home thirty minutes and have read both articles about the hit-and-run deaths on the *Brampton Chronicle* website half a dozen times. I tried searching online for more information, but perhaps because of our city's rocketing crime rate, the deaths appear not to have warranted any other mentions.

Plus, there's one major difference between these deaths and the ones Becca committed: The bodies were left behind. After each of her hit-and-run murders, Becca would call me, normally in the middle of the night, to "move furniture"—i.e., meet her at a remote location where she'd be waiting with a body wrapped in her murder carpet. We'd lug it and two shovels to a random spot, dig a grave, and hide the evidence. Rinse and repeat. Thirteen times. The lack of bodies is precisely how she went unnoticed for a decade. And because she said she planted something on each body that tied the death directly to me, I've never had the courage to turn her in.

According to the *Chronicle*, the first victim this time around was a man in his seventies named Darwin Harrow. The second, and most recent, victim was a woman in her twenties named Bindi Carmichael. I search online for Darwin but find no social media pages. Bindi has a Facebook account with three photos and a handful of brief posts, most accompanying pictures of either breakfast food or sunsets.

The two news articles are sparse, the stories downplayed, likely trying not to stir up more fear in a town that learned six months ago it was home to a serial killer who had buried more than a dozen bodies in our local park. I make a list of the few details they provide: Darwin was crossing a quiet street when a car sped through a stop sign and hit him dead-on. It was early afternoon on a drizzly spring day when someone heard the thud and went outside to find a man's crumpled body in the middle of the street. No one saw the car.

Bindi was killed in the parking lot of the local mall after hours. She was found with a shopping bag containing a new pair of jeans, her body ten yards from her car. There were no skid marks to suggest the driver had attempted to stop, which indicates that whoever hit her fully intended to do so.

The older man doesn't exactly fit Becca's typical victim profile. Approximately once a year her "feelings" would build, and she'd encounter someone who pissed her off enough that she decided to kill them. I don't know what an elderly man might have done to get on her bad side, but Bindi is a different story. Becca had worked in the jewelry store at the mall since high school and killed at least two people in that same lot.

My palms are sweaty, and the pen slips in my fingers, skidding across the page and digging a hole in the paper. If Becca were here, she'd mock me for being someone who even owns a notepad, but Becca was always able to find something about me worth ridiculing. Murder and getting under my skin were her best and only skills.

I let out a slow breath and count backward from ten.

The therapist said I needed to find a way to seek closure without finding a body, because if Becca is indeed another of Footloose's victims, it could be years, if ever, before she's found. I'd spent countless hours searching the city with no luck. I agree I need closure, but not for the reasons everyone believes. They think I need to accept the fact that she's not coming back, when what I really need is a guarantee. Without a body, I'll never be able to stop looking over my shoulder. These hit-and-run deaths are proof of that. And what's worse? Becca's alive and back to her old ways, mowing down innocent people when she gets the urge? Or that there's someone new out there with the same violent tendencies?

CHAPTER 4

Life as Novelty Concept Manager at a small stationery design company is not as exciting as the title might lead you to believe. It comes with an interior office and a cheap metal nameplate for my desk, but the respect of my peers has less to do with admiration for my accomplishments and more to do with the lingering fear that I had something to do with the death of our coworker Angelica, despite being cleared in the crime. I mean, Becca killed her, and I helped hide the body, but I had no idea it was going to happen. What's not attributed to fear that they might be next on my hit list is resentment that my newfound notoriety has brought in a ton of new contracts.

That Thursday, I'm working on my current project: a ruler in the shape of a foot, with bloody saw marks for the inches, painted toes at one end, and a jagged edge at the other. Ever since my name was leaked as Footloose's last surviving victim, Weston Stationery has been inundated with design orders, which would be flattering if not for the fact that all the new orders feature some type of unpleasant foot fetish. It's tacky but it pays well, and I'll soon have a down payment to make, so I'm not turning away the work.

I keep my door open so I don't feel completely excluded from the office, but it does little to help me feel included. When I step out to refill my coffee that afternoon, the murmur of office gossip immediately ceases, making my short trip to the break room feel like a walk of shame. I let out a breath when I enter the small room, out of sight of suspicious eyes, and prepare to rinse out my cup, freezing when I spot the newspaper abandoned on the counter. It's open to page 7, a single color photo on the otherwise black-and-white page. THIRD HIT-AND-RUN VICTIM DIES IN HOSPITAL.

The coffee cup slips through my fingers and shatters on the floor, the remaining half inch of brown liquid spilling across the tiles. The cheap fluorescent lights reflect eerily on the surface of the puddle, turning it black and red, congealed blood in my bathroom, in a carpet, in my freezer.

The fettuccini alfredo I'd had for lunch threatens to come back up, and I grip the counter, dragging in desperate breaths through my mouth. Blinking rapidly, I order myself to calm down. This has been happening since

Christmas, since I'd glanced out the window of my car and seen a familiar blond head bobbing by on the street, high ponytail, bright-yellow puffer jacket. Becca. There was an intense stabbing pain in my chest, horror at her return, guilt at having the audacity to have just bought a new sweater for Graham, wrapped neatly in gold and green, something for which I'd paid extra at the mall. For living. Moving on.

How could you? I heard her say, the words echoing in my skull like a death knell. *How dare you?*

And then a car horn had honked angrily, and the blond woman turned her head and it wasn't Becca, it wasn't anybody special, and I'd hit the gas so hard I flooded the engine and the car stalled in the middle of the intersection.

"Carrie?"

I blink black spots out of my vision until my boss, Troy, comes into focus, hovering uncertainly at the entrance, half an egg salad sandwich in his hand.

"You okay?"

I get the impression it's not the first—or second—time he's asked.

"Just fine." The edges of the room sharpen, the blood on the floor becoming coffee once again. "I dropped my mug—that's all."

I snag a piece of paper towel from the roll on the counter and crouch to blot at the mess, keeping my head ducked to hide my flaming cheeks.

"What's going on?"

I hear murmuring outside the room, and then the question repeats, like a chain reaction. Like they're all hovering out there, whispering about me, because no matter how many days and months I put between Angelica and Footloose and Becca, it's just not enough.

"Have you heard about this?" Troy taps his finger on the newspaper. He asks the question too loudly, like he's trying to drown out the gossip.

I stand and toss the paper towel in the compost. "Um, no."

"Three people dead from one drunk driver." He tsks disapprovingly.

"They know it was a drunk driver?" I cling to the word *drunk* almost desperately, hoping he doesn't notice.

"Well, no. But what else could it be? Three different people running folks over in the same month? One person doing it on purpose? C'mon. This town already had a serial killer. It's not going to have two. Lightning doesn't strike twice. I even asked Detective Greaves about it." He adds that last line with just a bit too much bravado.

Slowly, I look at him, and the bravado dissipates. "When did you talk to Detective Greaves?"

"Um, earlier today. He came by looking for you."

"I didn't know that."

"You'd stepped out. I thought I emailed you."

Heart pounding, I turn my back and grab a broom to sweep up the shattered ceramic.

"Watch your feet," I mutter. From the corner of my eye, I see Laverne from Promotions in the doorway, gripping her water bottle like she's here for the hydration, not as the office spy.

"Hi, Carrie," she says, when I return her stare.

"Hey, Laverne. Careful in here. It's dangerous."

She clutches the red string of beads that dangle from her glasses and fails to stifle a dramatic gasp. I sweep the broom over the toe of her shoe harder than necessary, catching a piece of broken ceramic handle, and she jumps back like she's been burned.

"Told ya."

"You, uh, you got this under control, Carrie?" Troy gestures to the small pile of mug pieces I've gathered.

"All good, Troy."

"Cool, cool. Then I guess I'll, uh, get back to work."

I shoot him a smile, and he backs out of the kitchen, shooing the interlopers away. Tossing the broken mug in the trash, I snatch up the paper and take it to my office, closing the door to read and panic in private. The third victim is an unnamed forty-year-old man, run down while jogging one evening. He was unconscious but still breathing when a dog walker found him and called an ambulance to the intersection of Laurel Street and Boone Road.

That's two blocks from my home.

I do a double take and read the article again, this time more carefully, but it doesn't include the date he was hit, saying only "a few nights before." I wake up my computer and frantically search the accident online, but as with the others, there are no results other than the *Brampton Chronicle* website, which has no further details. This story is even more bare-bones than the first two, as though the police are really trying to downplay April's third hit-and-run death. Maybe they, like Troy, think it's a drunk driver mowing down innocent victims. And maybe they, like Troy, think there was only ever one serial killer in Brampton. What nobody but me knows is that there were two killers in town, and one of them enjoyed running people over when she got mad. One who's supposed to be dead.

The room spins, and again my stomach lurches, my lunch determined to make an escape. I put down the paper and will myself to calm, though the possibilities running through my mind make that impossible. Becca's dead, I assure myself, over and over again. There are no such things as ghosts. She can't be the one doing this. But the same murder method and the proximity to my home feel like too much to be mere coincidence. It feels like a copycat. Like a message.

The implications are overwhelming, and I give up the fight and bend over, hurling my pasta into the trash can. I grip the edge of the desk, sweat beading on my forehead, eyes watering. *You're just sick*, I tell myself. *This is the physical manifestation of your fears and paranoia. There's no copycat killer in Brampton. No one knew about Becca but you. You're imagining things.*

My stomach twists again, calling me out on the lie, and I throw up the last vestiges of my lunch, gasping pitifully at the effort. When I'm sure the worst is over, I tie up the bag and lie on the floor, letting the coolness of the fake wood ease my nausea. I don't know how long it is before there's a soft knock on the door and Graham comes in, hurrying to kneel at my side.

"Carrie," he says, his voice a whisper, "are you okay? Troy called, and I was in the neighborhood on a sales call. He said you were sick."

"I'm fine," I mumble.

"Do you want me to drive you home?" When I nod, he nods, too. "Your place or mine? Troy said you can have the day off tomorrow to have space and time to recover."

I picture that stupid PTSD book on his nightstand, my boyfriend's sweet, pure intentions. *Sufferers need time and space, and only they can decide when they're ready for you.*

It's no good, I want to tell him, letting him lead me silently out of the office as my coworkers look on, their judgment palpable. Time and space can't help me, because I don't have post-traumatic stress disorder. I can't have post-traumatic anything when my trauma is still all too present.

CHAPTER 5

The Brampton Kill Seekers invited me to their meeting by sticking fourteen flyers in my mailbox, one a day for two weeks. *They're only lost until they're found* is their motto. I'd ignored them the way I ignored the journalists who camped out on my street after my name had been leaked following my escape from Footloose, ignored them the way I ignore the stares at the grocery store and the office and wherever else I go. And ignoring my problems has mostly worked. Until I finally went to a meeting and found myself in this mess. Now I spend my Sunday morning scouring the artlessly designed BKS website for any mention of the latest hit-and-run death. Somehow, despite calling themselves "kill seekers," they seem not to have even *noticed* the latest killing. What they are focused on, however, is Fiona's note. JUST IN CASEx.

Just in case what?

Fiona wouldn't have attempted to blackmail me, wouldn't have followed me up an abandoned hiking trail if she'd truly believed I posed a risk to her safety, would she? And if so, why? She was expecting $50,000, enough for a teenager to think she'd be set for life, but not really. And Fiona wasn't your typical teenager. She'd been in trouble lots of times before she met Footloose, and like it or not—like her or not—the experience changes people. She assured me that she'd made only one copy of the pilfered flash drive, and that was the copy she'd given me to prove it was real. The night I met her at the hiking trail, she'd given me the original, and that was supposed to be it. So what made her think "just in case"? And where the hell is X?

The police interviewed me following Fiona's disappearance, but there was no reason to believe I'd had anything to do with her second vanishing act because I was the whole reason she'd returned from the first. We'd spoken a few times following our return, since we had a shared traumatic experience few others—well, literally no others—had survived, but that was it. At least, that's what I told the police.

I read every news article I could and watched the ten o'clock news every night, poring over the information, my heart in my throat as I waited for the big reveal that they knew she was dead and they knew who'd shoved her off a mountain. But they didn't know that, and they still don't, technically. It wasn't until early February that they even found her car, and by then the hiking trail had been wet and frozen a dozen times, thawed and trampled by animals a hundred more, and there were no clues left at all. The back window of her locked car was shattered, which I'd done in order to retrieve the duffel bag of money she'd attempted to extort, but that was it. No body, no crime.

Now, almost four months after her disappearance, I'm once again hunting down every news article I can, printing them and putting them in chronological order. The disappearance was big news for weeks. Fiona was semi-famous for having survived Footloose, and people around the world wanted to hear her story. Her mother held them at bay, saying her daughter needed time to settle in and readjust, but before that day could come, Fiona had disappeared a second time. Permanently.

Except for when he's stalking me, Greaves is a man of few words. I have fifty different news stories in my hand, and he's quoted in only four of them. Three of those times he just says, "No comment," and the fourth he says, "We're working on it."

I read the stories again, noting the similarities and any differences in the articles. Fiona was last seen by friends with whom she'd gotten milkshakes on the day of her disappearance. Her behavior was normal, perhaps even a little more upbeat than usual. They noticed a positive shift in her attitude, like she was getting back to her old self. Her mother was concerned when Fiona didn't return home that night, but pre-abduction, she'd been known to vanish for days at a time, so while her mom made note of the absence, she tried not to panic. When there was still no sign of her daughter the following evening, she contacted the police. We'd gotten nine inches of snow, and Fiona's car was gone—perhaps she'd been in an accident.

The police looked for the vehicle, but there was no reason for anyone to venture out to the abandoned parking lot at Barr Lode Trail, and even if they had, the car was covered in white, blending into its surroundings. When the snow melted and the occasional person ventured to the mountain for some renegade snowshoeing, they assumed the car belonged to another winter sport enthusiast. It was only when a guy who'd been to the trail a number of times finally realized the same vehicle was in the same spot each visit and there was a hole in the window that he reported the car and the police belatedly swooped in.

The license plate identified the car as belonging to Fiona, but two months of exposure to Maine's winter weather made it almost impossible to identify much apart from a strawberry-patterned duffel bag tucked in the trunk. It contained several changes of clothes and toiletries, enough to suggest Fiona had intended to leave town for at least a week, if not longer. Why she stopped at Barr Lode Trail, nobody knows.

A measly three articles mention the JUST IN CASEx note, which was shared by Fiona's frustrated mother when the police refused to make it public. I search truc-crime forums online, the busiest one boasting more than two thousand comments. Following the failure to find X, the prevailing theory is that Fiona left the note as a red herring, an effort to distract her parents and any searchers from looking for her when they could be looking for X, which never existed. The duffel bag, nighttime excursion, and Fiona's previous predilection for disappearing supported that theory.

Pictures of the note are readily available online, and I enlarge one now, scouring it as though there might be something here that no one else has seen, but there's not. It's exactly what Emmett showed us: a piece of paper torn from a notebook, the words JUST IN CASEx encircled by a wiggly line ending in an arrow that points to the x at the end of the sentence. The only thing slightly unusual is the way the squiggly line appears to have been drawn with painstaking care as it winds its way to x.

I reread the article announcing the existence of the clue. *Heather McBride, mother of twice-missing teenager Fiona McBride, has shared this photo of a note she found under her daughter's pillow the day she was reported missing. Mrs. McBride contacted police and provided them with the note, but after months with no sign of Fiona and desperate for answers, she decided to make her daughter's last words public.*

I stare at the note like a lifetime of experience sharing a bedroom wall with a master manipulator will give me some insight, but all it does is remind me of the time we were kids and Becca came up with a scavenger hunt of her own. It was for me to find my birthday gift, a pair of earrings she'd seen me ogling and which she'd subsequently stolen from a cheap department store. Even at age eleven, I'd seen enough that I should have known the X at the end of her map was little more than a waste of time, but instead I'd played along, following the increasingly dangerous and painful clues.

I snuck into the backyard of our notoriously crotchety neighbor to find a note that led me to the collar of a nearby dog known for biting; slithered under a parked car to pluck a clue from its undercarriage, getting an oil stain on my new birthday shorts for my trouble; and was whimpering and coughing my way through our fiberglass-covered attic before my parents sniffed out the plot and put an end to the hunt.

Becca said I didn't get the prize, because I didn't finish the game, and made a show of wearing the earrings every day for the next week before "losing" them. It was years before it dawned on me that there had never been a reward for me in this game. Becca was always going to be the winner, and I'd always be the loser.

I sigh and contemplate Fiona's note. JUST IN CASEx.

Then I read the article accompanying the note again.

...shared this photo of a note she found under her daughter's pillow the day she was reported missing.

Found under her daughter's pillow.

Pillow*case?*

I scour the forum, looking for anything to indicate this particularly literal interpretation of things has already been investigated. It's not easy, since the words *pillow* and *case* appear 189 and 443 times, respectively, but eventually I locate a couple of comments from people asking about the pillowcase itself. Had it been thoroughly examined? Was there anything inside the lining of the case? Stuffed into the pillow itself? One random commenter chimed in to say that the police had looked into the pillowcase but nothing was found.

By the time you get to the end of the forum, no one has much else to say. They deduce that the note must be a hoax. If not Fiona's idea of a prank, then perhaps something Heather McBride invented to reignite interest in her daughter's case. From the look of things, it worked for a short while, though no one has had much luck with the investigation. But perhaps they're just not quite as motivated as I am.

———

The McBride house is in a nicer, newer part of Brampton, the homes five to six years old as opposed to a hundred. They favor brick facades and white shutters, and expansive green lawns. At two o'clock in the afternoon on a bright and cheery Sunday, it's the only one with the front light glowing.

I plaster on a pleasant smile as I park and hop out of the

car, channeling my inner Becca and discarding all thoughts of my crimes and thinking only of myself. What do I want? That secret flash drive. When do I want it? Now.

For months, I've gotten used to the sensation of being watched, a strange heat on the back of my neck, the signal that Greaves is nearby, calmly observing. It's annoying but nothing more. He can watch me every day for the rest of my life and he'll never see me do anything worse than toe the occasional ethically gray line. But today the sensation is different. Despite the blue skies and sunshine, there's a cold tickling between my shoulder blades, a feeling that something more sinister, more plotting, is nearby. I climb the steps to the house and ring the bell, glancing around casually as the tinned sound of chirping birds wafts out. Bare rosebushes flank the door, cars are parked harmlessly at the nearby homes, and a couple of kids ride bikes at the end of the street, a serene suburban tableau. But I know better than anyone that looks can be deceiving.

I shunt the feeling to the side, forcing myself to focus on my current mission and making sure my smile is in place when Heather McBride opens the door. She greets me with a polite hello. She's cut her hair, the red strands pulled back in a stubby ponytail, and wears a white button-up blouse and gray slacks.

I've met Heather just once before. She is her teenage daughter's doppelganger, a forty-one-year-old with a high-powered career and firm handshake that belies her frail appearance. We spoke once at the hospital when

Fiona and I were admitted following our escape from Footloose. Heather had tearfully and carefully hugged me, thanking me for saving her daughter. That's how she knows me: as the woman who rescued Fiona. Nothing more. Nothing worse.

"Carrie," she says now, smiling. "Nice to see you again."

I smile back. "Thank you for agreeing to meet with me."

She blinks as though startled by the very idea of my gratitude and then steps back to gesture me in. "Why, of course. Would you like some tea? Or something stronger? My husband's not home," she adds, like that's permission to start drinking.

"No, thank you." I try to ignore the guilt churning my insides when disappointment flickers across her face. "Well, maybe just one."

Her smile returns, and I step inside and remove my shoes, following her down a long hall to the back of the tidy, traditional home. Formal dining and living rooms feature vases of fresh flowers, and a third bouquet rests on the large kitchen island, the only splash of color in the sterile black-and-white room. Large windows frame the backyard, showcasing a garden that looks more like it belongs at a professional nursery than a suburban home with its neat rows of flowers and planter boxes stretching all the way to the fence. On the other side of the fence is a forest and steep ravine, ensuring they'll never have neighbors.

"Wow," I say, when Heather sees me gaping. "Your garden's amazing."

She flushes. "Green thumb. It's my hobby."

Pouring us both a generous glass of white wine, she takes a seat on one of the stools at the pristine marble island. I do the same, sipping my drink and shoving away memories of the nights Footloose poured the wine and I murdered Heather's daughter.

"So," she says, studying her pale-pink fingernails, "you heard about the note."

I'd decided the truth was the best approach when calling, explaining that I'd only just learned of Fiona's mysterious clue and that I, more than anyone, wished to know if there was more to it than a teenager's silly prank. Heather believes that there is, and with the police simply claiming they're "working on it," she was more than happy to have me come over to discuss.

"I don't know how I missed the story," I say. "I mean, I suppose I do. After so much attention, I just kind of stopped reading the papers and going online."

"You canceled your social media accounts." At my surprised expression, Heather smiles shyly and sips her wine. "I followed you. I mean, you were someone who'd been through the same ordeal as my daughter, and I wanted to know if I could understand."

"I'm sorry," I say. For the social media, the note, the murder.

"You don't owe anyone an apology. In fact, your call was the bright part of my week. Perhaps you'll offer insight no one else can."

"Please don't get your hopes up. I don't have any special skills. I just wanted to see things."

She nods hopefully. "Absolutely. The police still have the original note, of course." Her expression darkens, the way mine does when I think of Detective Greaves. "But I made a copy. I'll show you where I found it."

She takes a fortifying gulp of wine before hopping off the stool and heading back to the front of the house where a staircase leads to the second level. I scramble to follow, trailing her up the carpeted stairs, our footsteps muted, the house suddenly too quiet. Three thousand square feet, five bedrooms, four bathrooms. Finished basement. Well-maintained garden. That's how the press had described the home as they'd camped out following Fiona's return. They cited these facts as though the five bedrooms belied the possibility that there could be trouble in paradise. That Fiona could have been a teenager with issues.

At the top of the stairs, there's an office to our left, the other four rooms extending down to the right. Double doors mark the end of the hall and presumably the primary bedroom. Fiona's room is second from the stairs, twice the size of my own. It's unexpectedly bright and girly for a teenager known to take off for long weekends, skipping class, and being carted home from local drug dens by police. The room looks like it was never updated when she became a teenager, maturing from the smiling little girl in the pictures taped around the vanity mirror, missing front teeth replaced by braces and then a straight white smile.

There's a queen-size bed with a fluffy purple comforter, glow-in-the-dark stars plastered to the ceiling, and night-stands with matching lamps shaped like clouds. The closet doors are open, revealing a standard teenager uniform of jeans, T-shirts, and hoodies, boots and sneakers piled on the floor. It's obvious they haven't straightened the room since Fiona disappeared, have left it exactly as it was, willing her to return and for things to be normal again.

Heather's trying not to blatantly stare at me but she is, as though I might have a psychic revelation about what happened. All I'm seeing is proof that, while I knew Fiona as a girl I rescued from a serial killer's murder cabin and then the nuisance who tried to blackmail me, she was also somebody's daughter, a young woman still figuring out exactly who she was going to be.

No one, I'd decided for her.

"This is where I found the note." Heather crosses to the bed and gently touches her fingertips to one of the large purple pillows. "Under here. I, um, put the copy here, so you could see exactly how it was."

"Is this the only note she left?" I ask.

"Well, the only one like this."

"What were the others?"

Sadness crumples her features, and she swipes a hand across her face, smoothing it away. "After she...after she came back the first time, she started leaving notes. You know how we did before cell phones?" She laughs sadly. "Like, 'Going to the store, back at two.' 'Meeting so-and-so for dinner at the mall, will be home before ten.' After disappearing once, she didn't want to disappear again."

I swallow the lump in my throat. People have speculated that Fiona left the note as a hoax, or that Heather invented it to spark interest in her story. But neither is true. Fiona left it for exactly the reason she said: just in case. Just in case she didn't come back from her meeting with me. Despite her claim that she wanted to extort me so she could run away, deep down, she just wanted to be found.

I have a decade of experience shunting my guilt to the side, but my eyes are burning, and tears are trying to spill over. When I first started helping Becca bury bodies, I felt bad for the victims and their families, people who'd spend the rest of their lives asking unanswered questions. But this is the first time I've come face-to-face with a grieving mother, seeing the havoc wreaked by my actions.

The pause is getting awkward, and I swipe at my eyes. For the first time ever, I wish Greaves were here so he could set the example on how to investigate a scene. Shooting Heather what I hope is a confident, competent look, I cautiously approach the bed and lift the edge of the pillow like I'm expecting a spider to leap out. Instead, a color copy of the note waits, the gold text glowing under the rays of sun streaming through the window.

JUST IN CASEx

It's uncomfortable with Heather watching, but I slowly pat the pillow, knowing it's unlikely I'll find a flash drive no one else discovered but needing to do it anyway.

"The police checked the pillowcases," Heather confirms. "They say they looked everywhere, but obviously not everywhere, because they haven't brought her home."

"They say the same thing to me about my sister. And I have the same reaction."

A phone rings shrilly somewhere in the home, the sound quickly swallowed by the too-large space.

"I'll leave you," Heather says, backing out of the room. "Take all the time you need. Look at whatever you like. Whatever you think will help."

I count to ten after she leaves, hearing the slight squeak of the stairs as she descends, and then carefully squeeze all four pillows, feeling nothing of note. I toss them aside and flip up the purple duvet cover, shaking it so anything tucked inside would drop to the bottom. I grope the edges of the fabric but feel nothing more substantial than the zipper. Crawling onto the mattress, I dig my fingers into the edges, pressing against the seams in case Fiona cut an opening and slid the flash drive inside. Nothing. I heave the mattress up and peer underneath. Again, nothing. The white wooden headboard has no secret compartments I can discern, nothing taped to the back.

Getting to my knees, I use my phone to shine a light under the bed, the wooden slats of the frame speckled with dust and stray hairs but no further clues as to what Fiona may have hidden "just in case."

Inspiration strikes, and I close the curtains and the door, making the room as dim as possible as I squint at the stars on the ceiling, expecting a pattern, or at least an obvious X. Nothing. The theme for today.

Another squeak of the stairs interrupts my frustration, and I hastily toss open the curtains and the door, rearranging the comforter and pillows on the bed as Heather returns.

"Sorry about that," she says, as though she has anything to apologize for. "This house is too big. And it's so empty." Her voice catches, and she works to compose herself, forcing a smile. "I think about getting a pet sometimes, for company. But Fiona was allergic, and if—when—she comes back, I don't want to have to give it up."

The words are like acid on my guilty conscience. "I..."

"Sorry," she says, waving a hand. "I'm rambling. Did you find anything?"

I shake my head. "No luck."

Her smile wobbles, and my stomach lurches, like it wants to hug her and tell her the truth. Tell her we're both searching for something and the odds aren't good for either of us.

I scan the room. The posters on the wall are of pop groups; the stickers on the dresser are unicorns and rainbows. A little girl who still believed in magic. Even the clothes in the closet belie the destructive and manipulative woman Fiona had grown into, nothing to suggest she spent weekends passed out on the floor of seedy drug dens and the rest of her time plotting to extort me.

Just to feel like I've done all I can, I pace the perimeter

of the room, pressing on the posters in case there's something stuck to the back, feeling around the pictures taped to the mirror frame. Nothing. The light on my phone is still on so I aim it behind the furniture, finding only more dust. Hesitating, I turn to the closet. Closets are still something of a trigger because a serial killer once jumped out of mine, punched me in the face, and broke my tooth. With far more caution than a sunny little girl's room requires, I direct the light into the corners of the closet floor, hoping to spot something that might feel like a clue. A box, perhaps. A flash drive. An X carved into the wall. But there are just shoes, a couple of items of clothing that slipped off the hangers, a book bag, and a black suitcase with red polka dots.

I start to move away and then pause. Turning back, I study the suitcase more closely. They're not polka dots; they're strawberries. I'd read the articles about Fiona's disappearance a hundred times. They'd found a strawberry-patterned duffel bag in the trunk of her car, abandoned at Barr Lode Trail.

"Is this—"

Heather has moved up beside me. "That's not the bag," she says, and my heart sinks. "The police still have the one she took with her. They say it's evidence. Of what, I don't know."

JUST IN CASEx

I reach for the suitcase. "Do you mind?"

"No. Go ahead."

"Did the police look here?"

"Probably. I'm not sure. They made it clear it would be easier for me not to be present while they searched her room. They put things back the way they found them, mostly. And they said they didn't take anything."

I pull the bag out of the closet. It's the largest size you can buy, with a zipper that allows it to expand even wider. I open the compartments on the front, shining my light inside, seeing nothing. I feel with my fingers, but there's just smooth canvas. Laying the bag on the floor, I unzip it and lift the top, finding a small toiletry bag inside, its contents shifting when I pick it up. Heather crouches opposite me, watching closely as I open the small yellow bag and empty the contents onto the floor of the suitcase.

Disappointment wells up. A travel-size tube of toothpaste, dental floss, and a hair elastic. No flash drive. No clue. I replace the items and give the lining of the suitcase a cursory feel, but it's empty. Stifling a sigh, I close the suitcase and return it to the closet.

"Well," I say, "I guess the police checked there after all."

"They said she was running away forever," Heather says, a tear slipping down the side of her nose. "And I remember thinking, *If she was really going forever, why would she just take the duffel bag? Why not the bigger ones?*"

"Good question," I say, though I know. When you're desperate to get away, when nothing matters more than your freedom, you'll give up everything to get it. Then I ask, "Bigger ones? As in, more than this one?"

Heather sniffles and wipes her nose with her hand. "Yeah, it's a matching set. There's a carry-on piece."

"Where's that one?"

"Still downstairs, I think. We were going to go on vacation, just the three of us. Somewhere warm for the holidays, to escape the press, the memories. Just escape, in general. She'd packed a bag."

There's a tightening in my chest. Hope, maybe. "May I see it?"

"Of course."

I trail Heather back downstairs, where she opens a hall closet and pulls out a smaller version of the strawberry-patterned bag from Fiona's room.

"It was an early flight," she says, unzipping the case. "We put the bags down here so they were ready to go first thing in the morning. But Fiona never came home."

Fiona had been in a rush to meet me, to exchange the original flash drive for cash, to hit the road and never be seen again. She said it was because she didn't fit in here, her parents were smothering her, and she couldn't wait any longer. I didn't know she was trying to avoid a beach vacation.

"Did the police check here?" I ask.

Heather shakes her head. "No. I never even thought about it."

The bag contains two swimsuits, three tank tops, two pairs of shorts, a skirt, and a set of flip-flops. There are no toiletries, no phone charger, no electronics. Nothing to suggest she intended to get on that plane. But Heather doesn't notice any of this, her eyes shiny with tears.

"I'm sorry," I say, closing the bag. "I didn't mean to reopen—"

She cuts me off with a shake of her head. "Not at all," she says. "It's just... we wanted it to be over, you know?"

"I do." I unzip the small compartment at the front of the bag. It's where I keep my passport or the tiny lock to fasten the zippers. This one is empty, except for something loose and gritty. I press my fingers into it and carefully slide out my hand, studying the tiny flecks stuck to my skin.

"Is this dirt?" I ask, even though I can see almost immediately that it's not. The black bits are small but uniform, like miniscule flies.

"Lavender," Heather says, reaching out to pluck one between manicured nails. Recognizing my confusion, she adds, "Seeds. Lavender seeds. It's a beautiful plant. You start with nothing, end up with something magical. It's why I love gardening. You think you know what you're going to get, but sometimes you're surprised."

She thought she was getting a little girl who loved rainbows and unicorns; she got Fiona. My parents thought they were getting the perfect blond prom queen; they got a serial killer.

"You grow lavender?"

"Mm-hmm." She rolls the seed between her fingertips, like she's imagining what it might one day become.

"Why would Fiona have the seeds in her bag?"

"Oh, I don't know. When I'm planting, things get everywhere. She was always complaining if I tracked dirt into the house or the flowers I cut smelled too strong or the stamens stained her clothes. Usual teenager stuff. These were probably just stuck on something else when she put her things in here." She stands and wipes her hands on her pants. "Why don't we finish our wine?" she suggests. "Maybe inspiration will strike."

I stand, too, following her to the kitchen and retaking my seat at the marble island, the wine warm and too sweet. Apparently when Heather came down to take the phone call, she'd found time to arrange a wooden cutting board with a selection of crackers, fruit, and cheese, and now I'm obligated to spend the next hour snacking with the mother of the girl I killed. I feel guilty about that, sure, but the whole time Heather's talking, I'm staring out the windows into the backyard, contemplating her carefully maintained garden, the only thing that brings her joy anymore.

Being Becca's sister meant learning how to live with a million little swords stabbing you every day, when you least expected it. She never wanted to deal the killing blow, because that meant she wouldn't have easy access to a victim anymore. But she wanted to destroy or ruin anything that mattered to me—a piece of clothing, money I saved, a rare friendship. Not because she wanted those things, but because she enjoyed watching me suffer. I'd never gotten a pet, because it would have given her too much power, too much leverage. She would have gleefully harmed the defenseless thing I loved most because it would have brought her so much joy to see me weeping over its destruction.

Fiona hid the flash drive in her mother's garden. Somewhere, in that lovingly maintained expanse, is the key to my future. My freedom, waiting to be dug up.

Eventually, I turn the conversation to polite inquiries about the garden and even get a tour, nodding along as Heather describes the best growing conditions, soil pH, sun exposure, and more. Fiona would have buried the flash drive in December, and the months between make it impossible to see where the soil was disturbed, if anything is out of place. I ask Heather if she had issues with neighborhood pets or animals digging in the yard, but she says no, that the fence keeps them at bay.

By the time I leave, I've learned far too much about garden zones and nothing about where exactly X may be in the massive yard, only that I have to search for it. I give Heather a final wave and walk down the drive, lost in my thoughts as I dig my keys out of my purse. Somewhere nearby—too nearby—a car revs its engine and speeds away in the opposite direction, its taillights flashing red as it narrowly misses the kids still riding bikes in the street. Someone throws a rock after it but the car doesn't slow, and I watch until it's out of sight. I squeeze the keys tightly, feeling them bite into my skin. The sinister feeling of being watched when I arrived, the abrupt departure now. It could be Greaves, switching up his usual surveillance methods. It could be a coincidence, my paranoia turned up to high once again. Or it could be something more.

I jog down the street to the three boys discussing their near miss.

"Hey," I say, a bit breathless. "Did you guys see who was driving the car?"

They stare at me warily, like they've been told not to talk to strangers and have taken the warning to heart.

"Was it a man?" I try. "A Black man, maybe?"

One shakes his head decisively. "No. Definitely not."

"You're sure?"

"They were white."

"Was it a woman? With blond hair?"

The boys consult each other uncertainly before the same one shrugs. "I don't know. It was just a blur. I didn't see their face."

His friends nod their agreement, and I force a smile. "Okay, thanks."

Returning to my car, I pop the trunk and look inside. It's empty. The car doors were locked when I went into the McBride house, the windows rolled up, and it's the same story now. Maybe whoever it was just thought it was interesting that I was visiting the McBrides. A determined journalist, desperate to wring out the last details of this gruesome story.

Maybe.

But maybe not.

CHAPTER 6

I know it's a little outside of your desired area," says Misha, our real estate agent, "but a fifteen-minute drive gets you a lot more bang for your buck."

Graham and I turn back to study the small yellow house, two bedrooms, one bathroom, the front yard overgrown with suspicious weeds that scrape my ankles. We glance at each other dubiously. Not only did Misha give us the wrong address on two of the three houses we saw today, but she's consistently called Graham "Grant" all evening. With her platinum hair and fitted pink sweater dress, she's a lot like Becca, if Becca sold houses. She's terrible.

"You've given us a lot to think about," Graham says, shaking her hand because he's too polite to just push her into the large prickly bush that resides in the driveway.

She turns to me, hand extended, a gaudy bejeweled

butterfly ring glittering on her finger. I busy myself hunting in my purse for my phone and send Graham a quick text. *Tell her she's fired.*

We all hear his phone buzz in his pocket, but he doesn't check it.

Misha shifts on her dangerously high heels. "Well, um, I'll let you two mull over these great options and wait for your feedback."

You suck, I think.

As though he can read my mind, Graham takes my hand and gives my fingers a light squeeze. "Absolutely," he says. "Have a great night."

I tug him toward his car, parked at the curb between two abandoned bags of trash. "Let's go, Grant."

Misha's still waving as we drive away, and Graham makes it all the way to what remains of a stop sign at the end of the road before he bursts out laughing. "I can't believe you didn't shake her hand."

"I can't believe you did!"

"What can I say? I'm a gentleman."

"You're something, Grant."

He checks his watch. "Almost seven. Want to grab a bite to eat and take it to the park while it's still light out?"

We get burgers and onion rings and find a small, quiet park with picnic tables that overlook the Brampton River, its water rushing fast thanks to the winter thaw and spring rains.

"Okay," Graham says once he's downed half his burger.

"House one, too decrepit. House two, too small. House three, too dangerous."

"What are the odds the 'bang' for our buck was gunfire?"

He bites into an onion ring. "Hundred percent."

"I thought house hunting was going to be like it is on TV. Too big, too small, just right."

He nudges my knee with his. "It'll be worth it in the end."

"I hope the end's not too far off. My house has started to smell like burnt toast whenever the furnace turns on."

"And my downstairs neighbor thought his stray cat was just lonely, so he got another stray cat for company."

"Let me guess—you complained to the building manager? Oh no, wait. You're Graham Fowler. You bought them treats."

"Just twice."

I laugh, and he tosses an onion ring at me.

"Did you ever have pets growing up?" he asks. "You never told me."

I try to keep my tone light. "No pets," I say. "My dad's allergic." That's not true. My parents may never admit it, but they were wary of Becca's propensity for violence long before I was. Too many animals went missing in the neighborhood. They weren't going to let one into our home for her to torture under their roof.

"We didn't have any, either," Graham admits. "My mom said I had to prove I was responsible. By the time

I did, I was old enough for a car, and I wanted that instead."

"*You* had to prove you were responsible? What types of things did irresponsible Graham do?"

"Oh, y'know. Load the dishwasher front to back, squeeze the toothpaste from the middle, put tomatoes in the fridge instead of a bowl on the counter like a 'good son.'"

"And to think I was going to buy a home with you!"

He smiles. "Did you have a car when you were in school?"

"Yep. I worked at a diner and saved all my money to buy it."

"What about Becca?"

The question throws me for a second, but I nod. "Yeah. Graduation gift. My parents paid for it."

"What kind?"

I look at him in surprise. "Um, I don't know. It was black, I think. You know I'm not a car person."

"It's strange that Becca was."

"What do you mean?"

"How she was trading in her car every year."

"She always wanted the best of everything. Why is it strange?"

Graham's having trouble meeting my eye, fishing in the bottom of the paper bag for stray pieces of onion rings. "Sorry," he says. "I just…"

I wait, but he doesn't finish the sentence. "Just what?"

"You just never talk about her."

I stifle a sigh. We've had this conversation before. It's sweet that he reads the self-help books with the aim of helping me, but more than anything, it's annoying. Becca's death was jarring, but it was hardly the worst thing to happen to me. Or Brampton's pedestrian population.

"People grieve in different ways," I say, not for the first time.

"I know. I guess I just…" He watches the water. "I guess with her around, there was always something between us. I know she didn't like me, and now that she's gone, I'm realizing there's so much I don't know about you."

"Like what?"

"Like if you had pets."

"I just told you I didn't. What else do you want to know? I'm an open book."

He shoots me a sheepish smile. "Who was your first boyfriend?"

I blush. "Don't laugh."

"Uh-oh."

"It was my first year of college—I was an outcast in high school—and he was an exchange student from Italy."

"Sounds romantic."

"It might have been; I'm not sure. He didn't speak English, and I didn't speak Italian, so it was mostly just us smiling at each other a lot and translating things on our phones."

Graham laughs.

"I said don't laugh!"

"I was *breathing*."

"You're a terrible liar. I'm not telling you anything else." I toss my hamburger wrapper at his head.

He catches the balled-up paper and leans in to kiss my cheek. "That's okay. I know everything I need to know."

———

Shortly after midnight on a Tuesday, the McBride house is dark and still. I'm also dark, due in part to my black pants, jacket, and knit hat, but also the dirt covering my hands and at least half of my face after tripping no fewer than three times as I attempted to traverse the ravine that backs the property. Despite spending several hours researching the best route through, I appear, unsurprisingly, to have chosen the worst one.

The homes in this area boast large lots, and the houses on either side of the McBrides' are set well away and quiet. Heart pounding and right knee throbbing, I remove my backpack and crouch to unpack the collapsible footstools I'd bought at the hardware store, which will help me scale the six-foot wooden fence designed to protect Heather McBride's prized plants, if not her daughter. Adjusting the light on my headlamp, I retrieve my new garden fork, trowel, and gloves.

As has happened a hundred other times in the past hour,

something moves in the forest behind me—a squirrel, a falling leaf, the wind—and I whip around, expecting Greaves but finding nothing. The last time I was in the woods, I killed somebody, and the time before that I was wrapped in a murder carpet in the trunk of Footloose's car, and the time before that I was burying my coworker while a second serial killer looked on. I don't have a great history with the forest.

Flicking off my headlamp, I climb on the wobbly footstool and drop its companion into the backyard. Peering through the boards of the fence, I squint into the darkness, scouring the area for anything out of place, like an attack dog or Detective Greaves. I give it a minute and even attempt a low whistle, but nothing moves. I'm alone.

There's another crack of something behind me, and again I whip around, and again I see nothing. A light breeze lifts the hair from my neck and knocks branches together like a slow round of applause. I take a deep breath and turn back to the fence, the posts digging into my fingers through the gloves as I wedge my toes between two slats and hoist myself up. I've never been an athletic person; late-night walks in the woods carrying a murder carpet comprise the bulk of my exercise routine. It's a terrible struggle to get my left leg high enough to hook my knee over a pointed slat on top of the fence, and very quickly I realize that putting a footstool down for my exit provides absolutely no assistance with my entrance. For an interminable minute, I hang on the fence, my knee aching, my fingers slipping, and waste precious seconds trying to envision a better outcome than the one that's inevitable. Another snap of a branch in the woods makes the decision for me, my extended leg giving an involuntary kick and boosting me over, fingers scrabbling to hang on as my feet plunge into nothingness. I dangle for a split second before a glove slips off and I lose my grip, landing on my back on the soft grass. My breath whooshes out on a painful grunt, and pain radiates up my spine, but I ignore my extreme discomfort and stay very, very still as I listen.

Silence.

Somehow, blessedly, my shameful entry has gone unnoticed. I roll to all fours and push myself up to standing to retrieve my glove. My knee protests, and I'm pretty sure I'm bleeding from a puncture wound courtesy of the garden fork in my pocket, but I can't dwell on my injuries. For now, I do my best to navigate by the light of the full moon, picking my way between rows of blooming flowers, their perfume replacing the smell of dirt and trees. In preparation for the lavender hunt, I'd memorized photos of the flowers before learning it doesn't bloom until summer, rendering that research useless.

I'd searched online for any indication of why Fiona had chosen the lavender plant out of all the showier options in her mother's garden and found an article in a *Brampton Chronicle* gardening feature from a few years earlier. Apparently, Heather had added lavender, which is difficult to grow in Maine, to her impressive growing repertoire after a "stressful turn of events"—her daughter becoming a renegade teen—and had called the plant a "lifesaver." She'd even taken to drying bunches of the flowers and selling them, donating the income to local homes for troubled teens. Mystery solved.

I creep through the garden, but the tall, purple-headed stalks are nowhere to be found or smelled, as predicted. Metal spikes protrude at random intervals, naming the plants in their vicinity like street signs. GLADIOLUS, DAHLIA, BEGONIA, ASTER. I risk another look at the sleeping house before turning on my headlamp. ECHINACEA, RUDBECKIA, IRIS, DAFFODIL. The options are endless, and exactly none of them are lavender.

I move to the planter boxes, which feature mostly herbs and vegetables. BASIL, THYME, ARUGULA, CARROTS. Everything you can find at a farmer's market, but still no lavender.

I'd come tonight, guilt and trepidation warring in my gut over the inevitable need to destroy part of Heather McBride's beautiful garden to cover my tracks, but now I'm ready to whip out my garden fork and shred this whole over-the-top scene to pieces. It's absurd how many plants she grows. It's insane how little lavender she has.

I have the fork in my hand when a light flicks on inside the house, glaring yellow through the drawn curtains. Approximately half a second later, bright white flood-lights turn on, blasting every inch of the garden with a stark, incriminating glow. I dive behind a planter box, scuttling forward on my elbows to drag the tips of my shoes out of sight. I'm at least fifteen feet from the back fence and my footstool to safety and forty feet from the house itself. I'd done a drive-by prior to opting to skulk through the ravine, and the gate at the front was locked, meaning hopping the fence was my only option and still is. I just have to reach the fence. And climb it.

"Hello?" calls a male voice. It's accompanied by the creak of a door swinging open, and though I can't see him, I imagine Mr. McBride in a housecoat and slippers, rifle in hand. "Who's there?"

I don't answer, obviously. I couldn't speak if I wanted to. My heart's beating so hard it feels like I'm about to bounce straight up off the ground and expose myself.

"Seamus?" It's Heather. The garden fork digging into my stomach makes me feel even worse about my plan to destroy the only reason she has left to live.

"Stay inside," he says.

"Do you see anything? If it's a raccoon—"

"I don't—"

All of a sudden, a dozen birds start chirping, an irritating, discordant melody. Seamus curses, and Heather squeaks, masking my own startled yelp. At the same time, we all recognize the sound for what it is: the doorbell. Someone is calling on the McBrides after midnight. Anyone who's seen a horror movie knows they shouldn't answer, but I pray fervently that they do.

Seamus makes a noise of protest but I hear Heather say "Fiona," and then the back door closes. I count to five, unable to wait any longer, before clambering to my knees and peeking over the edge of the planter. They're gone. Not for long, I imagine, since it's probably Greaves at the front door, asking for access to the garden.

I race back to the fence, straighten my footstool, and launch myself over the wood like lightning. They'll find the stool soon enough, but by then I'll be long gone, my clothes and shoes burned, the matching stool tossed into the Brampton River. I scurry down the hill into the ravine, my feet skidding in the damp earth, hastening the process. I'm breathing hard when I reach my car and pause, but there's no one racing through the woods after me, giving chase.

The trees are silent.

CHAPTER 7

On Wednesday, Graham takes me to dinner at a fancy French restaurant in downtown Brampton, so popular we couldn't get a weekend reservation. I bought a new dress for the occasion and even wore heels, and Graham wears a suit and tie. He acts like it's no big deal, but I recognize that the kind gesture is meant to take my mind off the news that the McBrides had an intruder on their property and the now-rampant nonsensical speculation that Footloose is back.

Brampton has been reeling with the possibility, and Graham has convinced himself that any advances in my recovery will be set back by the rumors, despite my assurances that I'm fine. I'm concerned, of course, in a completely normal and believable way, but not afraid. I know firsthand the worst is behind us. Mostly. I think.

When the check comes, Graham tucks his credit card

into the billfold without even looking at it, and I have to resist the urge to peek. The menu didn't have prices, but based on the miniscule portion sizes and art gallery–worthy presentations, dinner wasn't cheap.

"You didn't have to do this," I say, not for the first time. Graham smiles. "I know. I wanted to." He reaches into his suit jacket and my mouth goes dry as I half expect him to pull out a velvet ring box. But he just checks his phone, frowning at the display. "Sorry," he says, when he misinterprets my disappointment. "Work drama."

"No need to explain. I design office supplies for a living. I know all about drama."

We collect our jackets and leave, stepping out into the spring evening. Downtown Brampton is a cluster of neat streets with the regular assortment of shops and services, and we'd parked a few blocks away. It's approaching eight o'clock, and everything is in the process of shutting down for the night, banks and clothing stores dark, fairy lights twisted in the small trees that line the road.

We pause in front of a jewelry store that's still open, one much nicer than the shop at the mall where Becca used to work, the kind that has security guards and a secret back room for really rich people to try on really expensive items, a room I'll never see. The window is well lit, diamonds and emeralds sparkling in their cases, black velvet and artfully placed rose petals rounding out the display. On the left is a collection of engagement rings, the stones the size of some of the food portions I'd eaten tonight.

"See anything that…appeals?" Graham asks. He's studying the rings and avoiding my eyes, but his cheeks are a little more pink than normal.

"They're beautiful."

He nods at a tasteful gold band with a small, clear diamond. "How about that one?"

"It's pretty. Classic."

Now he looks at me. "Not good enough. How about that one?" He indicates a white-gold band with a pink diamond so large I might have trouble using my left hand while wearing it.

"Perfect for grocery shopping."

He smiles and snags my wrist, studying my fingers as though visualizing the perfect fit. Then he frowns, tracing his thumb over the scratches on my knuckles from when I'd fallen while climbing the ravine. Three times. "What happened here?"

"Oh," I say dumbly, like I've only just spotted the angry red lines. "Work. Paper cuts. I was digging in my recycling bin for something and got scratched up."

"Ow."

I tuck my hand in my pocket. "What can I say? I live a dangerous life."

Graham stares at my hidden hand and then looks back at the rings in the window, as though doubting his intentions. Doubting me.

"I have to tell you something," I blurt out.

Slowly, Graham turns. "Okay."

"I went to a meeting of the Brampton Kill Seekers."

For a second, he doesn't move a muscle, but I know his brain is processing the words, twisting and reordering them, trying desperately to find a way they make sense. Finally, he settles on, "What?"

"The Brampton Kill Seekers. They're a group of amateur sleuths who think Brampton has too many missing people, and they want to find them."

"The *Kill* Seekers?"

"I didn't name them. I just...I went to a meeting. One. One meeting."

His expression is still impossible to read. "Did you find anybody?"

"No. It wasn't encouraging." I tell him about Emmett and the rock salt lamp, and when I'm finished, I've managed to make him laugh. "I'm sorry I didn't tell you sooner," I say. "I just...I knew it was stupid."

"Then why did you go?"

"I guess I just wanted to see what they knew. And then a friend of Becca's showed up."

"I didn't know she had friends."

"Yeah, well, I met him once, and now his wife is missing, so he got invited and decided to see if the Kill Seekers had any answers."

Perhaps I've surprised him all I can in the past ten minutes because Graham doesn't even look fazed by the admission. He looks relieved.

"I'm glad you told me," he says eventually. "You've

been acting a little off lately, and I thought maybe you were struggling."

"No more than normal."

He shoots me a small smile, and we resume walking. "Did your friend find out what happened to his wife?"

"Becca's friend," I correct. "And no, I don't think so. I haven't spoken to him since the meeting, but I checked online and there are no updates."

"And no Becca."

"I didn't say they were good kill seekers."

We reach our cars, parked side by side near the water. I'd changed at work and driven here to meet Graham, and now he takes my hands and looks at me in a way that makes my heart flutter. *This is why I need the flash drive*, I tell myself as he leans in to kiss me. *So I can have this forever.*

Graham kisses me and steps back. "We have to find a place soon," he says. "I'm ready to stop driving in opposite directions when we say goodbye."

"Me too. Shall we take the plunge on that haunted Victorian in the middle of the hellscape? Or the one with the bullet holes in the front door?"

He laughs. "I'm partial to the one where they found a skeleton in the wall."

We part ways, and I get in my car, giving the back seat a covert scan before starting the vehicle and driving home. When I reach the house, I sit in the car for a minute, contemplating the dark street. Apart from the two serial killers who frequented the area last fall, it's a safe neighborhood, so I get out and walk the two blocks to the intersection of Laurel Street and Boone Road, where the third hit-and-run victim had been struck down. I've checked the news, but there've been no additional mentions of the crime and no new details. The victim's name, occupation, and date of death are all conspicuously absent. I couldn't investigate even if I knew what I was doing.

The corner is quiet, lights on in a few front windows, but no one's out walking their dog or enjoying the cool spring night. It's just me, peering around strangely, looking for my sister or her copycat crouched in a bush snickering, and finding nothing. As expected, my investigation begins and ends on this corner.

Eventually, I give up and make the short walk home, where I find someone waiting not so casually at the end of his driveway.

"Hello, Mr. Myer."

Tonight he doesn't even have his broom, the prop he normally uses as a cover for his spying efforts.

"Good evening, Carrie. Everything okay?"

"Just fine," I say, keeping a straight face. Mr. Myer is in his nineties and looks like a mild breeze would knock him over.

"I saw you come home." He nods at my house, as though I don't know which one it is. "And then I saw you leave."

"I just wanted the fresh air."

"After everything that's happened, I wanted to make sure you made it back all right."

The thought of Mr. Myer trailing me through the dark streets, of Mr. Myer being the cause of the niggling feeling at the back of my neck, almost makes me laugh.

"That's very kind of you." I start to bid him good night but then stop. "Speaking of everything that's happened," I begin, "what do you make of that hit-and-run from last week?"

He blinks and scratches the sparse patch of hair at his temple. "Hit-and-run?"

"It was in the news. A jogger was hit at Laurel and Boone."

He frowns. "I don't know anything about it."

"There would have been police, an ambulance."

He shakes his head stubbornly. "That's not possible. I'd know."

While Mr. Myer does his best to make sure he knows everything, even things that are none of his business, he's not exactly the most reliable witness. He didn't, for example, ever notice Footloose entering my house, planting evidence and recording devices, and later, drugging and kidnapping me.

I can see this line of questioning is making him edgy, and perhaps more than a little offended, so I back off.

"Maybe I'm mistaken," I say with a placating smile. "Maybe it was somewhere else."

"It must have been," he says testily. "It couldn't have been here. Couldn't be."

"Have a good night."

I leave him with a wave, returning to my house and letting myself in. Mr. Myer watches from his own door until I'm safely inside before calling an end to his nightly vigil.

I lock the door and lean against it, trying to process what little I've learned. Three hit-and-run deaths with very little coverage. Kill Seekers who didn't think the deaths warranted a mention. And a neighborhood busybody who didn't hear an ambulance. It's almost like I'm the only one who cares about what's happening.

It's almost like I'm the only one who's supposed to.

CHAPTER 8

Two days later, I'm being followed. It's approaching 1:00 p.m. on a beautiful spring Friday, and the second I step outside the front doors of Weston Stationery, I feel it. It's not the warm, irritating tingle of Greaves's stalking, but it's also not the icy, sinister tickle of the other stalker. It's something uncomfortably in between.

The business park that's home to Weston is large and mostly desolate, a bunch of nondescript buildings with a view of the highway and little else. It's an eight-minute walk to Thai Me Up, and I appear to be the only person taking their lunch at this hour. My kitten heels click over the pavement as I check both ways before hurrying across the street against a red light, trying to convince myself I'm imagining things. I'm almost at the end of the block when I hear it. A second set of footsteps, keeping time with mine.

I whirl around to see a figure dart out of sight behind the edge of the building at the corner, maybe ten yards away. I walk in place for a few steps, careful to stomp loudly, hoping my follower thinks I've resumed walking and shows themselves. Nothing happens.

Maybe it was a shadow, I tell myself. Maybe it was a completely innocent employee walking from their car to the building, and I'm making something out of nothing. But the strange sensation tickling between my shoulder blades is something I've known most of my life, the warning that Becca was up to something particularly not good, to be on the lookout, to be wary. I'd done my utmost to dismiss that feeling when Footloose was around, mistaking his warning signs for Becca's, but they're both dead, so this has to be something—someone—new. And I don't want to wait until they jump out of my closet or take me to a murder cabin. I want to confront this particular demon on my own terms.

Removing my shoes, I tiptoe back to the corner, my sixth sense clanging louder and louder, like a warning bell in my brain. I'm two doors from the end of the block when the sun slips behind a cloud and the glare on the windshield of a pale-gray van shifts, revealing Detective Greaves behind the wheel. I trip over my own feet as the detective lifts a hand in greeting. Of fucking course. I glare back, preparing to put on my shoes and storm off to lunch, for which I'm already late. As though he's on the same page, my phone buzzes in my bag, and I tug it out, seeing the message from Graham telling me he got the booth in the back and is ordering spring rolls because he's starving.

I stuff the phone in my bag and then hesitate. I've come this far. Squaring my shoulders, I hurry to the end of the block and peek around the corner, jumping in surprise when I actually find somebody crouched there.

"Emmett!" I shriek, my voice echoing between the buildings.

He straightens awkwardly, his red hair covered by the same knit cap he wore at the meeting, his denim jacket paired with a new plaid shirt.

"Oh, hey," he says, failing terribly at sounding casual. "Carrie. What a surprise. I was just tying my shoe."

"What are you doing here?"

"Tying my shoe."

"In this business park!"

He glances down the road as though the answer might come to him. Or, if he knows Greaves is nearby, that he might come to his rescue. But that doesn't happen. "Just...looking," he says finally.

I raise an eyebrow.

"For you," he adds quickly. "Sorry—I know that's weird. It's just...we didn't have your contact info, and you're not on social media anymore, and Nikk said he didn't have your phone number, and we wanted to talk..."

"So you followed me?"

"Well, I was actually just going to go into your building, but then you started walking and I just...did the same."

His gaze drops to my bare feet, and I hastily put my shoes back on. "They give me blisters," I lie.

"Cool, cool."

There's a shuffling sound, and I turn to see Ravjinder approaching, her expression vaguely sheepish. Like the night we met at the library, she's dressed in a power suit, her hair and makeup impeccable.

"Ravjinder. You work here?" I ask. Her eyes flicker to Emmett, and I realize there's more to this stalking than I thought. "You guys came together?"

"I'm so sorry," she says. "You didn't answer our emails, and Nikk said he didn't think you'd be coming to the next meeting, and going to your house seemed weird—"

"You left fourteen flyers in my mailbox."

"Going to your house *again*," she amends, "and we just really wanted to talk."

They exchange another look, and my heart rate doubles. This can't be about me abandoning an old email address. Did they solve Fiona's clue, find the flash drive, and come to extort me as well? Back at the gray van, Detective Greaves has gotten out and leans against the tire well, purportedly checking something on his phone but most likely recording this impromptu meeting. That's the best-case scenario. Worst case is the back of the van is full of armed police officers ready to take me down because the Brampton Kill Seekers caught their first killer and have already handed over the flash drive.

"Talk about what?" I shift my purse on my shoulder, my sweaty palm leaving a smudge on the leather.

"Just if you had any thoughts or insight," Emmett says.

"We haven't made much progress on the Fiona clue, and it seemed like...you might?"

"Why would it seem like that?"

"Because you knew her."

"I didn't know her," I say too quickly. "I met her. A couple of times. Briefly. She didn't tell me about a clue."

Their shoulders sag. "Oh."

"Sorry," I mutter, risking another glance at Greaves, who's now openly staring.

"Did you hear about the attempted break-in at the McBride house?" Ravjinder asks hopefully.

I flush. "Yeah. I heard about it."

"They think Footloose is back."

"He's not back," I say firmly. "He's dead."

"Then who do you think it was?"

"Maybe it was a raccoon?"

"It was a person," Emmett clarifies. "Definitely a person. With a footstool."

I try to appear surprised by the reveal. "Wow."

"They said you were there," Ravjinder adds.

I freeze. "What?"

"A couple of days before. Heather McBride said you visited her."

I barely resume breathing. "Right. Yes. I did. For... closure." They look doubtful so I reluctantly whisper, "And to investigate the clue."

They lean in eagerly. "And?"

"And no luck." I feign disappointment. "I searched

Fiona's room, but the police had already been by and anything they found was gone. All I really got was a tour of the garden. Through the front door. In broad daylight."

Ravjinder laughs politely. "Lucky you. People pay for that."

My phone buzzes again in my bag, and I open my mouth to say my goodbyes, but Emmett interrupts. "People pay for a tour of the McBride garden?"

"No," Ravjinder explains, "the community garden. Where she grows the lavender. My sister used to buy it there. Before she…"

From the corner of my eye, I see that Greaves has gotten bored and started wandering our way.

"Which garden is this?" I ask. Then, because I don't want to sound like I'm interested for criminal reasons, I add, "I read an article that said lavender helps with relaxation and healing."

"Oh, yes. It's a beautiful herb."

"The big one over on Hartford Avenue," Emmett says impatiently. "Why don't you come to the next meeting and we can talk more? Maybe brainstorm?"

"I'll think about it," I lie. The lavender wasn't in the McBride garden, because it was in the community garden. Of course Fiona wouldn't have hidden the clue so close to home, in a place her mother would literally be digging. She hid it in public, where anyone could find it. Just in case.

Greaves is now a few feet away, squinting at his phone as though searching for directions. Copying him, I grab my own phone from my bag and peer at it.

"Sorry I can't talk more," I say, "but I'm meeting my boyfriend for lunch and I'm late."

Emmett is clearly ready to argue, but Ravjinder speaks up first. "Thank you for talking to us."

"Of course," I say, for Greaves's benefit. "It's nice to know people are still trying when so many others have failed."

———

I spend the next day researching the Brampton Community Garden for Health & Healing and that night dressing in dark clothes and packing a book bag with a spade and garden fork. It's just after one o'clock in the morning when I sneak out of my house. The back door is warped and swollen from years of disuse and bad weather, and it takes almost more time to get it open and then closed again than it did to prepare for tonight's mission.

Because his body was never found, the rest of the town is on high alert for the return of Footloose, but I know that threat is past and whatever threat has taken its place has its sights set squarely on me for reasons unknown. The real threat to my freedom, however, is the flash drive, and once I get it back, my unwanted mystery suitor can follow me until they realize their mistake and die from boredom.

I cut through my yard and then through the neighbor's, emerging onto the opposite street, pitch-black, quiet, and almost identical to mine. Old houses line the road and trees tower over them, their leaves whispering together in the light, cool breeze. The occasional streetlamp flickers as I hurry past, head ducked under the hood of my sweatshirt. I'm certain I look like a cat burglar, but there's no law against a late-night walk with a bag of garden implements, so even if Greaves does manage to tail me on tonight's excursion, I'm not technically doing anything wrong, just weird.

I make it two blocks without seeing or hearing anyone, freezing in place when a car passes by at the intersection ten yards ahead. The road doesn't have a stop sign, and the car is going suspiciously slow for the middle of the night, almost like the driver is looking for something. I crouch in the shadows and wait until they trundle out of sight. My recent spate of criminal activity has wreaked havoc on my nerves, every second glance and murmured conversation making me more paranoid than normal. It's probably someone tipsy trying to get home safely without being stopped. There's no one looking for me. There couldn't be.

I spot a couple more cars en route to Hartford Avenue, but they're all moving at normal speeds, and no one appears to notice my strange behavior. Hartford is a four-lane street lined with box stores, fast-food restaurants, gas stations, and, on a sprawling lot that used to be home to a grocery store, the Brampton Community Garden for

Health & Healing. I've driven past it a hundred times over the past five years but have never ventured in. According to my research, one third of the garden is devoted to Heather McBride's lavender plants, and the remaining space is available to rent to local gardeners with no land of their own who want to grow things in a raised box in a fenced-in block next to a Taco Bell.

I approach on the sidewalk from the west, the chain-link fence twice as high as I remember it and quite unexpectedly topped with barbed wire, presumably to keep out animals and people like me. The entrance opens onto the street, the gates padlocked shut and wrapped with what looks like a bike chain. Apart from our two serial killers and remarkably high missing persons rate, Brampton is not particularly known for crime, and the security measures feel like overkill.

Two cars speed past, one chasing the other, music blasting out the open windows. I surreptitiously tug on the padlock as I pass, in case it's not really locked, but it is. I hadn't anticipated this particular hurdle and hadn't procured another footstool to assist with hopping yet another fence. Moving on to the next street, I make a left and walk toward the back of the lot. The only light comes from the streetlamps on the main road, their weak glow barely stretching past the first row of planter boxes. An enormous structure looms at the back of the lot, closely resembling a haunted farmhouse. It's a two-story peaked building with double doors and a broken top-floor window. A loud *creak* slices through the night, and I jump, expecting again to be attacked or arrested, but nothing happens. Another creak, this one more faint, and I crane my neck to look up. Framed against the night sky is a rooster-shaped weather vane on the roof, rotating slowly in the breeze and gazing down at me with reproach.

I shiver, but I'm not cold. I continue walking and then stop again as I hear a footstep before my sneaker touches the ground. It's just a slight scuffing, someone touching their toes to the pavement, attempting to stop when I stopped, not quite fast enough. I whip around, but I'm alone on the side road, the garden at my back, a small library across the street.

You're hearing things, I tell myself. *And you're taking too long.*

I attempt one more fake step and hear nothing before giving up and hustling around the back of the lot, which features a small dirt parking area and the front of the farmhouse. This side has a sign that reads COMMUNITY GARDEN STORE.

There are no cars here at this hour, and the building, like everything else, is dark. A crescent moon hangs overhead, barely lighting the narrow path at the side of the store that leads around back along the fence. It's an uneven, rutted trail, like someone's regularly dragged a hose over the earth, and narrow enough that I have to remove my bag and carry it in a hand to fit through. I shuffle along, the wood slats of the building pricking at my sweatshirt, smells of dirt and mildew filling my nose.

Somewhere, a dog barks, and I trip, expecting a giant beast to leap out of the night and tear my face off, but when I calm down enough to breathe again, I realize it's far away. Still, I double the pace of my clumsy side shuffle until I emerge into the community garden, which somehow manages to appear even bigger from this angle. The Taco Bell looks like it's a mile away on the right, Hartford Avenue just a blip in the distance.

Like Heather McBride's garden, these raised boxes have little signs indicating what's being grown, but also who's doing the growing. JOHNSON: KALE, BEET, RADISH. HUANG: SUNFLOWER, ASPARAGUS, CHIVE.

At this hour, it's difficult to see much more, so I tug my phone from my pocket, make sure it's on silent, and tuck it into my sleeve before turning on the flashlight. Shining it through my sweater gives me enough light to see but hopefully mutes it enough that no one passing by notices. I definitely do not have a convincing excuse for being here at this hour with a backpack of garden tools and, if caught, would likely break down and confess to also being the McBride vandal.

The website said Heather's lavender occupied a third of the garden, so it seems like her section should be clearly marked, but I pace three long rows and find absolutely nothing to distinguish them from the others. Worse yet, all of these boxes seem to host herbs and vegetables, all of which have started growing, and the internet told me lavender wouldn't bloom in Maine until May.

Crouching low between raised beds promising carrots, I use my phone to navigate to the garden website and click the *lavender* link. It's so popular it gets its own page, Heather McBride's smiling face greeting visitors and making me feel guilty for too many reasons all over again. I skim the blurbs about lavender's health benefits, craft ideas, and recipes, stopping when I reach the pictures. There they are: rows upon rows of raised boxes bursting with purple blooms. So where the hell are they?

Finally, it hits me. I consult my phone and then my surroundings. The pictures on the website show no library, no Taco Bell, no road, no fence. And if they were taken *outside* when the plants were in bloom, it should have been almost summer, which means there should be at least a smidgen of sky. But there's not. The dim background in the photo is a wall.

Slowly, I turn to stare at the barn. Even more slowly, my gaze lifts to the second story and its cracked window. I don't even need to see the first level of the building to know the garden's on the top floor because that's just my luck. It's the worst.

There are two large barn doors back here, flanked on either side by small round windows, barely big enough for a cat to fit through, never mind a human. There's no ladder or anything to suggest access to the second floor from the outside and almost definitely no way for me to scale the side of a barn without being, say, arrested or falling off. I sit down and slump against a planter box, dejected and tired. Perhaps a better burglar would know what to do in this situation, but all I can think of is somehow returning in the light of day and somehow gaining access to the second level and somehow raking through all of the garden beds without anyone spotting me or calling the police. Otherwise—

I squeal when one of the barn doors slowly eases open, its hinges protesting the weight with a low, eerie moan. I stare in horror at its gaping mouth, the pitch-black void calling me in. The fact that going inside is exactly the thing I need to do is the exact reason this is so horrifying. I've known *two* serial killers. Nothing *good* happens to me. Nothing is *easy*. This is hearing a bump in the basement and going down alone to investigate. This is certain death.

There are three rows of planter boxes between me and the building and about thirty feet between me and the narrow path that leads to the front and freedom. Instinct tells me to sprint to the road and scale the fence, shredding my shirt and my skin on the barbed wire and telling Graham I had another run-in with the recycling bin, but I know that's not an option. When we were younger, Becca would play a game where she'd run upstairs ahead of me, turn off all the lights, and lurk in the darkness, waiting for me to try to come up to bed, knowing there was a monster waiting to pounce. I spent too much time hovering at the base of the steps, afraid of what waited.

I let fear dictate my actions, and that led to a future of carting bodies through the forest in a murder carpet.

Sometimes, I remind myself, the dark is just the dark. My imagination is the enemy.

I force myself to my feet and take a few cautious steps toward the building. It's completely silent. Even the wind has stopped. The door sways gently on its hinges, beckoning me forth. With my phone gripped in my hand, I approach warily, shining a light inside. The beam is immediately swallowed by the gloom, and it's only when I'm at the threshold that I can see enough to understand why: The garden store is split in two. The front, which has windows to the parking lot, is separate from this smaller back half, which is home to wheelbarrows and garden tools, stacks of fertilizer, watering cans, and other implements. On the left is a rickety wooden staircase that leads to the second floor.

I give the room a cursory check, shining my light behind a metal cabinet labeled SEEDS and even inside a large metal sink, but there's no one here, nothing to suggest how or why the door opened. Every muscle in my body is tight, completely on board with the plan to rocket right out of here and race home and take my chances with someone else finding the flash drive. But my brain is arguing with itself, making a case for the safe, sane logic of fleeing and the equally risky but reasonable argument for completing my mission when I'm so close to the finish line.

I pause at the base of the stairs and shine the light

up to where an open doorway waits. From here it smells like damp and dirt, and I tuck my phone under my chin before reaching over slowly to collect a shovel that's leaning against the wall, clutching it in front of me with both hands like a sword, ready to swing.

The stairs creak as I climb, the wood bowing under my weight as though trying to discourage me with each step. Still, I ascend, two steps, three, the dark cloying, shadows crawling over each other, tracking my progress. My heart pounds, a hundred unsteady beats for every step, the shovel slipping in my sweaty palms. *I'm not afraid of the dark*, I remind myself. *I'm not afraid.*

But I am, because I'm sane.

I reach the top and pause, peering in. The only windows are on the back wall, overlooking the community plot, the broken one on the far side of the room. I shift the shovel to one hand and grab my phone, shining the light over a dozen rows of raised beds, these much more high-tech than the ones outside, featuring what I imagine are watering systems and grow lights, the electricity quietly humming though the lights are off. There are a couple of work benches on one side, the walls peppered with flower quotes but no handy clues to indicate in which box I should start digging.

I settle on the closest box, take two steps toward it, and trip over a body.

CHAPTER 9

barely swallow my scream as I stumble, dropping the shovel with a deafening clatter. My eyes widen in horror as I fall onto the prone body, landing with an *oomph* that knocks the air from my lungs. Something crunches inside the legs I've landed on, making my stomach lurch and my senses shriek, nausea and panic fighting to take over. I scramble for the edge of the nearest planter box, trying to pull myself up, my fingers sinking into the dirt and failing to find purchase. I'm gasping and sweating, my limbs unwilling or unable to follow commands until eventually common sense penetrates my terrified haze, and I recognize that the body beneath me feels decidedly soft. Not like skin and bones and blood and fascia and muscle. Something like...hay.

Cautiously, I reach down and pat the body, feeling scratchy fabric and the occasional stab of dried grass through the flannel shirt and jeans. It's not a human; it's a scarecrow. I let out a shaky breath and swipe the back of my hand across my forehead, feeling it come away damp, the warmth in sharp contrast to the icy fingers tracing over my skin. The same sinister feeling that has been tracking me for weeks is back, tapping out the final beats of a warning I've been desperately trying to ignore.

"I know you're here, Becca." Angry and embarrassed, I get to my feet and collect my things, realizing all too late that holding a shovel next to a body in the middle of the night with my sister is the exact life I'd wanted to leave behind.

There's no answer.

"Just come out, you idiot. If you've been following me, then you know why I'm here, and you know what to do."

There's another pause before an all-too-familiar cackle rings through the room, making the hairs on my arm stand on end. It's a monster; it's my sister.

And she's back.

"Oh, fine," Becca says, stepping out of the shadows next to a storage cabinet. She pulls off the black hat covering her head and shakes out her blond hair like I'm about to take her photo. "Happy to see me, Sister?"

The thing about monsters is that, even once you think they're dead, there's a part of you that will forever wonder if you're wrong. If it's truly possible to slay the dragon, burn the witch, stab the vampire in the heart. They live on in the back of your mind, surfacing in nightmares and dark corners, the ghost that haunts you, even when you know better than to believe in ghosts. Even when they're walking toward you.

"What's your favorite food?" I demand. I clutch the shovel tightly, like I might need it to fend her off.

She manages to look perplexed but doesn't stop walking. "Popcorn."

I try to think of another question, something only the real Becca could answer correctly.

"Who stole my black lace bra in eleventh grade?"

That earns me an eye roll. "The pervert neighbor who was obsessed with you."

That's a lie. It was her, but for Becca, that constitutes a right answer.

I try again, the troll under the bridge, demanding the answers to three riddles before letting her cross.

"You stole my best friend in high school. What was her name?"

Her brow furrows as she thinks, but she's smirking, too, recognizing the game and knowing she'll win, because she always wins. "Tanya."

I close my eyes. Dammit. Fake Becca would know it was Sariah. Real Becca wouldn't care enough to remember.

"Jessica?" she tries again. "Louise? Vicki? Patrice?"

It's her. She's real.

"Yeah," I say, opening my eyes too late, as always. "All of them."

Now she laughs, a sincere laugh, her white teeth flashing. "You're hilarious," she says. "You didn't have five friends."

She's still walking toward me, but there's something off about her pace. She's slower, limping slightly, one hip dipped lower than the other.

I point out the obvious. "I thought you were dead."

"Yeah, well, I'm not."

I stare at her, but she appears not to think that statement requires elaborating.

"Why not?"

"Because you don't always get what you wish for, Carrie." She's reached the final set of planter boxes that separate us, but instead of coming down the aisle toward me, she continues across the room to the wall of tools.

"I didn't wish for you to die," I argue, only half lying. I wished her gone, by any means necessary, but I'd naively and optimistically assumed that meant a life in prison. "And I never get what I wish for."

She turns from the wall, shovel in hand, and ignores everything I just said. "Look at us," she says. "Just like old times. Digging holes, you whining, me helping anyway."

It's impossible for Becca to experience actual human emotions, but she sounds like she's genuinely pleased by this situation, that nothing would warm her cold, dead heart more than another illegal nighttime excursion with her sister.

"You've never helped me."

She cocks her head. "I help you all the time. How do you think you even got here?"

My mind races through the past decade, a careening roller coaster of terrible memories, murder carpets, dead bodies, serial killers, and worse. "It's a *bad* thing that I'm here."

"It's bad that you were working alone," she corrects. "But now it's better."

"It's not."

"You didn't even know she left a clue, Carrie!" The raised voice startles me. Becca's not a shouter. She doesn't experience enough emotion to shout unless she needs to be heard in a noisy room.

My knees start to shake, and I stab the shovel into the wood floor to anchor myself. "What would you know about the note?"

Becca was "dead" well before I first met Fiona. Before I rescued her, tried to reason with her, and then pushed her off a cliff. Becca doesn't know what I did. Becca doesn't know what Fiona knew, and she doesn't know what we're hunting for. She, like so many others, may have heard there's a "clue," but she doesn't know what it leads to.

"I know you didn't even know the clue existed," she says. "And I know that the second you learned about it at that meeting, you started acting weird and began trying to track it down. And I know it's very strange that Freda disappeared so soon after she returned."

"Fiona," I say automatically, though it's a waste of time. "She hated her life, and she wanted a fresh start without her *family* interfering."

Becca sniffs and misses the point. "If you say so."

"I do say so."

"Then what do you think you're going to find tonight?"

"I don't know. I'm just curious."

She arches a brow. "*Extremely* curious if you're vandalizing your second garden in a week."

The words hit me like a blow. Becca wasn't just the car. Becca was behind it all. She steered me here just like she steered me to the base of Barr Lode Trail to dispose of the first body—my first, her second—and ensnared me in this awful cycle of crime and murder.

"Where have you been for the past five months?"

"It's about time you asked."

"Where?"

"I've been recuperating at my friend Nikk's house. Not that you care."

It's the answer I was expecting, but still I sigh, dejection and nausea duking it out to see who should win this war. Of course Nikk's wife is missing. He might be a wife beater, but Becca's the one who kills. She's the one who makes people disappear. She knew about the Brampton Kill Seekers; she'd heard of Fiona's clue. And she knew that if I went to the meeting, I knew about it, too. Then she sat back and waited for me to do the dirty work. As always.

"Why are you doing this?"

"Because you need my help."

"That's not true."

"Really? You're going to dig up this whole place by yourself, looking for…?"

She trails off expectantly, but I don't fill in the blank. I'm not telling her I'm looking for an incriminating flash drive because she's smart enough to deduce that if I know there's a flash drive now, I knew there was one before, and Fiona's disappearance is probably connected. I'd never live it down if she knew I'd followed in her murderous footsteps.

She smirks at my stony stare. "Right. You didn't even manage to dig a hole in the McBride garden."

"Well, the clue wasn't there anyway…Wait. How do you know that?"

Yet another belated revelation hits me, and Becca's smirk turns into a full-blown grin. "See?" she gloats. "I helped you."

"You rang the bell."

"Well, that man was going to shoot you."

"He didn't have a gun."

She shrugs. "He could have."

"You followed me through the ravine?"

"Of course I did. Someone has to help you."

"For the last time, you don't help me."

She continues as though I hadn't spoken. "Though it wasn't easy." I expect her to reference her injured leg, but instead she says, "The number of times you fell…" She shakes her head, chuckling to herself. "I had to stuff my whole hand in my mouth just so you didn't hear me laugh."

"That's great."

"And watching you try to climb the fence, hanging up there like a stuck pig…"

I pry my shovel out of the floorboards. "Okay, you know what? Let's do what we do best and start digging."

Becca beams. "I thought you'd never ask."

Just like how we dig graves, we start on opposite ends of the room and use our shovels to dump mountains of dirt onto the floor, parsing through it for anything resembling a clue. I'm hoping desperately that Fiona put the flash drive in a box for safekeeping so it's easy to find, but it's also entirely possible that she didn't, that there is no flash drive, that there's nothing here at all but a bunch of now-dead lavender seedlings. I finish emptying my fourth planter, shining the light from my phone into the dirt as I rake through with my garden fork, finding nothing.

I check the time. Almost three o'clock. My eyes are stinging with fatigue, and my muscles burn from exhaustion. And we're not even halfway done.

"Huh," Becca says.

I straighten, my back protesting the sudden movement. "What did you find?"

"A key."

My heart sinks. "It's probably nothing. Someone just lost a key."

"In a plastic bag?" She holds up a plastic baggie by two fingers, using the faint moonlight filtering through the broken window to peer at it. "With an *X* on it?"

Confused and concerned, I pick my way around mounds of dirt until I'm standing next to Becca. She is indeed holding a bag with a gold *X* scrawled on it, and inside is a small, ornate key.

"Which planter was that in?"

She nods at the nearest box. "That one."

It's only half-empty, and now I frantically shovel the remaining dirt onto the floor, scraping through with my garden fork, searching for the flash drive. The key must be a hint, telling us we're getting close. X marks the spot…near the spot.

"What are you doing?" Becca asks. "We found the prize."

"That's not a prize. It's a key."

"It's got an *X* on it."

"What's it a key to?" I demand, my voice shrill. "There has to be more. That can't be it." But there's nothing left in the planter, nothing in the dirt. And half a room left to destroy before I pass out from exhaustion and nerves.

"Why do you think there's more? What were you expecting?" Becca sounds suspicious.

"I— Nothing," I lie. "But what kind of 'prize' is that? A key? Is there a map?" I snatch the bag out of her hand

and hold it up to the window, checking for more than an X on the bag, maybe another hint, an indication of what the key is for, but there's nothing. And even as I scour it, I'm thinking back to the moment I learned of the clue, when I decided it was a flash drive simply because that made the most sense. What else could Fiona have had that she found valuable enough to hide "just in case"?

"C'mon," Becca says, dropping her shovel against the wall with a bang. "Let's get out of here. Helping you is exhausting and thankless, as usual."

I want to protest, want the peace of mind knowing I'd searched every single planter box, but I know the more likely scenario is that I'll pass out in a pile of dirt and be woken up by a police officer in the morning.

Reluctantly, I follow Becca back down the stairs and out into the yard, the cool night air a boon after the humidity of the growing room. We shuffle along the fence to the front of the building, but when I start back to the main road to begin the walk home, Becca stops.

"What are you doing?"

"Going home. I walked here."

"I know. But I drove."

I think of the car passing too slowly through the intersection. "You followed me?"

"I mean, you had a head start."

"Where were you?"

"Parked in front of your house. Emilio told Nikk about the community garden conversation, and Nikk told me, and I figured it'd only be a matter of time before you tried to vandalize it, so I was waiting."

I'm pretty sure "Emilio" is Emmett.

"I went out the back."

"Yes, but you're not exactly stealthy, Carrie. I saw you moving around in your bedroom window so I knew you were awake, and then you made a ton of noise opening and closing your back door. I just cruised around until I spotted you and then drove over here to let you in."

I shake my head. "It doesn't matter. I'm walking home."

"Well, I drove."

"I heard you. Drive yourself back to Nikk's. Thanks for the 'help.'"

Becca looks appalled. "That's it? That's all I get? I found the key!" She's raising her voice again, but this time I know it's a technique for getting attention and trying to force me to do her bidding.

I start walking away. "Good night, Becca."

"The least you could do is invite me over."

"It's late. And I'm sure you'll invite yourself another time."

"I want to come over now."

I turn to stare at her. Her insistence is out of character. Even when she really wants something, she still acts blasé and uncaring.

I narrow my eyes. "What happened with Nikk?"

She chews on the inside of her cheek, something she always does when she's thinking. It's too dark to see, but it's easy to picture her lower lip stained with blood, as usual. "We had a falling out."

"Is he alive?"

"I don't see why he wouldn't be."

"Because there've been three unsolved hit-and-run deaths already this month, and perhaps he's number four?"

"I haven't hurt anyone this month."

"Stay in a hotel."

"I haven't worked since November, when I almost died trying to help you."

"Almost. But not really."

"I just need a place to sleep," she insists, pulling keys from her pocket. "Stop arguing with me. I'm tired."

There's no point in arguing with her—this I've learned. She never gets tired, and she always gets what she wants. If I don't let her in, she'll break in. And if I walk home, I can't rule out the possibility of her running me over.

"One night," I say.

"That's all I need." She grins and heads down the block. "And a shower. And maybe some popcorn. And a change of clothes. Do you have anything extra small?"

CHAPTER 10

Despite my fervent prayers that last night was a nightmare, Becca's still in my house the next morning. She wore one of my old T-shirts and complained relentlessly that she felt like it was smothering her. That didn't stop her from rifling through my closet this morning and choosing an expensive dress before downing three bowls of cereal and leaving the empty box on the counter. In six hours, she's managed to erase five months of emotional healing.

"So," I say, as we sit opposite each other at my kitchen table, cups of tea in hand. Hers has four teaspoons of added sugar.

"So," Becca says. The plastic bag with the key still inside sits between us, the final stop in a treasure hunt that provides only the hunt and no treasure.

"You want to tell me what happened?"

She sips her tea, winces, and adds more sugar. "I told you last night. I knew you were going to the community garden—"

"Five months ago," I interrupt. "Footloose told me you were dead. He had a picture."

"Well, that's what he thought. He ran me over, after all. But it's not like I don't know what a hit-and-run victim looks like. I just played dead."

"At the paint factory?"

"Yeah." She shakes her head in disgust. "He'd been listening in on our conversations and knew that's where I took Angelica. He said it was 'ironic' that the story should end there. Joke's on him, though."

"Is it?"

She shrugs. "He came to my apartment, said he'd spare your life in exchange for mine, and I said no. Then he drugged me and took me anyway. I woke up in the factory parking lot, and he gave me ten seconds to run. I'd been there half a dozen times, so I knew a bit about the area and sprinted toward the edge that has a drainpipe buried in the weeds. But he lied and didn't give me a head start. He hit the gas right away. I heard him coming and then…"

"He hit you."

"Yeah. He broke my fucking leg and a few other things, so I couldn't exactly get up and keep going. I lay there and played dead while he took pictures and whistled, and then when he went back to the car to get my murder carpet, I crawled into the weeds."

"He just left you?"

"Well, he looked for a while, but I hid in the drainpipe, and eventually he said I'd die from exposure anyway, and he had 'better things to do.' Then he left, taking my favorite coat. I passed out and almost froze to death."

She recounts this version of events as matter-of-factly as I'd recap a trip to the grocery store, sparing extra disgust for the stolen coat.

"How'd you get to Nikk?"

"Like I said, I know the area. It has an old pay phone, so when I regained consciousness, I dragged myself over, collect called Nikk, and he came and got me. End of story."

Despite the fact that my life is infinitely improved without Becca in it, I can't help but be offended. "Why didn't you call me? I thought you were dead. I made posters."

"I saw those. I don't know why you chose that photo."

"Because you didn't look insane."

She laughs. "You're funny, Carrie. I missed you." There's a pause for me to say I feel the same, but I can't make myself share the sentiment. "Anyway," she continues, "I'll need some cash to get supplies. Just a bit of clothing, toiletries, a new pillow. How old is the one in your guest room? It's basically a rock. It's like sleeping in the Flintstones' home."

"It's orthopedic."

"Fascinating. I think a thousand should do it."

"It sounds like you're talking about staying here."

"Where else?"

"Literally anywhere," I reply. "Anywhere else."

Becca tries to look astonished and hurt but can manage neither, so returns to her default setting of manipulative. "Where would I go?" she asks, touching a hand to the right side of her chest, like she thinks that's where a human heart is located. "I was evicted from my apartment, and you sold all my things."

"You weren't evicted, you were dead, and I had to spend four hundred dollars on a truck to take your unwashed belongings to the dump and another four hundred to clean the place. When was the last time you dusted?"

She laughs again. "You're funny. I missed you."

"You used that line already. You need to go. Call a friend; call the jewelry store and ask them for your job back. And if you didn't kill Nikk, call him and apologize for whatever you did."

"What makes you think *I* did something wrong?"

"Oh, I don't know, our shared history?"

"You've really changed, Carrie. And not for the better."

"Good."

She scowls. "It'll just be a few months."

"I won't be here in a few months," I tell her. "I'm moving."

"What? Where?" Her alarm is real. Becca is a parasite learning her host is no longer a habitable environment.

"I don't know yet," I admit. "Graham and I are buying a place."

"Ew. You're moving in with Graham?"

"He's my boyfriend."

"Well, that's one gross thing that hasn't changed."

I stand and put my mug in the dishwasher. "That's the end of this conversation. I'll give you twenty bucks and…That's it. Just twenty bucks."

"I searched online for those hit-and-run deaths you accused me of last night."

"So?"

"So they're not real."

"Yes, they are. I saw the stories."

She makes a strange face at that news. "Well, I couldn't find them anywhere."

"Well, your computer skills are lacking."

"I know what the key is for." I know what she's doing because she's always done this. When she doesn't get the answer she wants, she changes the subject and then later circles back to nag you until you give in. It doesn't matter if the new subject is an obvious lie.

"Do not."

"I have more ideas than you do."

"Do not."

"It's Graham's."

"Still no."

"Let me prove it. We'll go to his place and try the key, and if it works…I'm right."

I plant my hands on my hips. "I don't need to try that key to open his door because I already have a key,"

I remind her. "And it's not his; it's too tiny. And why would Fiona hide Graham's house key?"

"Because he's a sex predator."

I roll my eyes. "Nope."

"There's something off about him, Carrie. Admit it."

"Why would I do that? I grew up with you. If there was something 'off' about him, I'd have known right away. The thing you find strange is that he's kind, Becca. He's decent."

She taps her chin pensively. "No, that's not it."

"You have to go."

"I can't!" she snaps, her calm facade cracking for just a split second.

"Call Nikk—"

"It's not about him," she says. "It's just best if we don't tell anyone I'm back yet."

"Why not? What about Mom and Dad?"

"It's been five months. What's a few more?"

In a normal family, I imagine the parents would be ecstatic to learn their missing daughter has returned, mostly unharmed. In this family, it would be exactly like learning their psychotic daughter was back and things had gone back to their awful brand of normal.

"Why can't we tell anyone?" I ask. "The police have an open file—"

"You know they're not trying to find me," she interrupts. "Not only are they terrible at locating people, they don't even know when they're missing. But that's not it."

"Then what is?"

She sighs and gets up, hunting in my cupboards until she finds a new box of cereal and tears it open, plucking out the marshmallows and eating them dry. "When Nikk went to report his wife missing, he asked for Detective Greaves. Greaves was much less interested in Nikk's missing wife than he was in me."

"Why? He hardly looked for you."

"I'm aware. But he wasn't interested in my death. He was interested in my life."

I blink. "What?"

"Apparently, in his investigation into you, he also investigated me. And he noticed that three women with connections to the Brampton Mall had gone missing. And that I worked there."

I have a flash of Ravjinder, joining the Kill Seekers to locate her missing sister.

"That doesn't mean—"

"And he specifically asked Nikk if I'd ever mentioned someone named Shanna Lewis."

I actually gasp. Shanna's the dead body I saw, the one we carted up the mountain at Barr Lode Trail and dumped off the cliff. The same spot I brought Fiona.

"He has no proof" is what I come up with.

Becca sniffs. "Obviously. But until I figure out why he's obsessing over Shanna ten years after she 'went to Mexico,' I need to lie low. Here. In your house."

I pinch the bridge of my nose. "I don't want to do this anymore."

Her bowl is on the counter, still half-full of milk, but Becca gets a new one from the cupboard and fills it to the brim with fresh cereal. "Don't worry; it won't be much longer," she assures me, winking in a nonassuring way. "I'm here to help."

"Again, you are not helpful."

The too-familiar slam of a car door staves off an argument. I dart up front to the window, and sure enough, Graham is at the curb, a box of pastries in hand.

"It's Graham." I turn and bump into Becca, who's crept up right behind me.

She squints. "Are those donuts?"

"Go upstairs," I order. "And don't make a sound. No creaking floors, no ghostly moans, no sex noises."

"But I want—"

I grip her arm and drag her to the stairs. "Eat your cereal in silence."

"You know, Carrie, you've really changed."

"I know, Becca. You said that already. Now go."

She pouts. "Well, I don't want to go."

"Fine. Stand here, eat your cereal, and wave to Detective Greaves."

"What?"

We turn to look through the sliver of opening between the curtains. Greaves has joined Graham on the sidewalk, and the two appear to be making small talk. Graham offers him a pastry.

"You think Greaves is suspicious of *you*?" I say. "You're dead. He's been following me for months."

She frowns. "Why?"

"Angelica, Shanté, Fiona."

"I don't know who those people are."

The conversation outside concludes, and Graham starts up the driveway, waving to Greaves like it's any normal Sunday and they're two friendly neighbors. Sometimes he really is just a little too nice.

Becca stares at me, trying to gauge whether or not I'm serious. My heart is pounding, but I'm not about to let her know I'd strongly prefer for Graham—and Greaves—not to know about her spontaneous return from the dead, either. As soon as she senses weakness, she has to press.

Finally, she gives her shiny hair a toss and flounces up the steps, taking extra care to stomp on the yowling stair three down from the top. "Fine," she says, pivoting and heading for my bedroom. "I'll eavesdrop from up here. I didn't sleep well with your rock pillow, and your boring conversation should help me get some much-needed rest."

I ignore her and turn to beam at the door just as Graham lets himself in.

"Morning," he says, looking vaguely startled to see me waiting.

I kiss him. "I heard your car."

"You can just admit you smelled baked goods."

"Who? Me? No. What?"

He smiles and removes his shoes before heading for

the couch and sitting down, in perfect earshot of anyone eavesdropping upstairs. Oh well. What Becca said is true. Compared to our sisterly conversations, Graham and I talk about nothing that's not incredibly sane and dull.

"Golf," he says, right on cue.

I take the pastry box and lift the lid. "Huh?"

"My work golf tournament is today, remember? But because we couldn't see each other last night, I wanted to see you before I started playing."

"That's sweet. I wanted to see you, too."

He leans over and kisses me with far more passion than ten o'clock in the morning normally warrants. I'd be all for it, except for the fact that Becca's probably got her face pressed against the gap in the stair railing and is watching everything while gagging.

"Sorry," I say, when I pull back and a flicker of hurt crosses his face. "Late, um, late night."

He shrugs it off and bites into a croissant. "What'd you get up to?"

"I...Drinking" is what I come up with, biting into a donut. "It was a long week."

"Did you hear about Heather McBride's lavender garden?"

I almost choke. "What? No. I haven't been online."

"You don't even need to go online. It's all over the news."

He reaches for the remote and turns on the television, navigating to Channel 6, our local station. Sure enough, there's a side-by-side comparison shot of the lavender garden in glorious full bloom and the destruction wrought last night.

I gasp because I'm supposed to. And because in the glaring light of day, it looks far worse than I remember.

"This is a place of health and healing," says a woman with curly gray hair and glasses, a volunteer badge hanging around her neck. "Only a monster could destroy a charity garden. And after everything that poor woman has been through?"

The camera cuts to the tear-stained face of Heather McBride, who's being comforted by two more solemn volunteers in green smocks.

They cut back to the news anchor at the station desk, staring soberly into the camera as he describes yet another crime in which I've been involved. "This is the fourth time in six months that the McBride family have been made victims," he informs us. "First, when their daughter was abducted by the serial killer dubbed Footloose; again, when she vanished before Christmas; last week, when their home garden was broken into; and now, when the lavender garden Heather McBride lovingly maintains has been viciously vandalized."

"Why?" the first volunteer is asking as she wades through the mess. "Why kill these innocent plants? Who could murder a flower? Meant for charity?"

My hand trembles as I turn off the television. "Wow," I say awkwardly. "That's terrible."

Graham shakes his head and finishes off his croissant.

"It's insane is what it is. What's this city coming to? The highest missing persons rate in the country and now petty vandalism targeting a grieving family?"

I hear the floor creak upstairs.

"I mean, maybe they're not being...targeted."

"Then what is it?"

"An awful coincidence? It's easy to feel like the world's out to get you when you're already suffering an impossible loss. Every little thing..."

Graham pushes a piece of hair behind my ear. "Is this about our house search? Is it upsetting you more than you're letting on? I know you're still grieving your sister, and drinking alone last night..."

I flinch. "Oh, um..."

"Because I'll call Misha and tell her to raise the budget. It'll be a bit more than we're comfortable with, but we're both smart, normal, employed people. We can balance the books if we have to, right? What matters is that we begin our life together. A fresh start."

"Yes," I say, picturing Becca rolling around on the floor upstairs, silently laughing. "Whatever it takes. Let's start over."

He grins and kisses me again before getting to his feet. "I'll make the call. For now, I'm off to Newport Village to golf in the name of medical supplies. I'm probably going to make a fool out of myself. The people I work with have been training for this. Can you imagine? Training for a charity golf tournament?"

I follow him to the door. "They take their charity seriously."

"I guess after what happened at the community garden, giving back matters more than ever."

He leaves and I wave until he drives out of sight, closing the door and slumping against it as Becca comes bounding down the stairs. "Are there donuts left?"

"Help yourself."

She's already pouncing on the box like a leopard. "This is perfect," she declares.

"Eat your heart out."

She takes a bite of pastry and spits it back in the box. "Not the apricot Danish. The golf tournament." She finds a Boston cream that's more to her liking.

"Stay away from the tournament."

"Ew. Why would I go to Newport Village?"

I sigh. "I don't know, Becca. Why do you do anything?"

"Because I can." She licks chocolate off her finger. "And today, with Graham out of the picture and all his lame coworkers golfing for charity, we can investigate that guilty creeper."

"He's not a creep."

She retrieves another treat from the box and stuffs half of it into her mouth. "He brought you a bunch of pastries on a Sunday morning," she says. "He's definitely feeling guilty about something."

CHAPTER 11

Becca's never had a real relationship. The occasional boyfriend, sure, but in the end, they all broke up with her. Two families actually staged interventions to convince the men they were being mistreated. And it worked. They saw the light.

I've had no such intervention, just a lifetime of knowing better and being unable to do anything about it. Not even being run over by a serial killer and left to die in a drainpipe could keep my sister away, which is why we're driving to Graham's office at Brampton MedSupplies. It took all of my effort to convince Becca that we would not be visiting his apartment, despite her argument that, if the key we found in the garden didn't open the door, I could use the one in my purse. Instead, I compromised by agreeing to visit the office, which is closed on Sundays, and trying the key there. If it doesn't work, it proves that her "instincts" about Graham being a sex predator and/or a creeper are off, and we can move on to plan B, which is yet to be determined.

Brampton MedSupplies occupies the third and fourth floors of a tan-colored office building on the western edge of town. It's across the street from a series of box stores and surrounded by similarly generic shops and services. On a Sunday, the building is quiet, just a few cars on the first level of the underground parking garage. Almost immediately, we run into trouble when the elevator requires a key fob to open.

"Go ahead," I tell Becca, nodding at the mystery key clutched in her palm. "Prove Graham's a creeper."

She pivots and stomps her way up to street level, wearing a pair of my expensive leather boots and the freshly washed dark jeans and jacket she'd worn to accost me at the garden. When Becca's on a mission, she looks like a character in a TV show, blond hair gleaming in the sun, hips swaying as she makes her way to the revolving glass doors and waits impatiently for me to catch up. I'm breathing hard from the short trek from underground, and perhaps my nerves are getting a little unruly. I know Graham is a good person just like I know the key doesn't open his apartment or his office door or a secret sex-predator lair. But while Becca's instincts are bullshit, her ability to manipulate situations isn't. If she says she's going to find something today, she's going to find something. It's just a matter of what she can invent on a whim and what I can do to mitigate the damage.

We step into a nondescript lobby with a list of businesses on a pillar in the center, a security desk on the left, and a bronze elevator bank on the right. The guard does a double take when Becca enters, and though we've met a dozen times before, he doesn't even glance at me, following my sister's progress to the list of names and openly admiring her ass.

I stand next to her. "They're on the third and fourth floors."

"I can read, Carrie." She stalks toward the elevators and jabs the UP arrow with her thumb.

"You got an appointment?" the guard calls, remembering his job description.

Becca turns as though just now realizing he was there. "Yes," she says. "Lotus Massage. In five minutes. Do I need to sign in?"

He grunts and drops a notepad onto the desk. "Yeah." To me he adds, "What about you?"

I was entirely expecting to be recognized on this visit and had brought Graham a tiny trophy as my cover, preparing to say I wanted to leave it on his desk as a congratulations for participating in the golf tournament. Now I open my mouth to remind the guard we've met—multiple times—but Becca jumps in.

"She's my nurse," she says, crossing to the desk and scribbling something I'm sure is not her name. "Can't you tell from her outfit?"

Both the guard and I study my outfit of loose linen

pants and a comfy gray T-shirt—perfect for afternoon office break-ins with back-from-the-dead sisters. Unlike Becca, I'd dressed to be forgotten, but it seems I needn't have bothered.

"Sure, yeah." He takes back the book and nods the okay for us to proceed.

"Told you that shirt looks like pajamas," Becca says under her breath as we walk back to the elevators and she presses the button again.

"It's Egyptian cotton. It was expensive."

"If you say so."

There's a *ding*, and the doors glide open. Becca keeps her head ducked as we step into the car, so I do the same in case someone later has the bright idea to review the security footage. Becca presses the button for the massage parlor on the sixth floor, where we get off and take the stairs down to level four, her heels—my heels—advertising our whereabouts to anyone who might be wondering. When we emerge in front of the locked glass doors for Brampton MedSupplies, the floor is dim and deserted. Light spills in through the large windows on the exterior of the building, bouncing off an empty reception desk and boardroom table and otherwise confirming the office is unoccupied.

"You're sure Graham's office is on this floor?" Becca asks, retrieving the key from her pocket.

"Of course I'm sure. He's in the far corner."

She tries to insert the key into the lock, but it doesn't

go in more than a millimeter. "Huh," she says, sounding genuinely perplexed.

"Don't you dare break the glass," I say, when she lifts her foot.

"I wasn't going to."

"I told you the key wasn't Graham's. Now, let's go."

"Stop being such a quitter. We just got here."

"And we can't get in. Game over."

She shoots me a disdainful look and whirls on her heel—my heel—and stalks down a short hallway with a sign for restrooms. A handful of doors are marked with images for the men's and women's bathrooms, a storage closet, another stairwell, and an electrical room.

Becca tries each door, but only the bathrooms and stairwell are accessible. She peers into the men's room with some interest before shouldering open the women's door. "Aha," she says.

I don't bother trying to sound intrigued. "What?"

"That." She clicks her tongue and indicates a grate in the wall above the sinks, a couple inches below the ceiling.

"An air vent? What is this, *Mission: Impossible?*"

"It is with that attitude. Here. Help me up." She steps out of the boots and clambers gracelessly onto the counter in her socked feet. Standing on her toes, she uses her fingertips to pry at the edge of the vent cover until it pops loose, dust raining on our heads. We cough and sputter, waving hands in front of our faces until we can breathe again.

"Carrie," Becca says irritably, "help me."

"I'm standing here. What more can I do?"

"I can't reach the vent from here, so boost me up."

Becca's standing on a three-foot-high counter. The best I can do is push at her calves.

"That's not possible."

"You're too negative." She shifts to the end of the counter so the spot between the two sinks is free. "Climb up here and crouch like a table. I'll stand on your back."

"You don't even know where the vent leads or how big it is."

"If you would help me, I could look. Now, hurry up. My massage is only an hour, and you've wasted, like, forty-five minutes."

"It's been ten minutes."

"Whatever. Hurry."

I contemplate the vent, barely larger than a coffin that would perfectly contain Becca's body. It's as wide as her shoulders and maybe eighteen inches tall. It probably goes in a couple feet then turns, making it impossible for her to wiggle through heroically like she's imagining. If I don't help her realize it's impossible, I'll have to spend the rest of the day listening to her whine and plotting a return visit by herself during business hours.

"Fine," I mutter, hoisting myself onto the counter. My feet dip into one sink and the motion-sensor faucet turns on, blasting my ankle with lukewarm water. I curse and readjust and then get on all fours, Becca stepping on my back before I'm properly in position and nearly knocking my head into the opposite tap.

"Just as I expected," she says, her voice echoing as it disappears into the vent. "An access point."

"It is not."

"Is too. It goes straight ahead, and I can see a light from the room below. I bet it's Graham's office."

"I bet it's not." My retort is cut short when she jumps off my back and launches herself into the vent. I torque my neck to see her legs dangling out of the opening, her torso vanished.

"Help me," she says, her voice muffled. She kicks her feet, either to propel herself forward or to try to kick me in the head or both.

I dodge the flailing limbs and stand, wedging her into the vent, wondering how long it would take for her to smother in there and how much longer for someone to find her body. And how far I could get before that happened.

But Becca doesn't get stuck, because she's Becca and evil, impossible things are her forte. Slowly her thighs, then her knees, her shins, and eventually her toes disappear into the vent, and I hear her muttered progress as she makes her way through, a smug cackle ringing out when she presumably reaches the "access point."

"I'm looking at the reception desk," she calls back. "I'm going in. Meet me at the front door."

"How are you going to get down…" My voice trails

off as I realize I'm wasting an opportunity. I quickly hop off the counter, grab the boots, and dart down the hall back to the glass doors just in time to see Becca land in a crumpled pile on the floor inside Brampton MedSupplies. She hastily springs to her feet and tosses back her hair, wiping at a gray smudge on her forehead and pretending she'd stuck the landing while I try to keep a straight face. If she sees me laugh, she won't let me in.

"Good job," I say, which motivates her to unlock the door. I step inside, the office stuffy and uncomfortable because the air-conditioning is turned off on weekends. The receptionist left a paperback splayed open on her desk, ready to resume reading tomorrow. Other unoccupied desks are home to framed photos of people's kids, lunch bags, umbrellas—all the signs of people leading a nice, sane, normal life, the one I so desperately want.

The offices have glass walls, enabling us to peer inside without entering, but we pass a couple of locked doors on the way to Graham's corner. Becca tries the mystery key but has no luck, vowing with each failed turn that it's going to open something in Graham's office, just wait. A photocopier hums to life and we jump, peering into the niche in the wall that houses the machine, which does nothing more than coolly judge us.

"This isn't the place," I whisper. "Let's just go."

"We're too close to give up," Becca replies, zeroing in on Graham's door up ahead, his bronze nameplate gleaming in the sunlight. She hurries down the hall, and

I follow more slowly, my feet dragging. This is a huge violation of Graham's privacy, his trust. I've violated far more people's lives in far worse ways, all in the name of appeasing or assisting my sister, and resentment simmers as I enter the office behind her. She's already rifling through his desk drawers.

"Don't make a mess," I warn. "There are cameras in here. If anyone has reason to check, they'll see us."

"They'll only recognize you."

"Graham would recognize you. And so would Greaves."

She huffs but handles the paper clips with slightly more care.

I turn to study the room, the walls featuring artwork that looks generic but that I know Graham personally selected. He likes bucolic landscapes—rolling green pastures and sloping mountains, a tiny house nestled by a lake. He wants a life of peace and quiet, and I want that, too. It's why I'm here, I remind myself. Once we rule out Graham as the X at the end of Fiona's scavenger hunt, we can turn our attention to the lock that actually fits the key and put an end to things once and for all.

"Huh," Becca says after a moment.

"What?"

She looks perplexed. "It's like he's here."

"What? Who?"

"Graham. He's here, messing with me. Just when I thought he couldn't be any more boring, I find…this." She holds up a Rubik's Cube.

"So he likes puzzles. It means he's smart."

She lifts her other hand to reveal an adult coloring book with an outer space theme.

"And...creative," I add lamely, since I didn't know he was quite so, well, lame.

Becca snorts and drops the items back into the drawer, gives the office a derisive once-over, and heads for the door. "I'm going to look around. I know this key opens something."

"All keys open something," I counter. "Just nothing in this office."

She snatches the boots from my hand and trots out as I head to the desk, tidying the mess she'd made despite my warning. There's a framed picture of me and Graham next to his computer monitor, my head on his shoulder, us beaming for the camera on a weekend getaway to a sleepy beach town. Next to it is a second copy of the PTSD book he keeps on his nightstand. I check the door, but Becca's nowhere in sight. I know I told her not to damage anything, but if these windows actually opened, I'd hurl the book out.

I squash the urge and tuck the Rubik's Cube back into his drawer, straightening the pens and business cards around it. Then I stop. Poking out from beneath a protein bar is a slightly wrinkled business card, white with black text and an all-too-familiar logo at the top. The Brampton Police Department. Using the edge of my nail, I tug it out, heart thumping when I see one of the names I loathe

most stamped in the center in capital letters: DETECTIVE
MARLON GREAVES. I have two of his cards at home.

It's okay, I tell myself. *They've met. It's normal that he'd
have Greaves's card.* Still, I locate the stack of business
cards wrapped in a rubber band in the back of the drawer.
Graham collects them from basically everyone he meets,
cheerfully announcing that you never know who'll need
to buy medical supplies and they never know they need
to buy them from him until he tells them.

I remove the elastic and fan out the cards, of which
there must be at least a hundred. I zero in on the plain
white cards—lots of fellow salespeople, a few hospital
administrators, and pharmaceutical company names. But
there, in the mix, are two more cards from Greaves.
On their own, they're just three boring cards, something
Greaves probably passes out to everyone he meets, cheerfully hunting for but never finding murderers. Still, I've
seen them talking a handful of times over the course of
our unfortunate acquaintance and never once have I seen
them exchange cards.

I hear footsteps in the hall and shove the bundle of
cards back together with shaking hands. *It doesn't mean
anything*, I tell myself, yanking out the third card after
I mistakenly group it with the rest, the paper slipping
through my fingers. *You're overreacting.*

The card lands facedown on the desk, and on the back
is a series of initials written in Graham's impossibly tiny
handwriting. There are at least thirty initials on it, some

with two letters, some three, some four. All but one set is scratched out. *B.S.S.* It's circled in red.

My heart rate manages to skyrocket even more, and I grip the edge of the desk for balance. It's probably nothing, I know. A medical company, a device, a person he met. He just used the card to make his notes because it was handy. But it's small, and the ink is various shades of black and blue, suggesting he didn't write this all at once. He was working on something. But what? And why with Greaves's card? And why does he have so many?

I hastily flip through the stack of cards, but only two others have anything written on the back, both personal email addresses that match the names of the sales reps on the front. The other two cards from Greaves are bare.

The footsteps get louder, and I jump when Becca calls out from down the hall. "Carrie?"

She'll gloat relentlessly if she sees the card, if she thinks there's a chance in hell her little plan was successful, if Graham is indeed a sex predator or a creeper. Those are the things I should be fearing far more than three little letters, but they're not. I've learned the hard way that there's no such thing as a coincidence.

I toss the bundle of cards back in the drawer and stuff the annotated one into my pocket just as Becca appears in the doorway, eyebrows tugged together. She grips the frame and slumps against it. "Oh good," she says, tossing her head back dramatically. "You're alive. I thought you might have died of boredom."

"Ha ha," I say, my voice a little too high as I follow her out of the room. "Did you find anything?"

She sounds disappointed. "No. If he's up to something shady, he's not doing it at work."

"Told you," I say, as the business card burns a hole in my pocket.

———

"Surprise!" Graham says, when he opens the door to his apartment.

Surprise, indeed. I'd gotten his call about us needing to talk and had driven over here straight after work on Monday, edgy and uncomfortable, trying to determine how best to explain why I'd helped my sister shimmy through an air vent so we could break into his office. And now I'm faced with…a puppy.

Cautiously, in case this is the meanest trick anyone's ever played on a person, I crouch to reach the dog's head, a small black-and-white creature with enormous brown eyes and huge ears. It darts toward my fingers before skittering back behind Graham's feet. I manage to graze the softest fur in the world with my fingertips before the puppy yips and vanishes into the apartment.

I straighten. "What's going on?"

"Don't be mad." Graham gestures me in and closes the door.

Since I was fully expecting him to be mad and perhaps

accompanied by Greaves, my bewilderment is sincere when I ask, "Mad about what?"

"It's not official, but...it could be."

I stare at the darkened bedroom into which the dog disappeared. "What?"

"The dog. Felix."

"You're getting a dog?"

"Could be," he repeats. "I mean, if you want to."

This is such a tonal shift from the mayhem I was expecting that I have to shake my head and grip the wall for support. "I, um...Wow."

The puppy returns, gnawing on Graham's toe while eyeballing me in what can only be described as a deliberate challenge. Graham scoops him up and nuzzles his head, planting a kiss on the little pink nose.

"Totally your call," he says. "My coworker's been fostering a pregnant dog, and she gave birth a few months ago. It's a Boston terrier, and they're small dogs, and the puppies are ready to be adopted out, and when she mentioned it, I just kind of heard myself say...'Maybe?'"

Now both Graham and the dog are giving me puppy dog eyes, neither of which are necessary because my heart's already melting. I dip my head, and the dog licks my chin.

"When you said you needed to talk..."

Graham stares at me patiently, as though he doesn't know how those conversations normally end.

"...I thought it might be bad," I finish.

He blinks. "Bad? What could be bad?"

He hands me the dog, soft and squirmy, and even though little black hairs immediately glue themselves to the front of my best white work blouse, I forget for a second how there could be a single bad thing in the world.

"Are you allowed to have dogs in this apartment?"

"Well, not technically. But it's just a tryout, so I spoke with the building manager and he agreed to three weeks."

"Who needs that long?" I kiss Felix's impossibly soft head. "Who even needs one minute?"

Graham's beaming. "So it's a yes?"

I smile, too. "Of course it is."

He looks giddy. "Let's take him for a walk. I think I left the harness in my bedroom. They gave me a whole bag of puppy stuff."

He disappears to grab it, and I spot his phone on the kitchen counter. Without overthinking it, I swipe my thumb across the screen, punch in the password, and check his recent calls, scanning for anyone or anything that could be *B.S.S.* Nothing.

Sounds from the bedroom suggest he's still searching, so I navigate to his contacts and scroll down to the *B*s. There's a Bob Smith, whose details list him as an administrator at an urgent care clinic in the next town over, but no one that sounds suspicious.

"Found it," Graham calls. "And I should tell you that when I say 'walk,' he doesn't exactly…walk."

I turn over the phone and step back as he returns with a tiny harness and somehow manages to wrangle Felix's squirming body into the contraption before carrying him to the door. "We'll have to amp up our house-hunting efforts," he says as we leave the apartment and get in the elevator.

"And get a better real estate agent," I reply.

Graham laughs like I'm joking, and we exit into the lobby and step outside into the sunshine. "I can work from home for the next few days," he offers, setting Felix down. "Then you can keep him at your place once our three weeks are up. And hopefully not long after that, we'll move into a home together, the three of us."

I almost trip over my feet as reality comes crashing down. The reason we never had pets growing up was unspoken but understood: Becca was dangerous. And now she has keys to my house, no matter how many times I take them away. I don't think she'd murder Felix for fun, but as long as she's my secret roommate, he'd be something for her to threaten me with, and after five months sans serial killer, I'm not ready to be under her thumb again.

My nod is unconvincing, and it doesn't escape Graham's notice.

"What's wrong?"

"Nothing. I mean…I already love him," I admit. "I just don't know about shuffling him between our homes. And with work…"

"We've got three whole weeks."

I give him a look, and Graham returns it with a sheepish smile. Three weeks to figure out what Fiona's mystery key opens and to determine if Graham's annotated business card is something awful or totally inane.

"I'll keep him until then," Graham says, bending to scratch Felix's head. The puppy gazes at him adoringly and then promptly gets distracted by a blade of grass. "And if it's not the right time, I'll give him back. We'll wait until we find our dream home to expand our family."

I blink back tears. Everything he's saying—house, dog, family—is all the stuff I want, and with Becca out of the picture, I'd almost started to believe I could have it. But her return is the sword dangling over my head by a thread. She could snap at any minute, and the whole dream could be destroyed. The reminder recalls my actual mission tonight. Before spotting Felix, I'd been trying to determine how best to bring up the business card.

"Did Detective Greaves give you this pet idea?"

Graham looks startled. "What? No, you and I had been talking about—"

"Just because he walks his dog by my place quite a bit, and I saw you two talking yesterday."

"Oh. I mean, subconsciously, maybe? But no, I don't think so. That was just a coincidence."

"Do you see him a lot?"

We've reached a fenced-in little dog park that's

curiously empty on a cool spring evening. Stepping inside, we close the gate, and Graham takes Felix off his leash. The puppy immediately sits down.

"Now and then," Graham answers, retrieving a little ball from his pocket and waving it for Felix before tossing it into the grass. The dog doesn't move.

"Has he ever given you a business card?"

"Yeah, all the time. They must get paid for each one they hand out."

I laugh and relax slightly. "So you two...talk?"

He picks up the ball and shows it to Felix, who sniffs.

"Small talk, I guess. Why are you asking?"

"No reason. I just didn't realize you guys were friendly."

He scoffs and tosses the ball. This time Felix bounds after it, promptly losing focus and rolling in the grass. "*Friendly*'s not the word," Graham says, an odd note in his voice.

"Then what is?"

He gives me a strange look. "He's the detective who hasn't found your sister. He's the guy you talked to when you were afraid but who didn't actually prevent Footloose from kidnapping you. He's someone who's still following you around town, wasting his time chasing dead ends when he could be doing literally anything better. I guess he's just...human."

Human. The worst insult Graham can come up with. We walk to the middle of the park, and I scoop up the ball, shaking it to get Felix's attention.

Graham shrugs. "I don't know. It's not like I've given this a lot of thought."

"Okay."

"Though he did ask me about Becca a few times."

I freeze, recalling how Becca said Greaves had asked Nikk about her, too. I force myself to throw the ball. "Like, if you happen to know where she is?"

He laughs. "Like, how long have I known her, have I ever met her boyfriends, friends, coworkers, etcetera."

I'd answered those questions, too. No boyfriend at the time of her disappearance; the only "friend" I knew of was Nikk; she worked at the jewelry store, but I didn't know the names of her (living) coworkers. After I'd helped carry Shanna's body up a mountain and watched Becca dump it off a cliff, I didn't want to know any other names.

"What'd you tell him?"

"That I didn't know who he could talk to. The strange thing is that he didn't seem to want to know her current circle of friends or people he could meet with now. He wanted to know about her past."

My palms are sweaty, my voice weak. "Why would that matter?"

"I don't know. I told him I met Becca through you and don't know much about her past. I didn't even know if you guys had pets growing up, remember?"

I force a laugh. "Right."

"Did she have a lot of friends before? In high school?"

"Yeah," I lie. "Beautiful people always do." Though Becca didn't, not really. She had followers and minions, but no friends. No one who knew her the way I did. Or if they had the misfortune of really getting to know her, they didn't survive it.

"Maybe that's why he was asking," Graham suggests. "Did anything happen when you were in high school?"

"Not that I recall. It was a long time ago."

Graham hesitates before smiling and crouching to scoop up Felix. "It's probably nothing," he says, nuzzling the puppy with his nose.

I force a smile of my own. "Right," I echo. "Nothing."

CHAPTER 12

Becca has decided she needs a disguise.

"I don't see why you can't just announce your miraculous return." I sigh at the stack of packages that have accumulated in my living room all week and the inevitable credit card charges that will follow them. The curtains are drawn, and Becca's standing in a pair of boy shorts and a tank top, modeling her various new ensembles as a spring rain flings itself at the windows. This is how I'm spending my Friday night.

"I already told you," she replies, fiddling with a short orange wig that makes her look like an extra in an elementary school play.

"Think of the attention you'd get for surviving Footloose. The newspapers, radio, Channel 6. Greaves might even have to…apologize." I'm dangling the best bait I have, and Becca chews on her cheek as she mulls it over.

"No," she says finally. "That's a terrible idea. Until we know what Greaves is really up to, he can't know I survived."

"But he knows nothing about you or your…proclivities. He's just nosy."

"Who says *proclivities?* Is that even a real word?" She bumps the tower of boxes with her hip, and they tumble to the floor, knocking over my favorite lamp. I snag it before it meets an untimely demise. Nothing in this house is safe as long as Becca's in the picture. Not me, not Graham, not Felix. Certainly not anything as tenuous as hopes and dreams.

"I like this," she says, planting her hands on her hips and now modeling a long black gown that has no business in Brampton. She turns to admire herself in the full-length mirror she'd carted down from the guest room. "It's glamorous."

"I thought the point of a disguise was not to stand out."

"The point of a disguise is not to be recognized. Not to go unnoticed. That's only easy for some people."

I roll my eyes.

"Besides," she continues, "hiding in your house is boring. Just staying home and watching TV all night…It's like I'm you." She shudders in revulsion. "Plus, if we're going to figure out what that key opens, I need to be able to move around freely."

"How have you been getting around for the past five months?"

"I wasn't for the first two. My leg was very broken. Then I was on crutches for the next three months. And now I'm perfect."

I bite my tongue. I wondered if she was going to deny having a limp, and I know better than to mention it.

She adds a gaudy fake diamond necklace to her ensemble before sitting on the couch kitty-corner to me and thumping her feet up onto my coffee table. "So," she says. "The key." It's sitting in its bag next to her left foot, and we both stare at it. "If it's not pervy Graham, then what does it lead to?"

"What if it's nothing?" I try, knowing it's a bad idea but saying it anyway. "What if it's totally unrelated to me and we're wasting time and energy on a wild-goose chase? Or a scavenger hunt that leads nowhere interesting?"

Becca sits up and gapes at me. "Not related to you?" she echoes. "Are you stupid? The clue basically said, 'Carrie, this is for you.'"

"No, it didn't."

"I don't know what went on between you and Felicia—"

"I told you: I rescued her, and then she left town."

Now Becca rolls her eyes. "—but no one leaves a clue when they could just be, y'know, around to tell the secret."

"She's a stupid teenager. It was all over the news. She got in trouble all the time, and this is just a way to waste resources so we're not looking for her in California or wherever she went."

"Tell me where the body is."

I feel paralyzed for a second, but I'd been preparing to field this question since the night I pushed Fiona off a cliff, and the answer comes automatically, if not entirely convincingly. "I don't know where she is. But she's not a body. She's a person."

Becca stares at me, her gaze piercing my soul, like she can see its darkest parts. "Huh" is what she settles on. "You don't have to tell me now, but I know there was more to your relationship. Why else would she leave a clue about you?"

"For the last time, the clue wasn't about—"

She lets out a frustrated scream that startles me into silence and then snatches up her phone from the table, stabs at the screen, and holds it out for me to see a picture of Fiona's note.

JUST IN CASEx

I lift my hands. "So?"

Using a manicured nail, she taps at the gold line that leads from the top of the page and wiggles its way down to the x. "Are you really this dumb?"

"Apparently, Becca. I mean, I'm only the person who figured out what the 'case' was and deduced the key was at the community garden. I must be an idiot."

"It's a map, you moron!" She flicks the screen. "Ugh. I wish I'd printed this on translucent paper and then gotten a copy of a map of Brampton. It would have been so impactful."

"What?"

"This wiggly line? It's the exact route from the McBride house to yours."

I frown. "How could you—"

"You followed it in the reverse, from your place to hers. But the real X is right here at the top. You're X."

I take the phone and stare at the line I'd considered arbitrary and amateur, like Fiona. I've made the drive between here and the McBride home enough times that I'm able to recognize the curves and turns as the shortest route between the two destinations. The clue itself, as I'd discovered, led to the suitcase, which led to the lavender, which led to the mystery key she'd found and which we now hold. But as a backup plan, *in case* no one figured out the clue, she'd also left a glittering arrow that points directly to me. She knew I was guilty of something but not how bad that something could be.

"You think the key opens something in my house?"

Becca shakes her head. "Nope. I already tried."

"Then what's the point of this?"

"The point is she didn't know what the key was for, but she was worried about you and figured the two were connected."

"Well, they're not. The only thing Fiona and I had in common was Footloose, and his murder cabin burned to the ground. If the key opened something there, it's too late."

"As usual, you're asking the wrong question," Becca says.

I groan. "Then what is the right question, Becca?"

"Where'd she get the key?"

For a second, I falter. That's actually a pretty good question. The key could only have value—and a connection to me, a significant connection—if it came from somewhere interesting. The only places Fiona and I had ever overlapped, either together or individually, were her house, my house when she tried to extort me, Footloose's cabin, and Barr Lode Trail, where I killed her. We can eliminate Barr Lode as a possibility because she left the key before she came to meet me and I'll deny that night until I die.

I tell Becca about our three shared spaces, omitting Barr Lode from the narrative.

"Seems unlikely it's her own house," Becca muses, "since the map sends people in two directions: one to her house and the other to yours. If the suitcase was X, that clue is already solved."

"And I really don't think it's anything here. I don't have any hidden rooms or safe deposit boxes."

"Yep," Becca agrees. "You're as boring as I feared. That just leaves Footloose's cabin. Do you think you could find it again?"

"No, it burned down, and it was late, and I was afraid—"

"Yeah, yeah. I know what you told the police. Do you think you could find it?"

"No," I say firmly and because it's the truth. I have a vague recollection of approximately where we emerged onto the highway, but first I'd navigated my way along a roughly hewn trail through the forest and down a logging road. Plus, I really don't want to go back.

"It doesn't make sense that the key would belong to the cabin, anyway," I insist. "That place was a secret. Why would he lock the door?"

Becca mulls that over. "Okay. That's not terrible logic. Tell me again about how you found Frances. Could she have stolen a key from him?"

I shrug. "I mean, maybe. But if she did, she didn't mention it to me."

"And the only entrance to the cellar was the door you found?"

"Yeah. It was just a hole in the ground. I looked inside after Fiona got out, and it was empty." I stiffen. "Wait."

"What?"

"Your coat was in there."

"My favorite yellow one?"

"Yes. Fiona said she complained she was cold, and he threw it down there. What if the key came from your pocket?"

Becca picks up the plastic bag and studies the key. "I don't recognize it," she says. "And even if I did, you let them evict me and then threw away all my stuff. You saw for yourself: There was nothing incriminating in there. If this key was from me—and I don't think it was, because all mine were with my car keys, which you also threw away—then it leads nowhere important."

I sigh. If I hadn't personally searched Becca's entire apartment, I wouldn't believe there wasn't some evidence of her countless crimes in there. That's why I spent a weekend going through the place before calling a junk removal company.

"Unless…" Becca squints at the key.

"What?"

"It's dirty."

"So?"

"So what if she found it in the cellar? Like, maybe Footloose dropped it?"

"It doesn't matter. The cabin burned down—"

"You told me about that place. It was just a bunch of awful rooms. It wasn't a home. He had to sleep somewhere, right?"

My skin flushes hot and cold, and I think I'm going to pass out. Memories of my "date" with Footloose flash through my mind, mingling horribly with snapshots of my return visit, exploring his house—his safe suburban home—and seeing where he ate, slept, lived. Planned.

He had the cabin, where he brought people to torture them. But he also had a house, not too far from here, that looks perfectly normal to anyone who doesn't know what a serial killer looks like.

Becca's leaning forward, eyes drilling into mine. "You know something."

I rub my face. "I…I don't—"

"Tell me," she says. "We find what the key opens, and this whole thing goes away."

I prop my elbows on my knees, dizzy with fear. I'm already in a house with a serial killer, but the prospect of heading to a second location with her is making me nauseous.

"Carrie," she whispers. She covers my hand with her icy fingers and gives me goose bumps. "You can tell me. I'm your sister."

———

Forty-five Poplar Street looks much the same as it does in my frequent nightmares: a benign yellow two-story home with white shutters and neatly trimmed hedges lining the front. Unlike during my break-and-enter visit last December, the wreath on the door is gone, as are the Christmas lights that decorated the roofline. So is the silver SUV. What's new is the FOR SALE sign staked in the front yard with half a dozen metallic balloons floating above it, flashing in the sun.

I'd insisted we do a daylight drive-by instead of another midnight burglary. With the possibility of the clue belonging to Footloose being our only lead, I'd lied and told Becca that, before the cabin burned down, I'd snagged his wallet and learned his name and address. If I tell her he'd brought me here for date night, I'll never hear the end of it.

"It's for sale?" Becca presses her face to the window in the back seat and points out the obvious. If her "disguise" of short, curly dark hair and bright-pink muumuu wasn't noticeable enough, her staring is.

My heart thuds against my ribs as I stop the car across the street and stare, too. Because Footloose died in his murder cabin, the one I burned down and the one the police can't locate, no one has ever learned his true identity, except me. I'd kept that information to myself in case he, like Fiona, had had the genius idea of leaving something behind to incriminate me in his absence. Since then, I'd limited myself to one secret internet search a week to see if the disappearance of Daniel Nilssen, aka Footloose, had been noticed or reported, but I'd found nothing. Until now.

"I wonder how much it is," Becca says thoughtfully. "I need a place."

"What are you doing?" I demand when she climbs out of the car and picks her way across the street in too-high heels. She ignores me and approaches the sign, which has a little pocket for sales pamphlets. Taking far more than her share, she hobbles back and tosses a handful into the front seat where they scatter over my lap and slide to the floor. I ignore the mess and gape at the brochures. Real estate agent extraordinaire Misha Collins beams at me from the front pages.

In the back seat, Becca cackles. "Well, we're definitely on the right path. There's an open house in half an hour. It's a sign from God."

If there is a god, he's only giving one sign, and it only involves one finger.

"We're not going to an open house."

"You're the one who wanted to come in the afternoon. I said we should come in the middle of the night like normal burglars, but you had other plans."

I'd actually been under the naive impression that the light of day would tame Becca's more insane impulses and let me come up with a better plan for returning to the home of a dead serial killer, but it turns out she's insane no matter what time it is.

"The plan is just to scope it out," I say. "And then formulate a plan."

"'Formulate a plan,'" Becca mimics. "Who needs a plan when Misha Collins is about to arrive, open the door, and give us a tour? You should be ecstatic. This way our biggest crime is being lookie-loos."

That's decent logic, but Becca doesn't know I know Misha from my own house-hunting ventures, and the further away I can keep my 'Becca life' from my ideal life, the better.

"We can come back tonight," I say, knowing that'll appease her. "In a different disguise. Your pink muumuu is too memorable. If anyone reports our break-in, we don't want the real estate agent providing a description of people who visited the open house."

Becca harrumphs. "Fine. But I'm hungry. I want sushi."

"I'll take you to a gas station, and you can get some."

She laughs, and we both squeak when a loud knock sounds on the driver's side window. I turn in horror to see Misha grinning at me.

"Carrie!" she exclaims, delightfully oblivious. "Hi! I didn't know you and Grant were considering this neighborhood!"

"What the fuck?" Becca sounds intrigued.

I roll down the window. "Misha. Hi. Um, yeah. Yes. We are. Sort of. Graham's working, so I'm just here with my...friend."

Instead of simply waving like a normal person, Becca wedges herself halfway through the front seats and extends a hand to Misha to shake like a wealthy widow. "Diana Speedwell," she says. "Pleasure."

Misha's smile never wavers because Diana Speedwell is wearing a fake diamond necklace and could potentially buy a house today. She reaches in front of me and shakes Becca's hand, the giant butterfly ring on her finger scratching my chin.

"Why don't you two come in, and I'll give you the early bird tour?" Misha suggests. "The open house isn't for another thirty minutes, but you must be excited if you got here early!"

"Totally!" Becca chirps, hopping out of the car.

I grip the steering wheel and order myself not to scream in frustration. Plastering on a smile, I grab my purse and follow them across the street to Footloose's house. "Has this place been on the market long?"

Misha carries an enormous tote bag and digs inside until she locates a ring of keys. "Just a week. It's a foreclosure," she adds in a whisper. "The homeowner stopped making payments, and neighbors hadn't seen him since the holidays. He'd had a difficult life, so they think he just skipped town. Or worse."

Becca perks up. "Worse?"

"*Suicide*." Misha gets the door open and gestures us inside. My stomach lurches, and my knees go weak, and I have to grip the handrail to propel myself through the door.

Becca nods sagely. "The holidays are a difficult time for many people."

When I'd come here by myself, it had been dark and cold, and I'd entered through the back. Now, with the front curtains open and the house smelling like it's been freshly cleaned, it's a completely different experience. There are still basic furniture pieces, but anything personal is gone, just a vase of fresh flowers on the coffee table and a single pink pillow on the couch.

"Has this been professionally staged?" I ask. If they'd already cleared the house of Footloose's personal belongings and the key in my purse unlocks one of those items, then that item is likely buried beneath ten tons of trash in the Brampton dump and as good as gone. Mystery finished.

"Nope," Misha says cheerfully. "They're still trying to see if he has any extended family, so we paid to have the personal stuff boxed up and stored in the basement. We kept the furnishings because they were in pretty great shape."

"I'd say," Becca agrees, turning the knob on a door that looks like it should be a coat closet but leads to the lower level in which I'd watched Footloose's home torture movies. "Oh! Is this the basement?"

"Yep. People think it's a coat closet, but homes this age tend not to have them at the front of the house. There's a small mudroom at the back. Come take a look."

Becca winks at me before tottering after Misha down the hall, and I stare at the gaping door to the basement, swinging slightly on its hinges like it's calling me in for a third time. I resist the urge to run back to my car and leave Becca to handle this nightmare, and follow them to the kitchen and dining nook. They had gotten rid of personal items like books and photographs, but the kitchen still has a dish rack on the counter, a knife block, and a gleaming silver pot on the stove like Footloose might return any minute to boil pasta.

Another vase of fresh flowers sits on the table, not unlike the McBride home. All the signs of good and normal, when the truth is, nothing is normal. There's a serial killer in disguise in the home of a second serial killer whom I killed, and Misha's telling us that the roof was replaced two years ago and Becca's asking if it's a good school district.

"The house is walking distance to one of the best

schools in Brampton," Misha tells us, grabbing a plate from the cupboard and pulling a box of cookies from her extremely overstuffed tote, dumping them on the plate. A pair of pantyhose falls out, and she hastily scoops them up and crams them back in her bag before extending the plate of cookies in my direction.

I stare at it like it's about to morph into the shape of Footloose and scream, "You killed me!"

"Carrie?" I hear, shaking my head and forcing myself back to the present, where Misha's looking at me expectantly. "Would you like a cookie?"

The last thing I want is food, but she's holding out the plate and Becca's eating one, so I take an oatmeal raisin and thank her.

"Anything for a friend!" she trills. "Shall we check out the bedrooms? The homeowner updated the bathroom a year ago, so it's very nice. And all the original fixtures have been well maintained, so there's a beautiful blend of classic and modern."

"Classic's just a nice way of saying old," Becca informs her.

Misha falters at the base of the stairs. "Oh, well, I mean..."

"But I love old things!" Becca lies. "They have so much history. Houses from this period—were they known for having any...secrets?"

"Secrets?"

"You know. Nooks and crannies. Hidden panels."

Misha blinks, her blue eyes guileless. "Oh. Well, none that I know of. But then I guess it wouldn't be a very good secret if I knew, would it? Now, be careful on the stairs, Diana. They're a little uneven, and your limp might make things difficult."

She giggles as we follow her up, but she wouldn't be laughing if she saw the look on Becca's face.

CHAPTER 13

To keep myself from obsessing over the growing tally of crimes I've committed and the one I intend to commit in a few hours, I spend the evening trying to decipher the *B.S.S.* on the back of the business card I stole from Graham.

Google is either no help or too helpful, depending on how you look at it. Secondary schools, science degrees, and vague "support systems" dominate the first ten pages of results. The schools are a nice, innocent option since Graham's openly discussed our future and having a family, and our house hunt has included the consideration of being in a good school district. He has a degree in geography and has never mentioned returning to college, so I rule out science degrees. *Support systems* appears to mean companies that offer IT solutions, but Graham doesn't work in IT and, to the best of my knowledge, has no use for that particular type of support.

I narrow the search by specifying *Brampton B.S.*, which brings up six pages of message boards dominated by teens grumbling about how much they hate Brampton and how life here is bullshit. I skim through the comments, but they're the usual litany of complaints about how there's nothing fun to do in this town and how it has too many murders. I stop when I reach a message board named *Brampton B.S.—Missing People & Unsolved Mysteries*, run by none other than a user named EmmettBKS.

I click the link and wait for the page to load. The top post is a collage of photos of all of Brampton's missing persons from the past fifty years in chronological order. At the top of the list are Fiona McBride and Lilly Fiennes.

There's a thump from upstairs, and I quickly slap the laptop shut and stuff the business card in my pocket. I haven't told Becca about *B.S.S.*, and I don't intend to. The less she obsesses over Graham, the safer it is for him.

After a minute, I hear the toilet flush, and the floor groans as Becca shuffles back to her room and slams the door. Just to be safe, I sneak out of the kitchen and peer up the stairs, but she's not creeping down, trying to catch me in any illicit act.

Returning to my computer, I revisit the forum and scroll through the comments, searching for any from Graham. The posts all relate to the Brampton PD's failed investigations into the cases, many of which have gone cold, with a much-repeated chorus of how Footloose managed to hunt in Brampton and the surrounding towns for a decade, burying bodies in our local park without the police ever catching whiff of a crime.

I do a search for Graham's name, but nothing comes up, and no posts read like they might be from him. A search for my own name brings up nothing, and a search for *Becca Lawrence* generates three results, but they're just mentions on lists of missing people.

I leave the message boards and visit the local business directory website. It doesn't let me search alphabetically, only by business name and location, so I try *BSS Brampton* and score zero exact matches. There's BS Johnson Notary, BS Dental, BS Automotive Repair & Windshield Replacement, but no BSS. I try searching without the *B*, in case *B* does indeed stand for Brampton, but *SS* generates a similar variety of results that have no meaning without proper context.

Scanning the back of the card, I look for the most unusual set of initials in case I'm able to determine a theme. I settle on *W.I.S.* and type it in, watching the results populate. There are just two pages of results, but again, a huge variety of options. Welling Income Strategies, Westside Industrial Storage, Winks Information Source, Women's It Styling.

I click on them in order, hoping against hope that

one will sound familiar or ring a bell. Maybe Graham mentioned it in conversation, something totally innocuous that makes perfect, harmless sense.

Welling Income Strategies is exactly what it sounds like, an investment management firm that promises to improve your rate of return or your money back! Westside Industrial Storage lives up to its name, a facility on the west side of town that offers storage units for large items. Mainly tractors, if the photos on the home page are any indication. Winks Information Source is a now-defunct local website that thought it was a good idea to compete with other search engines, and Women's It Styling is a personal shopper service that guarantees to make you the next "it girl" at school, work, or in the world and uses a blurry image of Kim Kardashian to inspire us.

I sigh and prepare to click the next link—Wonder Indonesian Spa—when Becca stumbles into the kitchen, rubbing her eyes and wearing the Diana Speedwell wig. I snap the laptop shut, and she smirks.

"You don't have to hide your porn habit from me," she says, opening the fridge and gulping down half a carton of chocolate milk without bothering to use a glass. "'Google, show me dirty pictures of people kissing with their mouths closed!'"

"You got me," I say, reopening the laptop and quickly clearing my search history.

Snagging a bag of chips from the cupboard, Becca

munches them by the handful while gazing contempla-
tively into the backyard. "How many boxes of Footloose's
stuff do you think there are to go through?"

"No idea. A lot, I imagine."

"Well, how many boxes of my stuff were there?"

"I don't know. I used garbage bags and lighter fluid."

She glares at me. "Did you keep anything? To remember me by?"

I drum my fingers on the table. "I took back my
Michael Kors heels, the ones you swore you hadn't stolen.
And I found my gold necklace, the one with the pearls.
And strangely, I stumbled across the card Graham had
given me for our first anniversary, the one you said I must
have recycled after vomiting on it."

"You're a jerk. Let's go break into a house."

"I don't need mementos, Becca. I have a lifetime of
beautiful memories."

She stares at me, and because she's a psychopath, I
know she can't tell if I'm being 100 percent sarcastic
or not. "You're welcome" is what she settles on before
heading to the front door and putting on sneakers. She's
changed out of Diana's pink muumuu and heels, her limp
less pronounced with more practical footwear.

I follow and gesture to her face. "Are you planning to
go out like that?"

"With my head? Yes."

"With the wig."

"Of course I am. I'm also intending to wear sunglasses

and keep my head down while you drive your usual ten miles below the speed limit so anyone who later checks video of us crawling through the intersections can't see my face."

"But it's okay if they see mine?"

"It's your car, genius. I'm the one who's dead."

I'd already changed into an all-black ensemble similar to Becca's and now pull on a black wool hat before we head out to my car. We make the trip to Footloose's house in silence, Becca squinting at one of the listing pamphlets as I drive. True to her word, she keeps her head down, and because I'm now paranoid, I do my best to make sure my expression is completely innocent for anyone who may later review the footage.

"Pull in here," Becca says as we pass an all-night diner at the edge of Footloose's neighborhood. "Park next to the dumpster."

"What? Why?"

"Because it's out of sight of the security cameras at the front and we're walking the rest of the way. We don't need any neighborhood vigilantes noticing a strange car and memorizing the license plate."

"Is that how you—" I stop myself. I don't want to know how Becca's gotten away with murder for a decade.

The spring night is cool, and I shiver in my black hoodie as we make the ten-minute walk to the quaint little home that housed a serial killer and his sick delusions. The street is quiet, only a few windows glowing yellow at this hour. Becca checks the handful of cars parked at the curb, but they're empty. No witnesses.

"All right," she says, snagging a large rock from a garden two doors down and striding purposely toward the house. "Let's do this."

I grimace before pulling a key from my pocket. "We don't need the rock," I say. I still hadn't told her that not only did I remember my date at Footloose's house, but I'd kept the key I'd used to break in last time, and I don't know how I'm going to explain it now.

She glances back. "How else are we going to—" She spots the key in my hand. "Did you steal that from the real estate agent? Good job, Carrie."

"Um," I say. "Yes. Thanks."

She drops the rock, and I almost trip over it, scrambling to keep my balance. After one last covert look around, we slip along the side of the house and approach the back door, tugging on gloves and gearing up for more criminal mischief. I know Footloose is dead and the house is empty, but my hands still shake as I fit the key in the lock. The click of the tumbler turning sounds painfully loud in the quiet night, the faint whine of the door making the hairs on the back of my neck stand on end.

"Hurry up," Becca whispers. "I'm cold."

I reluctantly step inside, and she follows, closing the door behind us. The interior of the house is barely warmer than the exterior, the only light coming from what little manages to filter in through the living room curtains from the street. Becca insisted we leave our phones at home in case anyone ever had reason to check our whereabouts for tonight, so we can't use the flashlight app and I don't own any actual flashlights, so we have to wait until our eyes adjust to the darkness. I peer around the kitchen, the silence interrupted by the snick of metal sliding free of the knife block.

I whirl around to see Becca holding a large carving knife. "What are you doing?"

"We'll need it to cut the tape on the boxes."

It's not a bad answer, but it's still horrifying to see her creep stealthily through a dark house, giant knife in hand. She goes directly for the basement door, snapping on the bare bulb that dangles overhead to illuminate the unfinished stairwell. Footloose built a dining room down here, complete with fireplace and hidden panels for his video equipment, but the other half was still unfinished, and the smell of must and damp earth is strong.

My stomach lurches as I follow Becca down, the light not doing much to ease my nerves. Despite my vast experience, criminal enterprise is not my chosen profession, and I'm sweating profusely.

"Ugh," Becca says when we reach the bottom. "I was afraid of this." The tour with Misha had not included the unfinished laundry room, and though Becca had tried to peek in, Misha had done an impressive job of blocking her.

Becca's never been afraid a day in her life, probably

not even the day Footloose mowed her down and she
hid in a drainpipe. The fact that she's even attempting
to use the expression heightens my anxiety as I peer past
her at the enormous tower of unlabeled boxes stacked
almost to the exposed ductwork in the ceiling. I flip on
the light as we approach, checking out the full scope of
the work in front of us. The tower is five boxes high,
eight boxes wide, and three boxes deep.

"Do the math," Becca orders. "How many is this?"

"A hundred and twenty."

"Who has that much stuff? They should have done
what you did and just tossed it."

"I told you that was the sensible approach."

Her tone is icy. "It was rude."

I stand on my toes to reach a box on the top. There's
not much room in here to work, so after a split second's
hesitation, I cart it over to the dining room, which still
has the enormous wood table from date night. They've
left the artwork on the wall, an oil painting Footloose
made himself to remember a sailing trip with his wife
and daughter, killed by a drunk driver. The television
still hangs over the fireplace, and even though the screen
is blank, I can still see the home torture movies Footloose had shown me, people writhing in fear and pain as
they died.

Becca drops her box on the table opposite me, the bang
making me jump. "Relax," she says. "This is going to take
hours. You're going to give yourself a heart attack."

"I'm in the home of a serial killer with a second serial killer, trying to find the 'clue' you're convinced Fiona left especially for me," I say. "It's normal for me to be tense."

"It's weak."

I ignore her and use the knife to slice open the tape, finding a box of women's shoes. I'd seen them lined up neatly in Footloose's closet the night I'd come back, as though he hadn't dared touch any of his wife's belongings after her passing. I dig through the pile with my fingers, but there's nothing in here that requires a key, so I close it and set it aside, returning to the laundry room to grab another box.

"Just clothes in mine," Becca says from over my shoulder. "Let's try from the opposite end in case that's just bedroom stuff."

It's a crapshoot, but I grab a box from the other side and take it to the dining room, finding it filled with towels. I grope through it in case someone thought to wrap a mystery box in terry cloth, but no such luck. Becca's box is full of soap, shampoo, and toothpaste, and we head back to try again. Ten boxes later, our black gloves are gray with dust, and we're sneezing so much we had to tie T-shirts around the bottom of our faces, courtesy of Footloose's daughter's clothing box.

"Who has so much stuff?" Becca grumbles as she kicks at the boxes in the laundry room. We'd eventually deduced that whoever had done the packing had placed the lighter boxes on top, which are mostly clothes and linens. Becca toppled them off to give us access to the heavier boxes on the bottom, and now I drag mine into the dining room and kneel on the floor to cut it open, Becca doing the same next to me.

"Tools," I announce, giving an involuntary shudder. Footloose had been a carpentry and engineering enthusiast, putting his skills to good use building a fun house in which to torture his victims. I dig through, squinting at items I don't recognize, but still nothing requiring a key.

"Toys," Becca scowls, tossing a stuffed unicorn across the room. I'd seen the toys and dolls arranged neatly on Footloose's daughter's bed, the room dusted and clean, as neat as the day she'd died.

We shove the boxes to the side and return to the laundry room. My feet are dragging because it's late and I'm tired, my eyes watering from the dust. Becca's limp is more pronounced, and she looks annoyed but otherwise unaffected. We cart two more heavy boxes into the dining room and squat, slicing them open with the carving knife and revealing more things from the daughter's room.

"This is cute," Becca says, holding up a beaded lamp.

My box contains the contents of the top of a dresser—a little metal mouse with giant ears for holding earrings and a matching silver hand, its fingers decorated with cheap rings. There are headbands and school photos, a wreath of plastic flowers, and a medium-sized wooden jewelry box with intricate floral scrollwork. I try to lift the lid, but it doesn't budge. I give it a shake and a solitary item rattles inside.

Becca pauses her search to watch. "Does it need a key?"

I turn the box over, but there's no keyhole. Scanning for latches or hinges, I see nothing.

"If it does, I can't find the keyhole. But there's definitely something inside."

Becca takes it and gives it another shake. The item tumbles around, but nothing comes loose. "It's one of those puzzle boxes," she says. "Like they have in Japan or wherever. Except it's homemade."

She's right. The more we handle it, the more I realize the finishes are not as smooth as I'd first thought, the scrollwork less polished. Footloose made this box for his daughter. I'd seen them before. They're impossible to open unless you find half a dozen or more hidden spots to press, slide, and lift until you get to the secret inside.

She passes back the box, and I rotate it in my hands, pushing carefully on a series of small, raised wooden panels on the right side. Nothing happens. There's a matching set on the left, and after a second of fiddling, one shifts, just a little. I peer at it closely and see a tiny gap into which I can wedge my fingernail and lift out the panel. As soon as that one's out, the one above it slides down to reveal…more wood. I turn the box again, looking for its next secret.

"What are you doing?"

"Trying to open the box."

"We're not here to do puzzles. We're here to open something and then go home."

"That's what I'm trying—"

"There's an entire box of tools right in front of you!" Becca snaps, reaching past me to dig inside and retrieve a hammer. "Stop being such an idiot."

Snatching the box from my hands, she drops it on the floor and swiftly smashes it into a million tiny pieces. I gape as wood fragments fly everywhere. We don't even know if this is the item the key opens. We don't know if the thing inside is fragile. We don't—

"Aha!" Becca exclaims, reaching down to filter through the rubble with her gloved fingertips, revealing something sleek and silver. "It's a…"

My jaw drops.

"…key."

"Is that our key?" I ask. "Did it fall out of my pocket?"

Her brow furrows. "Hmm."

I dig in my jacket until I feel the familiar press of Fiona's key, still in its plastic bag, and tug it out.

"Nope," Becca says.

"We don't even know if our key opened the box!" I exclaim. "That key could be just any random key."

Becca combs through the wood shards some more, eventually raising a hand triumphantly. Clutched in her palm is a chunk of wood with a keyhole and locking mechanism. As much as I want this scavenger hunt to

be over, I don't want this to be the right answer. I
don't want our hunt for a locked item to reveal another
fucking key. And I really don't want to listen to Becca
gloat that her destructive tendencies worked. Still, I pull
the key from the baggie and slide it into the lock. It
goes in easily. And when I twist, the catch turns, opening
what would have been a box, if Becca hadn't bashed it to
smithereens.

"Well," she says, beaming. "Mystery solved."

"Nothing is solved!" I snap. "Why would he hide a key
in his daughter's toy?"

"Because she's dead?" Becca guesses. "And she's never
going to find it? One hiding place is as good as any."

"Well, this has been a waste of time. There's no
way Fiona knew what her key opened. She found it in
Footloose's dungeon and saved it, just in case. Now here
we are, with another key and no idea what it's for."

"It somehow relates to you."

"How does that make sense?"

"Because her little clue pointed directly to you, Carrie!
And you can play innocent for the press and Detective
Gráves—"

"Greaves."

"—but she knew something you didn't want her to
know, and I don't think her disappearing act is something
she had a say in."

"You're insane. Oh, wait—I already knew that, because
you've been murdering people for ten years."

"So have you."

"Have not!" I get to my feet and wipe dust off my knees.

"Well, you buried the bodies."

"I buried the bodies because you blackmailed me!"

"No, you did it because we're sisters, and sisters help each other!"

"For the last time, you've never helped me!"

A gasp at the door interrupts the fight, and we whirl around in unison, emitting our own gasps. Wearing an oversized Brampton Real Estate Corporation T-shirt and a pair of sleep shorts, blond hair a tangled mess, is my real estate agent, Misha Collins.

"Carrie Lawrence!" she squeaks, eyes wide with terror at all the confessions of murder she's just overheard. "Diana Speedwell!"

"Shit," Becca mutters, forcing the new key into my hand and gouging my palm in the process.

"Misha," I begin, "were you sleeping here?"

She blinks rapidly, tears spilling down her cheeks. "It's hard selling houses," she whispers. "This is just until I get my first commission check."

"I'm so sorry. I—"

She wipes her nose. "Were you ever interested in buying a house?"

"Of course we are. We're very interested—"

"Shut up, Carrie." Becca shoves me out of the way, and both Misha and I screech in alarm when we see the giant carving knife in her hand.

Misha bolts back up the stairs, bare feet thundering on the steps.

"Becca," I say, because it's one thing when the deed's already done and I bury a person I never could have saved, but this is different. Misha's still alive. She's my real estate agent. And that's a huge knife.

Becca spares me a furious look before racing after her.

I stuff the new key into my pocket and follow, not wanting to stay in Footloose's dining room but also really not wanting to witness what's happening upstairs.

"No!" I hear Misha scream, footsteps pounding over the floors.

"Carrie, block the door!"

I reach the landing just as Misha comes racing back down the hall, where she'd apparently fled to the kitchen when Becca chased her and then sped past her back to the living room. I freeze instinctively, arms spread, barricading the front door.

Misha skids to a halt in front of me. Her mouth moves in a silent plea, one single, desperate syllable. *Please.*

Becca emerges from the kitchen, her Diana Speedwell wig askew, the trickle of moonlight through the window glinting off the knife edge.

"She won't say anything," I blurt out. "Will you, Misha? We were arguing and things got out of hand. None of that stuff you heard was true. This is just a…misunderstanding."

Tears stream down Misha's cheeks. "I…I know,"

she says between sniffles. "I know you were joking. I won't...I won't tell anyone about your jokes. It's fine. Everything's fine."

"See?" I shoot Becca a pleading look. "Everything's fine. We can just go home. No questions asked."

"None," Misha agrees. "No questions. No anything."

My heart is pounding so hard it hurts. I've never had a chance to save one of Becca's victims before. I've always been part of the cleaning crew. Now I can make a difference. There's always the risk that Misha's lying and will tell people about what she heard, but she can't prove anything. Apart from, perhaps, the breaking-and-entering bit.

Becca sets down the knife. "You really trust her?"

Moonlight reflects off the tear tracks on Misha's cheeks. "You can trust me," she whispers.

"Yes." I nod, my head bobbing manically. "I do."

A muscle tics in her cheek, but finally Becca nods. "Okay, then. If you say so. Misha, go upstairs and forget you heard anything. Carrie, go get the car. I left my jacket in the basement."

My knees are weak with relief, my hand shaking when I reach for the door. "Right. I'll meet you outside, Bec—Diana. And Misha...see you at the next showing."

Misha's walking backward up the stairs, her fingers gripping the rail, eyes locked on mine like maybe this is a bad dream and she'll wake up and none of this will have happened. I've had the same dream, I want to tell her. And it's always worse when you wake up.

Becca pushes past me on her way to the basement, and I listen to her footsteps descend before I open the front door and step out. The street is dark and quiet, unaware. I reach for the car keys in my pocket, but my fingertips barely graze them before there's the sharp snap of a bolt being turned, a door locked.

A muffled scream rings out, and I whip around, staring in shock at the red-painted door. I don't need to guess what's happening on the other side because I know. What I can't believe is that I fell for it. That Becca would actually give Misha a second chance when it meant her own freedom was at stake.

I reach for my phone, remembering too late that Becca insisted we leave them at home so they couldn't be used to trace our movements later. I'm supposed to do something, I know. To run around to the back of the house and let myself in, stop this, stop my sister. But it's too late. I picture the knife Becca put down, and then imagine her picking it right back up.

I could race next door, ask them to call the police and say it was a break-and-enter gone wrong. But getting Becca arrested for this crime is the same as sealing my fate in all the others. She'd planted something on each body we buried, something that tied me to the murder. Hair, a business card, my phone number. Something. Enough. This time, I'm more culpable than ever before.

I'm trapped.

CHAPTER 14

Becca sleeps through most of the next day. I'd woken at 5:00 a.m. and checked her room, finding her sprawled on her stomach, one foot hanging off the edge of the mattress. The Diana Speedwell wig was gone, as were her clothes from the night before. I'd stripped out of mine as soon as I'd gotten home, running through the streets to ditch them in various garbage cans. After a hot shower and a Valium, I'd managed two hours of sleep, and I look like it, gaunt cheeks and bloodshot eyes evidence of my crimes. Or it could be because I've done little more than sit in a ball on the couch in my sweatpants, refreshing the local news cycle on my phone and waiting for the SWAT team to blast through the door.

But nothing happens. The most exciting thing on the *Brampton Chronicle* website is a goose that scared an elderly woman outside the library, and not a single brutal murder. At 5:00 p.m., I hear the floor groan upstairs, and a minute later, Becca makes an appearance, dressed in a pair of my old skinny jeans and the Egyptian cotton T-shirt she'd criticized days earlier.

"Morning," she says, stretching her arms over her head and cracking her back. "Or afternoon. Evening, maybe. Whenever. I'm hungry!"

She heads into the kitchen, and I stare at the space where she'd been standing, wondering if I'm the one who's crazy, if the past sixteen hours have been one big nightmare and last night's misadventure was nothing more than a figment of my overworked, overstressed imagination.

I follow her to the kitchen and find her staring into the empty cupboard that normally contains a selection of cereal.

"Did you hide it?" she asks without turning around.

"I haven't had time to go the store."

"Well, I'm hungry."

"Well, eat something else."

"Like what?"

"A salad?"

She glares at me over her shoulder. "Right." Abandoning her clean bowl in the sink, she proceeds to open three more doors until she finds a bag of popcorn. Tearing off the cellophane wrapper with her teeth, she sticks it in the microwave for seventeen minutes.

"That's going to burn."

"I'll know when it's done." She calmly examines her nails as the microwave hums, and my prickle of irritation grows into a full-fledged panic.

"Are you just going to stand there?"

Becca blinks. "Where else should I stand? Ugh. Don't tell me you're suddenly concerned about radiation poisoning."

"You killed someone last night," I whisper.

"I know," she whispers back.

"And that's it? You just...slept it off?"

"What else was I supposed to do? I was tired."

"She was my real estate agent. You said we were going to trust her not to tell—"

"Stop being so naive, Carrie. Of course she was going to tell. Why the fuck wouldn't she?"

"We don't even know for sure that she heard anything more than you destroying the box with a hammer!"

Becca plucks the bag of popcorn from the microwave, peeling it open to release the steam. "It's a little late for second-guessing. Plus, she definitely heard."

"Did you hide the body?"

"Um, no. It's not easy to hide that kind of...mess."

I gag.

"Listen." Becca tries to sound sympathetic but winds up sounding like someone who's trying to imitate someone sympathetic she saw on TV. "I know you're still a loser about this type of thing, but if you were more of an optimist, you'd see the bright side."

"Of murder?"

"Specifically that one. Graves—"

"Greaves."

"—has been obsessing over you and me because he has nothing better to do. Now he's got a real crime to investigate and fail to solve. Everything's back to normal. Consider it a welcome diversion."

"I'm not calling it 'welcome.'"

"Well, at least you're coming around to my way of thinking. Now let's have dinner and figure out what the new key opens."

When she says "dinner," she opens the fridge, snags a bottle of wine, and sits down at the table with her bag of popcorn to complete the meal. I'm not hungry, but I grab two glasses and sit opposite her, not complaining when she fills mine to the brim.

"What are your ideas?" she asks.

I gulp my wine. "I have none. We got incredibly lucky figuring out what the first key opened."

"No, we were incredibly smart. We just have to be smart again. What would Footloose have found so valuable that he'd lock away the key?"

I exhale. "I don't know. Another murder cabin?"

"Could be. But he's been gone for five months. Anyone he had in there is long dead."

"And we're not that lucky."

"Did he mention a job? What if *he's* the sex predator with a secret office?"

"He said he was retired." I open my mouth to mention that he'd driven cancer patients to appointments as a volunteer but stop myself. We've already broken into Brampton MedSupplies and murdered a real estate agent—I have to draw the line at vandalizing a volunteer service.

"Mailbox?" Becca guesses.

"Maybe. But how would we find it?"

"Why don't you suggest something, then?"

I sigh. "The puzzle box was included with his daughter's things. Maybe it relates to her somehow."

"You said she'd been dead for, like, seven years."

"Yes, but if he was still carrying the key to the box, it could be relevant."

"No. Hiding things in plain sight is the best way to hide them. No one was going to look in the box because it was obvious."

"That's all I've got."

Becca thuds her head on the table. "This is exhausting. I'm going to bed."

"You just got up."

"Well, I worked harder than you. Someone had to make sure we didn't leave any evidence behind after you ran away last night."

"You said we were leaving!"

Shrugging like that's somehow debatable, Becca gets up and flounces out of the room with the bottle of wine.

Impulsively, I get to my feet and grab my car keys, hurrying out of the house and driving to the nearest grocery store. In their floral department, I overpay for a brightly colored bouquet of flowers with a rainbow print wrapping and then head to the cemetery. It's warm and quiet on a Sunday evening, and I use the map on my phone to locate Angelica's grave. She's my former coworker, the one Becca killed and Footloose dug up, the body that started us down this particularly gruesome, precarious path.

Eventually, I spot her gravestone, the white marble still bright and gleaming in the waning sunlight as though someone comes by and regularly wipes it down. The grass is soft beneath my feet, the grounds well maintained, and I hesitate before crouching in front of the stone. There's no one in sight, the markers around us small and gray and offering nowhere to hide. Reaching out, I trace my fingers over the etching in the marble, a clumsy caricature of a serene angel resting its chin on its hands, Angelica's name and birth date written beneath it. She was twenty-five when she died.

I turn and sit, cradling the flowers in my lap and resting my back against the warm stone, feeling some of the tension ease out of my shoulders. I'd had nothing to do with Angelica's murder, but she was another young woman whose face I'd known, whose voice I'd heard, and who's no longer with us because of my sister's murderous impulses. My sister who believes she *helps* me.

"I'm sorry, Misha," I mumble down at the bouquet. "You didn't deserve it. I should have known better."

The words are as useless as my actions, and I flush with shame when I hear them. I take a breath, but the perfume of the flowers is too strong, making my stomach twist. I've done a lot of bad things in the past ten years, kept a lot of secrets, and this is just one more. Misha is just another name on an unwritten list, another Brampton murder victim, another poor woman that didn't make it because she met the wrong person on the wrong day.

"Carrie."

The flowers shoot into the air and launch themselves three rows over, and I flip onto all fours like an animal, not sure if I'm ready to fight or flee. I still don't know how I feel when I see Graham standing two graves away, his phone clenched in his hand, his face stricken with grief.

Almost immediately, my heart slices itself in half. He knows. Somehow, he knows what I've done. I stand as he crosses the space between us, his face crumpling as he wraps me in a too-tight hug, sobbing into my neck.

"I'm so glad you're okay." He pulls back and clasps my face in his hands. "I…I don't know what I'd do without you."

"I…" I'm confused. "How…What?"

He hugs me again, and I struggle to breathe as I pat his back in what's supposed to be a reassuring way but is just mystified.

"How did you find me?"

"The tracking app on your phone."

I stifle a groan. For Graham's peace of mind, I'd agreed to install the app after Footloose kidnapped me. I'll be uninstalling it later tonight.

"I know I promised to only use it if it was an emergency, but this is." His eyes are wet with tears. "You'll want to sit down."

I *need* to sit down. Adrenaline makes my legs weak, confusion stamped on my face. We take a seat on the grass, Angelica's tombstone next to my shoulder, like she's watching.

"What is it?" I ask as Graham wipes his eyes. "Did something happen?"

He takes a deep breath and shows me his phone, already on the *Brampton Chronicle* website. The giant headline screams what I already know: LOCAL REAL ESTATE AGENT FOUND DEAD. It's accompanied by the same full-color headshot of Misha from the listing brochures.

"No," I whisper. Even though I already knew this, knew other people would find out, am indeed at a gravesite apologizing to her ghost, only now that Graham knows does it feel real.

He shakes his head. "I can't believe it. They think she was at a listing appointment yesterday, and someone just…snapped."

His hands shake so badly that I can't read the smaller print, so I take the phone and skim the article as quickly as I can, desperately searching for any mention of Carrie Lawrence or Diana Speedwell.

Local real estate agent Misha Collins was found murdered today, her body discovered by a fellow real estate agent who thought it odd she hadn't shown up for an open house this afternoon. He checked her local listings and, upon letting himself into the presumably vacant Westchester property, found the home completely vandalized.

Police were called to the scene and shortly after, the body of Misha Collins was discovered in an upstairs bedroom. An unnamed source described the carnage as the "worst thing they'd ever seen," and added, "Only a monster could do this." Two senior officers were taken to the hospital to be treated for shock.

Stunned neighbors describe the area as quiet and peaceful, many of whom had met Collins at the open house the day before. Called "lovely and promising" by her coworkers, Collins was born and raised in Brampton. Her motto was "Live your best life forever."

The phone slips through my fingers. "Oh my God."

Graham takes my hand and stares earnestly into my eyes. "I know you were worried about Footloose from the start, and I didn't take the whole idea of Brampton having a serial killer seriously, but this... This is different. This is someone we knew. This is too close to home."

I manage a nod.

"We need to find a place," he continues. "We need to do whatever it takes to buy a home. You, me, and Felix. If this... horrible crime teaches us anything, let it be that life is short and Brampton is a dangerous city. We'll be safer together."

"I agree," I say, even as I know that's not quite true.

"And the police... What are they doing, really?" Graham's practically vibrating with frustration and injustice, which is very at odds with his even-keeled personality. "Walking their dog past your house? Following you to the movies? I mean, we've seen Brampton's missing person statistics. What are the chances they actually find the person who killed Misha?"

That's what I'm banking on. "It's awful," I murmur.

"Until then, I know what we can do."

I look up. "Huh?"

Graham folds my fingers in his and peers deep into my eyes. His voice is somber when he says my name.

My heart's pounding. "Yes, Graham?"

He gives Angelica's gravestone a serious nod, like they're making a pact. Then he turns back to me. "I think we should join the Brampton Kill Seekers."

CHAPTER 15

"Where are you going?"

I pause midstep and give myself one second to grimace before fixing my face in an innocent stare and turning to see Becca framed in the door of her bedroom. It's shortly before 7:00 p.m., and through the window behind her, I can see the final rays of sunshine vanishing beneath the horizon.

"Hmm?"

Her eyes narrow, and she steps toward me, flicking a finger in my general direction. "You're dressed up on a Wednesday night. Why?"

By "dressed up" she means I'm wearing jeans and a long-sleeve shirt and I haven't washed my face for bed yet.

"I'm meeting Graham."

"Why?"

"Because he's my boyfriend."

"On a weekday? You only see him on weekends because he spends the rest of his time with a dominatrix."

"It's a long commute."

"And you have your purse," she continues, tapping her finger against her chin. "So you're going out. But it's two hours past Graham's dinnertime…"

I sigh.

"…so you're going somewhere else. An eight o'clock movie means Graham would miss his nine o'clock bedtime…"

"Would you stop?"

"Tell me you're not going back to that house." She doesn't say "without me," but it's implied.

"The crime scene?" I exclaim. "Of course not. That's something you would do."

She looks offended. "It certainly isn't."

A car horn honks outside.

"I have to go."

"I'll come with you."

"Graham still thinks you're dead, remember?"

"Tell me where you're going."

"To get a coffee," I lie.

"You don't drink caffeine after noon."

"That's not true. Stop stalking me."

Becca does exactly the opposite and pounces, snatching my purse from under my arm, running past me into the bathroom and slamming the door. The house is too old and the crystal doorknobs don't lock, so she leans against it from the inside while I batter it from the outside, not terribly unlike our teenage years.

"Give me my bag!" I holler.

She yanks open the door, and I nearly fall in. "You're going to the Kill Seekers meeting?" she demands. My phone is in her hand, the screen still on the website where I'd confirmed tonight's start time.

I grab back my things, stuffing the phone in my bag and stomping down the stairs as Graham honks again.

"Graham wants to join," I mutter.

Becca coughs out a laugh as she follows. "What?"

"He thinks Brampton is too violent and we can't trust the police."

She laughs louder. "And *he's* going to put an end to the crime spree?"

He honks a third time, and I text him to say I'm on my way.

"Here's a tip," Becca says. "Look in your girlfriend's spare room!"

"Shut up." I jam my feet into boots. "This is important to him, and I'm being support— What are you doing?"

Becca's also putting on boots. "What do you think I'm doing? I'm going to the meeting."

"You can't go to the meeting. The meeting's about you."

She preens.

"Because you're a murderer," I clarify.

She shrugs. "All the more reason for me to attend. How can I stay one step ahead of the investigative dynamo of Graham and the Kill Seekers if I don't have the inside scoop?"

"I'll tell you the scoop."

"I'd rather see it for myself." She grabs a red wig from one of the boxes she still hasn't brought upstairs and yanks it on her head.

"Is that supposed to be a disguise?"

"They're looking for a gorgeous blond, not a stunning redhead."

I purse my lips before getting out my phone and sending another text.

"You're not telling Graham, are you?"

I give her a tight smile and reach for the door. "Nope."

I'm rewarded by the tiny flicker of uncertainty that flashes across her face, but before she can steal my phone again, I scurry outside and join Graham in his car.

"Sorry," I say, buckling in. "I couldn't find my bag."

"Worth the wait," he says, leaning over to kiss me.

I smile as we pull away from the curb, though we're barely at the end of the block when I see a figure dart out of my house and beeline it toward my car. I check my phone, but there's no reply to my text.

"Everything okay?" Graham asks.

"Yep," I lie. "How did you learn about this meeting? I forgot to ask."

"Hmm?" He reaches over to turn down the radio, which is nonstop reports and conjecture about Misha's murder, none of which come close to the truth.

I shunt that memory to the side. "This meeting. How did you hear about it?"

"Oh. Facebook."

"You just happened to visit the Brampton Kill Seekers page?"

He peeks at me, chagrined. "Well, after you first told me about them, I looked into the group. And some of what they were saying was pretty interesting."

This is alarming. "Really? Like what?"

"I thought you went to a meeting."

"One meeting. And I didn't do any research." I catch a glimpse of bright-orange hair as Becca stops next to us at a red light. Casually, she reaches up to scratch her nose using only her middle finger.

"Patterns and stuff." Graham presses the gas when the light turns green. "They've been documenting all the missing or suspiciously dead people from Brampton and towns within a fifty-mile radius and establishing patterns. Demographics, times of year, when and if the body was found, manner of death. It's kind of fascinating, if you like horrible things."

"Which you don't."

"I'm not insane, so of course not. But if the police can't protect us, who will?"

"You?" I guess.

"Don't laugh at me. I'm just saying, knowledge is power. Let's arm ourselves."

I remain silent, grateful Becca's not here to eavesdrop.

"I just heard how lame that sounded," Graham says. "And I take it back."

A few minutes later, we pull into the library parking lot. Like last time, it's dark and quiet, but there are at least twice as many cars as before. I shiver when we climb out, sparing a glare for Becca as she eases into the lot and turns in the opposite direction to park. I check my phone again, but there's no response and we're the only people in sight. Resignation makes my shoulders sag as we head toward the building and a car door slams behind us.

"Carrie!" Nikk calls.

Graham and I turn to see Nikk smiling widely as he jogs up to meet us, slightly breathless. He must have already been planning to attend and then waited for us when he got my text.

"Nice to see you again. I wish the circumstances were different, but..." He shrugs helplessly. As before, his hair is perfectly mussed, and he has the effortless, annoying air of just being superrich and handsome.

"Hi," Graham says. "Graham Fowler."

"Nikk Boulter," says Nikk.

Over his shoulder, I see Becca sauntering up, freezing comically when she hears Nikk's name. Her heels click on the pavement, and the two men turn at the sound, seeing nothing but two dozen silent cars and not the serial killer in an orange wig crouched between them.

"Thanks for your text," Nikk adds, directing the comment to me. "I'd been debating whether or not to attend, but when you said you were coming, I knew I wanted to be here, too."

Graham's expression of surprise is nothing compared to Becca's expression of rage when she sticks her head up over a car to glower at me. A second evening with Nikk wasn't high on my priority list, but it still beat out watching Becca road test her latest stupid disguise.

"Nikk's wife is missing, too," I explain to Graham as we make our way to the meeting room.

The murmur of hushed voices spills into the hall as we reach the door, the room still as brightly decorated as before. This time the chalkboard says LIVE YOUR BEST LIFE FOREVER like it knew I was coming and thought I wasn't feeling bad enough.

"That's beautiful," Graham whispers as we take our seats, with him on my left, Becca's wife-beating friend Nikk with a missing wife who was killed by my sister on my right.

I spot Emmett, Ravjinder, and Todd, and they give me solemn nods. There were fourteen people at the last meeting, and tonight there's easily twice as many. The circle of chairs has been rearranged into five straight rows, and Emmett stands at the front with a laptop and a large computer monitor, likely hoping to avoid a repeat of last meeting's embarrassing technical difficulties. Ravjinder and Todd appear to be helping him, and after enduring awkward small talk between Graham and Nikk about missing women, I'm grateful when the lights dim and

Emmett uses the app on his phone to cast an ominous but still ridiculous glow on his face.

"Death," he says in his deep cult leader voice. "Disappearance. *Yearning.*"

Beside me, Graham flinches. Nikk coughs into his fist.

"Brampton!" Emmett shouts. I'm ready for it, but Graham jumps in fright and clutches my arm. "Population: two hundred thousand. Missing? One hundred twenty-three. Unsolved deaths? Seventy-three. People who truly care?" He makes a show of pointing at each of us in turn, which he obviously hasn't thought through because there are way more than last time and he clearly loses track of his counting. "Many!" he booms, to make up for it. "Many, many people care. The last time we met, there were seventy-two unsolved deaths in the city. Tonight, there are seventy-three. And after tonight? None!"

The room breaks out in applause, though literally none of us are qualified to make such a statement and certainly can't be counted upon to ensure it.

From the corner of my eye, I see a flash of orange dart past the door and stifle an aggrieved sigh. As long as Becca only lurks in the hallway, we should be okay.

"Misha Collins," Emmett continues, clicking something on the keyboard. A copy of the same photo from the listing brochure appears on the larger monitor. "Twenty-six years old. Bright, beautiful, ambitious. And dead."

Graham actually gasps, though he knew all that.

"Slaughtered in an empty house by a vicious monster."

Another click and a new picture materializes, this one a pretty, slight woman with huge brown eyes and dark hair in a sleek bob. "Lilly Fiennes," Emmett says.

Next to me, Nikk makes a strangled sound, and a tear slides down his cheek.

Another click, and a new picture. "Becca Lawrence." It's the same unflattering one as last time, and I cover my mouth with my hand because I don't know if I should laugh or cry or run out of the room. Emmett's hosting a Kill Seeker meeting, has no idea the murderer pictured on his screen is creeping in the hallway, and has very likely added himself to her hit list for using such a bad photo.

The next click reveals Fiona, and then Emmett works his way back through a dozen more images of men and women I don't recognize though probably had a hand in burying. He only stops when people begin stirring, either from discomfort or boredom, and hastily skips through at least thirty more images without offering names until he comes to a graph with far too many colored bars for anyone to possibly comprehend.

"That's what I was talking about," Graham whispers.

"What is it?"

"Patterns!" Emmett bellows. Anyone who had dozed off during the slideshow now lurches awake. "Over the past fifty years, Brampton and its surrounding areas have had more than four hundred unsolved mysteries and homicides. The Brampton Kill Seekers have developed a proprietary database that allows us to track the victims by age, race, social status, and more. It allows us to note the date of their death or disappearance, the manner in which they left us, and the outcome of the case."

Graham looks riveted.

"To determine a pattern, we must have a starting point. And fortunately—or very unfortunately, depending on how you look at it—we have a starting point: Footloose. Not all the bodies uncovered in Kilduff Park have been. identified, but the earliest known disappearance was twelve years ago. And we know he preyed upon society's most vulnerable." Emmett punctuates those statements with clicks that take the number of bars on the screen down to just a handful. "And we know he killed them."

Graham is leaning forward as if this is spellbinding news, but I'm waiting for the punch line. All the information on the screen is stuff we already know, some a little more intimately than others.

Emmett hits a few keys, and a new chart appears, less busy than the first but considerably busier than the second. "If we narrow our window of investigation to the past fifteen years—to the timeframe we know Footloose was hunting—and we remove Footloose's contribution"—a click, and the chart becomes less cluttered—"we uncover a new pattern."

The room gasps, and so do I. Because with fewer colored bars, the text becomes more visible, and I see the pattern Emmett has been building up to.

"By removing the people whose bodies have been found," he continues, tapping a few more keys, "we're left with a decade of unsolved disappearances. Twenty-six, to be precise."

The screen populates with twenty-six pictures of missing people. Among them are Missy Vanscheer, the first person Becca killed; Shanna, the first body I helped hide; at least three people I recognize from having carted their bodies to unmarked graves; Becca; Fiona; and now Lilly Fiennes. I feel sick. Hiding one body a year is bad enough, but with approximately twelve months between each of Becca's "urges," I'd somehow managed to convince myself that maybe it wasn't *that* bad. Seeing so many of those faces gazing back at me is like being judged from beyond the grave.

I peek at the door and see Becca peering in, admiring her handiwork. Everyone else is engrossed in it as well and manages not to notice the murderer in their midst.

"You're suggesting Brampton has *another* serial killer?" Todd demands as Emmett finally turns up the lights, the presentation over.

"It looks that way."

"We didn't know what it looked like the first time," someone in the audience calls. "How could we know what it looks like now?"

Emmett taps the screen. "We didn't know about Footloose until we found thirteen bodies in Kilduff Park."

"So we're searching for a burial ground?"

Ravjinder sniffles, and Todd pats her shoulder.

Emmett calls up another chart. This one lists only the women who went missing in the past decade. The good news is that Becca kills whoever annoys her when she's having a particularly bad day, regardless of gender, so it's possible she didn't murder all of these women. The bad news is that Emmett is on a mission, and he's actually making a good case.

"Missy Vanscheer, high school student. Shanna Lewis, jewelry store employee. Harlowe Beam, barista. Jennifer Ting, dental hygienist." He reads through more names, showing their smiling pictures and noting jobs that run the gamut from entry-level to executive. "Kamaljit Kaur Bains," Emmett continues, "accountant. Angelica Holbrook, graphic designer. Becca Lawrence, jewelry store employee."

There's a notable murmur at the second mention of a person who worked at a jewelry store. I slouch in my seat.

"Fiona McBride, student. Misha Collins, real estate agent."

The screen ends on a collage of all the missing or dead women, and the room is positively vibrating with energy.

"Angelica Holbrook was one of Footloose's victims," Nikk calls out helpfully.

"Or was she?" Emmett counters. "Footloose targeted

people who were at the lowest points in their lives. Angelica Holbrook was young, successful, and up for a promotion. Becca Lawrence was thirty and beautiful. Fiona McBride was just seventeen and from a wealthy family with all the opportunities of the world available to her. Misha Collins was building her career as a real estate agent."

"But they never found Becca Lawrence, Fiona McBride, or Lilly Fiennes," someone says. "Why are we assuming they're dead?"

"Because of this," Emmett says, tapping a key so Brampton's obscene crime statistics appear on the screen. "These statistics are freely available online. If you wanted to murder indiscriminately and without notice, where would you go?"

"Brampton" is the quiet, unfortunate consensus.

"I dare say Brampton does have a second serial killer on its hands," Emmett says, his bravado increasing with the audience's rapt attention. Graham's gaze is glued to the screen, and it looks like he's stopped breathing. "And I think he's escalating."

He switches back several screens to return to the picture of Misha Collins. "Misha was known for never being seen without her treasured rainbow butterfly ring," he tells us, clicking to a new image of the gaudy ring I'd seen on Misha's hand every time we'd met. "And I have it on good authority that the ring was nowhere to be found at the crime scene. The whole house was vandalized, but nothing was determined to be missing…except the ring."

"A memento," Nikk whispers. The room is so quiet the softly spoken words are impossible to miss.

Emmett nods authoritatively. "That's right. I think our killer meant to make Misha Collins disappear the way the other victims vanished, but Misha was a fighter. She wanted to live her best life forever, and she fought for that opportunity. In the end, she lost the battle but left us a clue: her body. We now know for certain that there is a murderer in our midst, and that person took the ring as a token to remember their crime."

While everyone is fixated on the butterfly ring picture displayed up front, my eyes slide slowly to the doorway where Becca crouches, gaze locked on mine with laser-like focus. But unlike her usual flat stare, this time there's something I've never seen in her face before: panic.

Witnessing a human emotion from Becca is enough to send me into a flustered spiral, making it almost impossible to concentrate on the rest of the meeting. Graham wants to stay and mingle when it wraps up, but I tell him I have a headache and need to get to bed early. I'm pale and clammy thanks to the Kill Seekers' surprisingly competent investigation, and my visible illness convinces Graham to take me straight home.

"This was a great idea," I lie when he parks at the curb in front of my house. My car is back in the driveway, and I see Becca peeking down from my bedroom window. "I mean, it's terrifying, but you're right. The public needs this information."

Graham takes a breath. "I know you said you wanted to wait on the house hunting, but I think we should dive in headfirst. Life is too short."

I open my mouth to explain why we should wait—because my serial killer sister is back and I think we're in more trouble than usual—but his expression is so open and sincere that I hear myself say, "Okay. Let's do it."

Graham smiles and kisses my forehead. "I'll make the call."

I hurry to the house, Graham watching until I'm safely inside before honking and driving away.

I shut the door and drop my bag to confront Becca, who's stomping down the stairs. "Did you steal that butterfly ring?" I demand.

She's removed the orange wig, and her normally perfect blond hair sticks out in half a dozen different directions.

"That's not even the point, Carrie!" She stalks to the kitchen, and I follow.

"It sounded like an important point," I reply, squawking in alarm when I see the ring sitting on the table. "Jesus! We have to flush this. Why did you put it here?"

"Because I forgot I had it. But the ring isn't the issue. Try to focus."

I'm bewildered. "On what?"

"When you threw away all my stuff—"

"Not this again."

"—did you also throw away my keys?"

"No," I reply with certainty. "I used my copy to let myself in, and when the landlord asked for both copies back, we couldn't find your key ring. I had to pay thirty dollars for a replacement."

"Footloose came to my apartment the night I disappeared."

"I'm aware."

"And I thought all he took was me. I mean, who would take a key ring? What was he going to do? Check my mail?"

I look around, as though the answer's written on the wall. "No?"

I hadn't realized her hands were balled up into fists until she extends one and slowly uncurls her fingers to reveal the most recent mystery key.

"I know what this opens," she says.

CHAPTER 16

It's 11:00 on a weeknight, but five minutes after getting home, we're back in my car and making the forty-minute trip to the outskirts of Brampton, a desolate industrial area with a few gas stations and all-night diners playing host to truck drivers, prostitutes, and two murderers.

"Did they ever find the feet?" Becca asks, staring out the passenger window as she drums her nails anxiously on her knee.

"What?"

"Footloose. The feet he chopped off. Did they ever find them?"

"Um, no." I decide not to tell her about the one he left in my freezer that I later chucked off a bridge.

"Those must have been *his* mementos. I bet that fucker searched my apartment to see if I kept anything, and when nothing turned up, he took my keys."

"But how would he have known this one was important?"

"Process of elimination. There were only five on there. My apartment, my car, my mailbox, the store, and this storage unit."

"Well, if he kept it in a lockbox, that's a good sign, right? It means he never figured out what it opened."

She lifts a shoulder. "I'd just paid the bill for the storage unit. I never logged out of my accounts, so he might have checked my online banking history. You said my laptop was missing, right? One of the few things you didn't just throw away?"

"Wouldn't throwing away things have prevented this whole situation?"

Becca has no response to that so she ignores me and, after a minute, says, "This is it, up ahead." A giant neon sign glows in the night, announcing TOPLINE SAFE STORAGE in bright-pink letters. This far out of the city, we can see stars winking in the sky.

Becca's head swivels, orange wig bobbing, as I navigate the quiet lanes between outdoor storage lockers to park in front of the entrance. I'm wearing a wig, too, this one a dirty-blond bob that smells like chemicals and makes my neck itch. Becca insisted on fake glasses for each of us and stuffed her shirt with a pillow to make it look like she's pregnant. Inside, she uses her own pen to sign in with an indistinct scribble, and the guy at the desk gives us a cursory once-over before buzzing us through the heavy door to the interior storage units.

We keep our heads down as the security cameras follow our harried progress, and I have a flashback to Footloose's fun house, the red eyes of the cameras recording my every move for his later enjoyment. My breathing turns shallow as we navigate the maze of corridors, the concrete floor and high warehouse ceiling making our footsteps echo off the walls like unwelcome company.

"All right," Becca says when we stop in front of unit C969, a blue roll-up door with a silver lock. "Don't overreact when I open this."

"It's just a collection of tokens you kept from your victims to commemorate their murders," I reply. "Why would I overreact?"

She gives me a look. "You know what you're like."

For some reason, I'd taken Becca at her word when she told me the key was for the storage unit, but as I watch her bend to insert it in the lock, my heart pounds double time, uncertainty taking over. Just as quickly as that fear arrives it flees, the key slipping in easily and the lock tumbling open, the fear of actually seeing what's inside swiftly taking its place.

Becca grunts as she heaves up the door halfway and steps under into the dark. I wait for the smell of rot and decay to waft out, but it just smells like cold and concrete and dust, and a second later, she turns on the light, and I duck to follow her into her lair.

When she'd told me the key opened the unit and she'd used it to store her "tokens," I'd envisioned a creepy shrine with melted black candles and blood-smeared walls, clumps of hair and cobwebs in the corners. In reality, it's boring. In fact, if she had actually died and I'd never learned of the unit's existence and it had been auctioned off, I'm not sure the unlucky buyer would have known they'd stumbled onto a serial killer's treasure trove, thinking it was just someone's odd idea of a collection.

A set of cheap wooden tables line the walls on three sides; two tables have four items, the third has five. More than anything, the room has a thick layer of dust, and I sneeze before I take two steps in.

"Shh," Becca says, though we're the only people around and certainly the two most dangerous, despite appearances.

The first item on the table to my left is a small silver pin in the shape of a cheerleader, the letters MV affixed with tiny red gemstones. The silver has tarnished, now black in most places, and dust covers the rest. Still, I recognize the initials as belonging to Missy Vanscheer, who had the misfortune of being Becca's first victim. Missy was a cheerleader Becca had bickered with in high school who was rumored to have gotten pregnant and run off with her much older boyfriend, something that was never proven because it was completely untrue. I'm not sure if Becca killed Missy first or the fall did it, but Becca definitely pushed her off the cliff at the top of Barr Lode Trail.

Next to the pin is a tiny, dust-free patch of table that bears the imprint of an object, but no object. The third space is occupied by a college bus pass dated ten years earlier, and fourth is a pair of tortoiseshell glasses, the right lens shattered. The next two tables have similar tokens, some of which I recognize, some I don't. There's a high-heeled shoe with a red sole, and I know I'd carried the foot that still bore the matching shoe because I'd noted the pricey designer footwear before burying her out at the old corn field. A 2014 ticket stub for a movie confirms it was from the guy Becca told me had cut in front of her in line for the film, and a refund receipt for a jewelry store purchase suggests I've found the token for the woman who'd harangued Becca at work and tried relentlessly to get her fired until Becca permanently ended the argument. The last item is a red binder clip with white polka dots. Angelica, my former coworker, used to wear one on a chain around her neck because she was a kiss ass who wanted to show our boss how much she loved office supplies.

I take in the macabre reminders of my sister's hobby, the dust confirming her claim that she only visits when she has something to add, that she doesn't make a "habit" of this, though the thirteen tokens suggest otherwise. When I finish my perusal, however, Becca's not enjoying a sick walk down memory lane. She's standing next to the first table and staring at the empty space in spot number two.

"What was there?" I ask, still naively hoping everything might be okay, that Footloose had found the key but not its lock, that he'd never located her morbid stash.

"Guess," she says.

"I have absolutely no idea. Why would you take it?"

She turns slowly and fixes me with a gaze meant to imply that I'm the world's biggest idiot.

"You didn't take it?"

She shakes her head.

"Then what was it?"

"Guess," she repeats.

"How could I—" I cut myself off because the answer to this game has been the same all along. "Another key?"

A stiff nod, and the empty spot becomes even more ominous. I'd learned that Becca had killed Missy Vanscheer after my sister called me out to Barr Lode Trail to help her with something a week before my eighteenth birthday. That something had been carrying the body of Shanna Lewis, her coworker at the jewelry store and victim number two, up the mountain and watching Becca toss it over the edge.

Her nostrils flare as she inhales, and though I've known her to be a monster my whole life, it's the first time I've seen the mask fall off to reveal her at her most evil. If Footloose were still alive, he'd be dead very shortly.

"Let's go," she says.

She refuses to say anything more, but simmering rage wafts off her like a perfume as we lock up and I trail her back to the front, fearing she might take out her fury on the poor desk guy. The worst thing she does, however, is not say thank you as she stalks out the door and sticks out her hand for my car keys.

"I don't think that's a good idea," I say, clutching them in my palm.

"Why the fuck not?"

"Because I don't want to be an accessory to murder."

"Since when?"

"Since ever, Becca."

"Give me the keys. I'm not going to hit anybody. I just want to drive at the speed of a non-octogenarian."

The thing about Becca is that she lies all the time, the same way people breathe to live. But she doesn't lie about murder to me because I'm the only person she has to talk to about her favorite pastime. Right now, however, she's so angry that I'm actually a little bit afraid for myself, so I reluctantly pass her the keys.

She barely waits for me to get into the passenger seat before she yanks the pillow out of her shirt and we're peeling out of the lot, tires squealing. I grip the door with one hand and the dash with the other, and while she doesn't drive like an octogenarian, she doesn't drive like someone with a license or a respect for life, either. She also doesn't drive far. The six-minute trip brings us to another storage facility, this one just as desolate as the last. Except this time, she doesn't stop in front of the well-lit entrance. She drives a minute past the building and parks on the shoulder of the road.

I glance around warily. "What are we doing?"

"Let's go."

I'm loath to get out of the car while Becca's in the driver's seat in the iciest rage I've ever seen. As though she can sense the reason for my reluctance, she throws the keys at me as she gets out and stomps back toward the storage center.

I get out and hurry after her, not sure if I'd feel less safe alone in my car on the side of a road in this remote area in the middle of the night or trailing after my serial killer sister in this remote area in the middle of the night. "Why are we walking?" I whisper.

"Just keep your head down," she orders. It's gotten cold enough that her breath comes out in white puffs, the clouds hanging in the air.

I've never accompanied Becca on a kill before, but I imagine this is what it's like. She moves, stealthy and fast, back straight, shoulders square. She's focused on something, and she's furious. I feel innately horrible for whatever her target might be and keep the keys clutched in my hand, ready to sprint back to my car at the first sign of trouble.

She walks past the storage facility, the warm yellow light from the lobby showcasing its lone employee as we pass. There are no trees out here, only silent, single-story buildings, the ground mostly dirt and concrete, a light breeze whistling between the dark structures.

"Becca," I whisper again, "please tell me what we're doing."

In response, she turns abruptly and stomps back toward the storage facility, this time approaching from the side that won't allow the worker to see us. The exterior units are here, a maze of garage doors illuminated by the occasional fluorescent light buzzing overhead. Becca never slows as she winds her way through the sea of identical units before stopping at one in the middle of a row of indistinguishable doors.

"The missing key's for this unit?" I ask.

She nods sharply.

"Well, how are we going to open…"

She crouches, uses the hem of her sleeve to cover her hand, and raises the door approximately two inches. Pulling her phone from her pocket, she sticks it underneath and takes a picture. The flash is unexpected in the night, and I blink spots from my vision as Becca does it twice more, before straightening to study the screen. Her murderous expression doesn't change as I tentatively approach and stare at three pictures of an empty storage unit.

"Um…" I say.

She closes the door with her foot and strides back toward the road, me hustling along behind again. As always.

"Tell me what's going on," I plead when we reach my car. I get in the driver's side, and Becca doesn't argue, which is a terrible indicator of just how dire this situation is.

"I knew I shouldn't have kept it," she says eventually. "But I really liked that car."

It takes a second for the words to sink in, for me to realize she's referring to the car that waited at the base of Barr Lode Trail, the one in which I'd first seen Shanna's broken, dead body.

"That was your second...token? Your car?"

She nods. "The key to the unit that held the car."

"And now the car's gone?"

"It appears to be."

"Because Footloose found it?"

"That's the only thing that makes sense."

"And he left the door unlocked for you?"

She's chewing on the inside of her cheek, and I can see a smudge of blood at the corner of her mouth. "Someone did. That's why I didn't open it all the way. If they were waiting for me to show up, they might have wanted to document it."

I picture the cameras in the lot capturing our shadows darting past the closed lockers and then another camera waiting inside, triggered to go off when its motion sensor was activated. I feel dizzy.

"Why would he do all this?"

"You're asking the wrong questions, Carrie."

My palms are clammy on the steering wheel. "Okay, what would he have done with the car?"

"Wrong again."

I sigh in frustration. Becca's idea of the right question tends to be terrible. "Please, Becca. Tell me the question."

"The question," she snaps, "is if he has the car, then what the fuck is he waiting for?"

CHAPTER 17

I've been waiting for a long time. Waiting for my parents to recognize Becca's strangeness, to do something about it. For Becca to tire of the game, to tire of me and move on. For the police to catch on. For her to really be gone. For my life to begin. And yet, somehow, after a lifetime of waiting, I'm still not ready for the knock at the door before I leave for work the next day, to open it up and see Greaves on the other side. His well-honed poker face can't hide the worrisome glint in his eye.

"Good morning," he says. I'm wearing sweats and a T-shirt, and the half cup of coffee I'd had for breakfast immediately turns to pure acid in my stomach. "May I come in?"

"I don't think that's a good idea."

"Why not?"

There are a million reasons I don't want Greaves in my

home, but the serial killer in my guest room tops the list. And if the creaking floorboards overhead are anything to go by, she just woke up.

"Because I have to go to work."

"I'd like you to come to the station."

I clench the doorknob and catch Greaves's eyes flickering to my white knuckles.

"Why?"

"To talk."

Predictably, Mr. Myer chooses this moment to lurch out of his house, broom in hand, and hastily sweep his way down the drive. Greaves follows my stare and turns back to me with a small smirk, like he knows he's won. Mr. Myer has likely already called his neighbor Mrs. Wong, and she's probably polishing her binoculars.

"Fine," I tell Greaves, holding up a hand when he makes a move to step inside. "I'll come to the station."

Surprise flashes on his face before he quickly hides it, and I grab my bag and phone from the hall table, darting a glance up the stairs. I don't see Becca, but I know she's there, that she's listening. What I don't know is what she'll do if I let Greaves inside.

I trail Greaves downtown, his eyes catching mine in his rearview mirror at each red light, like I might be brave enough to make a run for it. But soon enough we're parked, and he's holding open the door to the police station, gesturing me through the squad room and leading the way to the too-familiar hall of interrogation rooms.

The last time I was here was the night Fiona asked to meet, and Greaves had given us a private space to talk while he eavesdropped on the other side of the two-way mirror. Now he's probably doing the same thing, letting me stew while he watches me squirm.

It feels like a lifetime but is probably an hour before he returns to the room, two paper cups of water in hand, an apologetic smile on his face. "Sorry for the delay," he lies. "Got caught up."

"No problem," I lie, too.

This room doesn't have a table, just two cheap plastic chairs positioned opposite each other, and now Greaves takes a seat, his knees a foot away from mine. I sip the water, my mouth dry with nerves I try desperately to hide. He probably thinks I'm trying to figure out my next move, but really I'm thinking about Becca and what she might be getting up to. Raiding my kitchen? Skipping town? Using my car to kill someone along the way?

Greaves wears a plain white T-shirt that showcases his unexpectedly muscled arms and leans in toward me like we're two friends about to have a friendly conversation in a police station, though he doesn't talk—he just waits. This is a technique Becca uses. Let you fill in the blanks, let your overactive imagination contemplate the worst-case scenarios, let you do the talking so she can pick and choose which words to use against you. Unfortunately for Greaves, I have a lot of worst-case scenarios to consider, and I'm not about to ruminate on any of them out loud.

"I'm sorry," he says.

Startled, I squeeze the cup and douse my knee with tepid water. "What?"

"I'm sorry," he repeats, this time on a sigh. "I've done—we've done—everything we can to locate your sister, and I know no answers can sometimes be harder to accept than the worst answer."

I stare intently at my knee, the cotton of my sweatpants clinging to my skin as my mind races.

"I've tried retracing her steps," Greaves says. "Speaking to her neighbors, her coworkers, her friends. We're still working to figure out exactly who Footloose was, if he had a second, um…"

"Burial ground."

He nods. "I know it's taking a while, but I wanted to let you know that we haven't stopped looking. We never will."

I'm thinking of Becca's stupid disguises, her most recent murder, her storage unit. I'm not sure how long the game can go on with these two playing the leading roles.

"Why did you ask me to come here instead of just telling me this at my door? I'm late for work."

"Your neighbor," he replies dryly. "Mr. Myer."

"What about him?"

"Every time I'm in the neighborhood, he asks me to help with something at his house. He's got a stuck window, he heard a possum in the basement, can't find his car keys. It drives me nuts."

He's smiling, but he's lying, too. He wanted Mr. Myer to snoop. He wanted me to let him inside so *he* could snoop. And if that didn't work, he wanted me to come here.

"I also wanted to run something by you," he adds. "You know about the Brampton Kill Seekers?"

I nod because he knows I do.

"Their recent, uh, studies, have revealed some interesting patterns."

"You didn't already know about the patterns?"

A ghost of a smile. "We knew. But having them posted online means we're receiving a lot more calls. A lot of people getting the idea that there's a second Brampton serial killer on the loose."

"Yeah. That was their thought."

"What were your thoughts?"

I blink. "My thoughts? Why would that matter?"

He shrugs. "I'm covering all angles. You're the only person we know who encountered Footloose and survived. Maybe you have some insight."

I'm already shaking my head. "I don't."

"What about your sister?"

I shiver instinctively, like the temperature in the room just dropped twenty degrees. "What?"

"Did he give you any indication that he was responsible

for her disappearance? Anything you can think of that might suggest where he…put her?"

"No. I mean, I told you this already. I told everyone. He implied that he'd hurt her, but he never actually said what he did. Or where she was."

"And Shanté Williams?"

"I told you. He said he brought her to the fun house and she…didn't make it out."

"It's odd that we can't find those bodies."

"Well, there were thirteen in Kilduff before anybody found one. Maybe it's just a matter of time."

He finishes his water and carefully crumples the paper cup in his hand. "Who else is there?" he asks, drumming his fingers on his leg. "Fiona McBride."

"Have you found her?"

He shakes his head. "It's unlikely that a seventeen-year-old girl managed to skip town without a trace."

I'd read the papers. I know the theories. The abandoned car at Barr Lode, the bag of essentials. "They said she met up with her boyfriend and took off."

"She didn't have a boyfriend."

"Well, you're the police. You would know."

Greaves leans back in his chair, the plastic creaking. "Imagine my surprise when I learned Misha Collins was your real estate agent."

I'd already started to see where this line of questioning was heading, but my shaky intake of breath is entirely genuine. Not a day has passed where I haven't relived that horrible night on a sick, endless loop. My naive belief that Becca would follow me out the door and leave Misha alone. Alive.

"It's terrible," I say. "She was so young."

"You know what I noticed?" Greaves reaches into his back pocket and pulls out a square of shiny folded paper, opening it to reveal the listing brochure from the open house, Misha's pretty face smiling out from the front.

"What?"

"She looks a lot like your sister."

I do a double take. Objectively, I know what Becca looks like. She's tall and thin and blond, pretty enough to turn heads but cold enough that those same heads often whip right back around, knowing instinctively it's better for their gazes not to linger. But when I think of Becca, the way you think of anyone you know well, she's not just a collection of physical attributes. She's more. She's manipulative, she's cruel, she's frustrating, she's funny, she's insane. Misha was merely incompetent.

"I guess," I say doubtfully.

"Blond hair, blue eyes. Slender. Pretty."

"Dead."

Something flickers in his stare, and the energy between us shifts, reveals its true self. "Now you're hanging out with Nikk Boulter."

Another involuntary shiver racks me. Any logical person would have to agree that I'm the obvious thread between these cases. The obvious threat.

"We're not hanging out."

"I saw you together."

"That was one—"

"Twice," he interrupts. "You attended two meetings together. You went out after the first one. And you met him at the second."

I don't ask how he knew that. "Well, his wife is missing."

"No kidding. Angelica was up for the same promotion. Shanté stole your thunder at a funeral. Becca stole the spotlight your whole life. Fiona got all the attention after *you* beat Footloose. Misha Collins flirted with your boyfriend while showing you houses. And now Nikk Boulter's wife is missing, just in time for you to become his newest friend."

I drop the cup of water, the remaining inch splashing across the floor. Greaves doesn't move.

"He's not my friend. I don't know what happened to those women. That's your job."

His gaze is hard. "That's why you're here."

"Because you can't protect the women in this town?"

"Because I know more than you think I do."

"Prove it."

"A black 2009 Pontiac Sunfire stashed in unit G178 at a storage facility at the edge of town, paid for by a fake account for the past ten years, with the DNA of Rebecca Lawrence, Carrie Lawrence, and Shanna Lewis all over it."

It's his trump card, and my stunned expression rewards him for playing it perfectly.

I shake my head stupidly. "That— I— No—"

"Shanna Lewis hasn't been seen since she left her shift at Robson Jewelry on May 8, 2010. Becca Lawrence, also employed at Robson Jewelry, hasn't been seen since November of last year."

"That's—"

"As I understand it, you accused Ms. Lewis of stealing your high school boyfriend. Is that correct?"

"No, I didn't have a boyfriend—"

"Oh, that's right. He didn't feel the same way."

"That's not—"

"So someone slashed her tires."

"I didn't—"

"And now we find this car with her DNA beneath the front bumper and her blood all over the interior of the trunk."

"My sister reported her car missing. Someone else—"

He leans in. "Was Becca helping you, Carrie? Did she know what you did to that poor girl and try to help you?"

My face is wet with sweat or tears or both. "She never helps me."

"Maybe she got tired of keeping your secrets, especially after what happened to Angelica. You got that promotion in the end, right?"

"I had nothing to do with those things."

"I get it," Greaves says kindly. "High school's hard. Hell, life's hard. And some people…they just make it harder."

I'm shaking my head. "You have no idea."

"Tell me. I'm here to listen."

I'm vibrating with frustration and indignity, guilt and horror. Becca caused this whole mess, and once again I'm left to clean it up.

My nose is running, and I wipe it on my sleeve. Greaves doesn't grimace, just waits patiently, the way he's been doing all along. Chipping away at my story, at the obstacles that keep landing in his path, getting to his final destination.

Somewhere in the building, someone is shouting, causing a commotion, and I want to be that person. I want to be stronger and braver and better than I am, not this sniveling, pathetic mess. My lower lip trembles as I open my mouth, trying to figure out how to begin. Wanting this so badly to be over, the way I always have, but not like this. Not when I was so close to the end.

A knock on the door makes me jump. Greaves sucks in a breath, his irritation palpable. Another knock, louder than the first.

"Yeah," he says, his voice cold.

There's a click, and I watch the silver knob turn, everything moving in slow motion as the door pushes inward and a man in a brown suit steps through, his expression pinched. He's quickly shouldered out of the way by a familiar blond in a sweater and jeans, her eyes shiny with tears.

"Carrie!" Becca cries, collapsing into my lap and flinging her arms around my neck, sobbing desperately. "You...You're okay!"

Slowly, I wrap my arms around my suddenly alive sister. I've known about her not-dead status for weeks, but my stunned expression is entirely genuine and mirrored in Greaves's own face as he watches me, a muscle in his jaw ticcing.

"Becca," I say stiffly, patting her back. "You're alive. I can't believe it."

Hovering near the man in the suit is a frail brunette with huge, brown eyes, peering uncertainly at the scene before her, like it's too real and raw to witness. Greaves looks away from the moving reunion and stands to approach the woman at the door.

"I'm Detective Marlon Greaves," he says.

"Lilly Fiennes." Her voice is small.

I do a double take. The last time I'd seen her picture was on the Brampton Kill Seekers' slideshow of missing women, certain my sister had killed her.

Slowly, Becca's trembling form releases me, and she makes a grand show of gathering strength and straightening. Her hair hangs in front of her face, the two-way mirror at her back. I'm the only one who can see her eyes, the only one to record the smug flicker of triumph in their murky depths before she collapses to the floor.

CHAPTER 18

"It was a bit last-minute, but it worked out perfectly in the end," Becca says as she brings three cups of piping-hot tea to my kitchen table and takes a seat with me and Lilly. We're both looking as shell-shocked as we did at the police station, while Becca's "distress" had vanished the second we were in my car driving home, one not-arrested woman and the two women she hadn't murdered.

"So last night..." I say, not for the first time.

Becca blows on her tea and nods at Lilly to drink hers. "I told you," she says. "I gave it some thought and figured the most likely scenario was that the storage unit was a trap. Footloose couldn't be certain I'd died, so he prepared a backup plan and sent the second storage unit key to the police."

Greaves had flinched when Becca told that part of the story, confirming that they had, in fact, been given the kcy like a gift. It wasn't something they'd uncovered as part of their excellent police work in her case.

Becca adds a spoonful of sugar to her cup. "Then when I heard Greaves stop by this morning, I went to get Lilly."

Lilly is, perhaps, the most unbelievable part of this whole story. Becca had indeed sought refuge at Nikk's home during her recovery because she knew his wife was a nurse, and Lilly had been so kind during her stay that Becca had actually started to *like* her. Like her so much that she could no longer overlook Nikk's wife-beating tendencies and had come up with a plan to help her. The two had taken the many expensive pieces of jewelry Lilly had collected over the years, and when Becca was well enough, she had driven Lilly to stay at a remote bed-and-breakfast half an hour outside of town, paying in cash with the money from the pawned diamonds so Nikk— and the police—couldn't track her.

Lilly has nodded along agreeably with this story and looks at Becca the way Felix looks at Graham: with pure trust and innocence. The only false part of the story they told the police—which they appear to have rehearsed on the trip back to Brampton—is that Becca had spent the past weeks with Lilly at the B and B, not at my house. Greaves trained his frosty stare on me during the entire conversation, but I'd been just as astonished by the development as everyone else and had no trouble appearing engrossed in the recap.

At length, and very reluctantly, Greaves had stalked out of the room, leaving it to a different detective to tell us we were free to go. They wanted to talk to Becca more about her encounter with Footloose, but she was feigning amnesia and claiming to recall nothing apart from opening her door to "Detective Schroeder"—aka Footloose— and later waking up in Nikk and Lilly's spare bedroom. She'd be sure to call if she remembered anything else.

"I'm glad you came when you did," I say, sipping my tea. "Greaves had really convinced himself the town had a second serial killer on its hands."

"He's right," Becca says.

I drink too fast and burn my tongue. "What?"

Lilly's eyes widen in horror, and her cup clatters on the table when she sets it down.

"Do you want to take a nap?" Becca asks. "I know it's been an eventful day."

Lilly blinks. "I, um…Maybe I'll just go to the restroom."

"Sure thing. It's at the top of the stairs."

We wait until we hear the third step from the top let out its mournful howl, followed by the click of the bathroom door.

"What the hell?" I demand. "Why would you say that in front of her?"

"Because I'm not talking about me, you idiot. You said before that there were three new hit-and-run deaths."

"You said you didn't believe me!"

She ignores that. "And when Nikk reported Lilly miss-ing, Greaves asked him some very specific questions about me. Then the hit-and-runs. Then Shanna's car." She stares at me like she's made a valid point. Or any point at all.

"What?"

"Someone knows too much!" She slaps her hand on the table in a rare show of emotion. "Someone knows about me. So unless you'd like to admit that you've suddenly learned how to use the gas pedal—"

"I drive safely."

"Then there's somebody out there that's trying to frame me for these new deaths."

"It's not 'framing you' when it's true."

The toilet flushes, and we both grow quiet, listening for footsteps on the stairs. Nothing yet.

"It's still consecutive life sentences for both of us," Becca counters. "How long do you think Graham will visit you in high max before moving on?"

I scowl and sip my tea, the drink suddenly bitter.

"Look." Becca reaches over to touch my hand, making me flinch. "Footloose shone a light on this town, and neither one of us can afford to be caught in its glare. The only reason we've gotten away with this for so long—"

"You got away with it. I'm a victim of blackmail."

"—is because no one was looking. Now they are. And if someone's out there imitating me, it's because they want that light to get even brighter. We have to figure out who they are and stop them."

"Assuming you're right and this isn't all just the work of your very overactive and very vain imagination, how are we going to do that? The last time we tried to find a killer, he very nearly killed us."

"But failed," Becca replies. "So we learn from past mistakes and—"

"He's here," Lilly says from the doorway.

"What?" I clutch my chest. "Who? Greaves? He—"

"No," Becca says, getting to her feet as her expression darkens. "Nikk."

Lilly's gone even more pale with fear, and when the doorbell rings, she somehow manages to pale even further, her eyes huge. I hate to admit it, but this is one of the rare occasions on which it's good to have Becca around. Whatever Nikk's got planned is no match for my sister.

"Basement," Becca says, herding Lilly toward the door I never use. The basement is gross and dank, home to the growling furnace of nightmares and a few boxes of dusty Christmas ornaments.

"What do I do?" I whisper when Nikk gives up on the bell and begins pounding on the door.

Becca glares at me like this is somehow my fault. "Answer it."

"And say what?"

"Just not the truth." She closes the basement door and leaves me standing alone in the hall as Nikk appears in the living room window, his hands up to shield his eyes from the glare of the afternoon sun. I freeze like an idiot until he spots me and gives a small smile that doesn't reach his eyes. I return the gesture and unlock the door with clammy hands.

"Hi," I say awkwardly. I hadn't changed out of my sweats and the stress of the morning—of my whole life—means I look convincingly exhausted. "You caught me, uh, napping."

"I guess a morning at the precinct would be tiring."

I blink. "What?"

He's wearing black pants with a pristine white button-up shirt and a dark tie, a silver name tag reading NIKK BOULTER, GENERAL MANAGER still pinned to his chest. A gold Rolex glints on his wrist, and his hair is as impeccably tousled as ever. But the tearful, concerned husband I'd met before is gone, and in his eyes is a hard gleam, its intention impossible to miss because I'd seen it in my own sociopath sister's eyes too many times before. It takes just that second, my startled, unguarded response, for him to slip the benign mask back in place and fasten it at the edges, his eyes suddenly soft and blue, the malice gone.

"I'm sorry," he says with a bashful smile. "I'm just…" He takes a breath. "I heard from a friend at the station that Lilly and Becca had shown up this morning. And that they'd left with you."

"Um…" I spot movement behind him, Mr. Myer, sweeping his driveway for the second time today. He drops his broom and takes his time picking it up, eyes trained on my house. "Yes," I say. "That's true. They asked me to answer some questions. Did Detective Greaves tell you this?"

"It's true? Lilly's alive? She's okay?"

My mind is racing. "She seemed fine. At least, she was fine when...I dropped them off."

That catches him off guard. "What?"

"I was going to bring them here—obviously I wanted to spend time with my dear sister—but they asked me to drop them at Brampton Plaza."

"Why?"

I shrug and resist the urge to look at the Rolex. "They said they wanted to buy something. No, not buy. Sell. They wanted to sell something."

Nikk's eyes narrow, and that hard gleam is back. "Pawn something?"

"That's not the word they used, though I guess there is a pawn store in the plaza, isn't there?"

"And then what were they going to do?"

"I don't know. Becca was acting a bit strange, to be honest. She seemed to recognize me at the station but then said she didn't remember anything else."

"What about Lilly? What did she say?"

I shake my head. "She spoke to someone in a different room. I didn't hear."

"We'll have to go to the pawnshop."

I stop shaking my head. "What now?"

Becca telling me that Nikk beat his wife and apologized with jewelry is one thing; there's always the possibility she made it all up just to hear herself talk. But the terror on Lilly's face when he knocked on my door put any doubt to rest, and despite his convincing performance now, I'm not buying it. I know all too well how it feels to be manipulated and mistreated.

"Let's go," he insists. "We have to find them. If Lilly's okay, I need to see her."

I mentally curse Becca for not suggesting I hide in the basement with them. "They're probably not there anymore," I try. "I mean, I dropped them off at least an hour ago."

Nikk's pacing on my stoop, and now he pauses. "You're right. We should wait here."

Instinctively, I move to barricade the door with my body, which earns me a suspicious stare. Mr. Myer has abandoned the sweeping gimmick and is openly waving over his neighbor, Mrs. Wong.

"Now that I think about it," I say loudly, "we should go to the pawnshop."

Nikk flinches at the volume. "We should?"

"Yes. Because there's a hair salon in the same plaza, and Becca mentioned something about dyeing her hair. For a fresh start. And that takes a while. She's probably in the chair next to Lilly, getting a makeover. I'm sure Lilly wants to impress you."

Nikk appears to mull this over, but I know I've won. It's the easiest way to thwart Becca: play to her vanity. Nikk might not be a serial killer—that I know about—but he's definitely vain, and the technique works here, too.

"You're right," he says. "That's probably it. Maybe we'll get some flowers on the way."

I'm still in my sweats, but I grab my bag from the hall table and follow Nikk outside and into his car. He's silent as he drives, tapping his fingers on the steering wheel and cursing under his breath when we hit a red light, his impatience clear. And not the desperate, naively hopeful impatience of someone anticipating a great reunion. The kind of impatience Becca displays when too many months have passed between kills and you can sense the invisible, murderous tension building.

"So," I say brightly, "this is a great day, huh? For you, for me, for the Brampton Kill Seekers."

Nikk glances over, his gaze steely. I think he's going to snap at me, but then his shoulders slump. "There's something I should have told you," he says as we accelerate through the intersection. "The reason I went to that first Kill Seekers meeting wasn't because I thought they would find Lilly. It's because Emmett texted and said you'd shown up. And I wanted to meet you—honest—but...I also wanted to find your sister."

I blink at the admission. "Why?"

"I'm sorry to tell you this, because you seem like a good person, but Becca's a"—he shakes his head sadly—"thief."

That's not the word I thought he was going to use.

"After her so-called run-in with Footloose, she came to my house to recover. Her leg was broken, and she needed some stitches on her forehead, and she knew Lilly was a nurse. She asked us not to tell anyone she was alive because she wasn't convinced Footloose was truly dead, and we respected her wishes. We took care of her, and when she was recovered, she vanished. With a lot of expensive jewelry."

I gasp dramatically. "The pawnshop."

"Yep."

"But what about Lilly? Was she really missing?"

"At first, I thought Becca had hurt her, but now that she's back, I can't help but wonder if maybe they were in on it together."

"Why would they steal? From you, of all people?"

He seems genuinely baffled as we pull into the plaza parking lot, half-full on a weekday afternoon, and stop in front of Silver Pawn Savers, its orange awning flapping in the breeze.

"Beats me." Nikk hops out of the car and jogs to the store as though Lilly might actually be inside.

I hurry in after him, the shop the predictable mishmash of instruments, artwork, jewelry, and weapons secured inside glass cases. The man at the counter looks like he builds motorcycles for fun, a leather vest covering his muscular but otherwise bare chest, and a blue bandana on his head.

He gives me a cursory nod before eyeballing Nikk.

"Were there two women in here earlier?" Nikk asks, turning in a circle like he might spot them ducked behind one of the displays.

"Lots of customers," the man replies.

"But two, specifically. Selling jewelry. An hour ago."

He shrugs.

"They might have come in separately," I offer helpfully. "What about a blond woman about this tall?" I hold my hand at a perfectly average height.

The man stares.

"Or…a brunette? Of the same height?"

Nikk has pulled out his phone and now shows the man the screen, which is a picture of Lilly. "Was she in here earlier?"

"Don't recognize her."

Nikk looks at me expectantly, so I grab my own phone, call up the only photo of Becca I kept out of obligation, and show it to the shop owner. "How about her?"

"Nope."

"Anyone selling fifty thousand dollars' worth of diamonds?" Nikk asks.

I do a double take at the number. So does the man.

"Definitely not. You cops?"

"Definitely not." Nikk scowls and stalks out of the store.

"You all right?" the man asks as I turn to leave. "With him?"

I force a smile. "Just fine."

We repeat the process at the hair salon two doors down, with the same results. When we're back on the sidewalk, Nikk stares at me accusingly.

"You said they were here."

"I said I dropped them here. It's what they wanted. I don't know what they did after I left."

He squints at me, jaw twitching, before jerking his head toward his car. "I'll take you home."

The return trip is even more uncomfortable than the one over, and all I can think is that Becca better have used the time to drive Lilly back to the bed-and-breakfast and get herself a room, too.

"They have to come here," Nikk insists as he turns onto my street. "Where else would they go?"

"I don't know. To be honest, they didn't seem..." I trail off as I see Graham sitting on my front step. I check the time: 5:30 p.m. Dammit. I forgot we had plans after work.

Graham's trying to teach Felix how to play tug-of-war with a stuffed carrot. Felix, for his part, does not seem to understand what Graham is doing, and Graham definitely doesn't know what I'm doing when I step out of Nikk's car.

"Hi, Graham," Nikk calls through the open window.

Graham scoops up Felix and gets to his feet. "Nikk, hi. How are you?"

"I'll let Carrie catch you up. You didn't, uh, see anyone at the house while you were waiting?"

Graham's expression remains blank. "No. Carrie wasn't home. Obviously."

"Right. Well, good seeing you."

Nikk drives off, and I stand stiffly at the curb for a second before approaching the house, stopping a few feet from Graham and Felix.

"So," Graham says.

"How long have you been here?"

Felix launches himself at Graham's chin, nibbling heartily.

"I don't know. Half an hour? We had plans to walk Felix, but you weren't home…"

I study my house. The door is closed, and there's no sign of Becca peering out the window, watching the awkward display. My car is still in the drive, but they used their own vehicle to get to and from the B and B, so all I can hope is that they used my diversion to make their escape.

"Did you go inside?"

"I opened the door and called out but didn't go in. Felix isn't exactly a good houseguest." Graham shakes his head, as though remembering the real issue. "What were you doing with Nikk?"

Becca's return and Nikk's arrival had prevented me from planning how best to explain the situation to Graham. I certainly don't want to tell him about my near arrest and all the very good evidence leading up to it, but the tiniest movement in my bedroom window catches my eye and I know I don't have a choice. If I don't do it, Becca will do it for me.

"Becca's back," I blurt out. "And so is Nikk's wife."

Graham gives a startled jolt and looks around. "What? Where?"

"We don't know. I, um...I was at the police station this morning, answering some questions Detective Greaves had about, um, Misha."

"Why would you know anything about that?"

"I don't. That's what I told him. And then Becca showed up with Lilly."

Graham's expression is strangely neutral, the way it is when I know he's trying not to be upset until he has all the facts. But the fact that the news that my dead sister is, in fact, not dead doesn't produce more of a reaction feels very un-Graham-like.

"Are you okay?" I ask, reaching for Felix when he starts to squirm. Graham backs away, and my fingers close on empty air.

"Maybe you should tell me everything. Inside," he adds, shooting a look over my shoulder. I don't bother turning. I know Mr. Myer is en route.

"Um...sure. Yes. Of course."

I glance at the window again, but whatever I thought I saw is no longer there. Which, of course, is no indication at all of whether or not it's hiding somewhere else in the house.

We go inside and sit on the couch. Graham puts

Felix down and steps on the handle of the leash, letting the puppy explore without disappearing altogether. The dog immediately turns in a circle and plops down, writhing around on his back before gnawing on the coffee table leg.

I recap my visit to the police station, opting for most but not all of the truth. I stop before the part when Greaves brought up the discovery of Shanna's vehicle and my notable links to too many missing and dead women, segue into Becca and Lilly's arrival and their odd request that I drop them at the plaza, and finally Nikk's visit and insistence that we head to the pawnshop in search of his wife. I don't know if we'll run into Nikk again, but Graham's not much of a liar and I want him to back up my story if it comes down to it.

"Whoa," he says eventually, blinking at the empty space over my head. "That's a lot."

"I know. Just when it felt like things might be settling down…"

Felix jumps on Graham's leg and gazes at him hopefully, and Graham scoops him up, studying his shiny, little eyes. "I thought we were settling down," he says quietly.

"We are. We are. Just our own version of settling."

"Or Becca's version."

A chill sneaks over me, and I resist the urge to look over my shoulder to make sure she's not creeping down the stairs. "What?"

"Let's be honest, Carrie. Can we do that?"

I bristle, a bit hypocritically. "Of course we can."

"The reason we didn't do it sooner—find a place, get a dog, move on with our lives—is because of your sister. Because she was so fucking…I don't know. Weird? But she had a hold on you. And of course I wasn't glad when she went missing, but her absence made a space for me. For us."

He's holding Felix, and it's impossible to miss that "us" doesn't just mean me and Graham, or me and Graham and Felix. It means our future. The intangible dream of a life together, the thing I want more than anything.

"There's always been a space for you. For us," I insist. "And I know she's a lot, but things are different now. I'm different. I have boundaries." I add that for Becca, who I imagine is eavesdropping through the floorboards.

Graham exhales. "I made some more appointments to see houses. The real estate agent's a man. He's six two. They said so on the phone. Three times."

"That's very reassuring. When do we go?"

"Are you sure you want to?"

Felix reaches out a little paw in my direction before wiggling madly, determined to reach my lap. After a second, Graham relinquishes him, and he flops onto my thighs, breathing hard. I rest my hand on his round little belly, feeling his heart beat.

"I'm positive," I say.

We get up and head outside, taking Felix for the planned

walk and getting takeout, eating in the park and researching the houses our new six-foot-two real estate agent has
lined up for viewing on Saturday. They're at the top end
of our newly increased budget, but unlike the hovels we'd
been seeing with Misha, they look promising, and I can
tell my enthusiasm goes a long way toward reassuring
Graham. We part ways on a good note, and I kiss both boys
before they leave and I let myself back into my house.

Becca and Lilly sit in the kitchen eating bowls of cereal.
"Why do you never have any decent food?" is Becca's
greeting.

"Why are you still here?"

Lilly studies her bowl intently, so Becca speaks for both
of them. "We're here because your stalker showed up
two seconds after you and Nikk left and waited on the
doorstep like a lunatic."

"He's my boyfriend, and we had plans. And we were
just gone for an hour and a half—why didn't you make
your big escape then?"

"Because Nikk's a psycho who's lurking around the
corner?"

"You don't know that," I reply, before reconsidering
my audience. "Maybe you're right. Well, what are your
plans, then? When do you leave?" My walk with Graham
put my priorities back into perspective, and getting roped
into Becca's petty mind games and actual murder games
is not something I'm willing to do. Anymore.

"Where would we go?"

"Literally anywhere. Back to the B and B, for example."

"That's not an option."

"Why? What'd you do?"

"Those places aren't free."

"Do you or do you not have fifty thousand dollars' worth of stolen jewelry?"

"It's Lilly's," Becca retorts. "And we spent the money."

"You spent fifty grand?"

"No! We spent five. You can't pawn that much jewelry without getting noticed, and we have to lie low. Now that Nikk's on the pawnshop trail, he can probably trace us back to the B and B, or close enough."

"I think you're giving him too much credit."

"She's not," Lilly says, her voice small. "He's done it before. I...I've tried before. But he always found me. Somehow, he always did."

In a millisecond, I feel enormously guilty. For her life, her husband, my sister, the pathetic meal options. "Sorry," I say, knowing it's not enough. "But there's got to be a way."

"She just needs to stay out of sight." Becca eats a stray green cereal loop off the table. "While we take care of the rest."

I give her a warning look.

"Moving furniture," she clarifies.

"Yeah, I got it."

"Good."

"But I'm tired of moving your furniture," I add. "In

the future, I'm only moving my own furniture. My couch, my table, my bed. Furniture."

"I don't know why you'd take those things. They're hideous."

"They're my furniture. You move your own furniture."

Lilly looks bewildered at the overuse of *furniture*.

"Fine, I will."

I open the cupboard for a wineglass. "Fine."

"In the meantime, Lilly stays with Graham."

I whirl around. "What? No."

Becca's pale gaze is steady. "Yes. Nikk doesn't know where he lives, and the biggest threat Graham poses is boring someone to death."

"You just called him a stalker."

"He is."

"No," I say again. "Leave him out of this."

Becca gets up and takes her still half-full bowl to the dishwasher, dumping it inside. Pink-tinted milk drips over the edges onto the floor. "Too late. It's decided."

"Incorrect," I say. "Graham is not a part of this. Drop it."

Holding my gaze, Becca says, "Lilly, get your things."

Lilly stands uncertainly.

"You said Nikk was outside," I remind her.

"We'll go out the back."

"Don't open that," I say, when she walks to the warped door and twists the lock. "It took me forever to get it closed the last time."

"So leave it open."

"No," I say, something in my voice causing Becca to turn, head cocked inquisitively, like maybe I'm not the gossamer obstacle she's used to plowing through.

"Or what?" she asks. I imagine all of her victims got the look I'm getting now. A cold, dead, calculating stare that says I'm not a person, I'm a thing that's in her way, and if I don't figure out how to move myself, she'll do it for me.

"I'll tell Nikk."

Slowly, her mouth opens. "You wouldn't."

"Try me."

"You would sic that man on an innocent woman?"

Any friend I'd ever had Becca had either stolen or driven away. She'd never had any friends of her own, no one she cared about, no one she could lose. This role reversal is a first for us.

I shrug. "She's your friend, not mine."

Something shifts in the pale depths of her eyes, a tiny but seismic glimmer of understanding, of the woman who complained that I'd "changed" upon her unwelcome return finally understanding that those words weren't just inconvenience but fact.

"Um," Lilly says. "What am I doing?"

Becca releases the doorknob. "Yeah, Carrie. What's she doing?"

I take a breath. This is my moment to say something dramatic, to really make a statement.

But the truth is, I don't fucking know.

CHAPTER 19

Our real estate agent's name is Beau Briggs, and he's every bit the six two his profile promised. He was a college football player turned real estate agent following a knee injury, and like Becca, he walks with a slight limp he denies. He's got a big smile and bigger plans for me and Graham and has apparently taken our increased budget as an indication that we're now willing to sell our souls in search of the right home, showing us houses that get our minds spinning and our bank balances screaming.

"Wow," Graham says as we stand in the foyer of a newly built home in a subdivision that's still under construction on the east side of town. "This is remarkable." His voice echoes off the marble walls and floors, bouncing down at us from the twenty-two-foot ceilings. The builder appears to have a strong preference for shiny things. A brass stair rail matches an enormous chandelier, and the kitchen cabinets are so slick I can see my stunned face reflected in the doors.

Graham catches my eye as Beau leads us onto a deck with a built-in firepit on one side and an outdoor kitchen on the other. He beams at us, and we smile politely in return.

He adjusts his bolo tie. "Pretty impressive, huh?"

"Very," I say, as Graham studies his shoes. "Three places to cook, just six feet away from each other."

"An abundance of options," he agrees.

He inhales deeply as though the air back here is as opulent as the house, which it's not, because both the home next door and the one on the opposite side of the lot are still half-finished, which means it smells like paint, plywood, and debt.

"Onward and upward!" Beau announces, pivoting on a heel and leading us back inside and up the grand staircase to the second floor with its four bedrooms, three bathrooms, and a bonus room so large it could double as a school.

"Nice, right?"

"It's...a lot," Graham offers.

The bathrooms show us where all the world's marble has wound up, the primary bedroom is the size of Graham's entire apartment, and Beau's smile is somehow bigger than everything. He plants his hands on his hips as he stands in the bonus room and faces us. "We'll have to move fast if you want to put in an offer."

"We don't," I interrupt, before Graham can politely deflect the question and we wind up spending the day touring homes we can't afford. "This is too big. We need something half the size. With one-tenth the marble."

Beau's face falls. "I see."

"It's also at the top of our budget."

His shoulders slump. "Right. I'm sorry. It's a difficult market right now, and if it was hard before, it's only gotten harder since Misha's...Misha's"—his voice breaks—"passing."

Graham shoots me a panicked look. "I'm sure we'll find something," he says, patting Beau awkwardly on the shoulder. "What else do you have lined up? That's more...suitable?"

Beau squares his broad shoulders. "Why don't I make a few phone calls?" he asks, tugging his phone from his pocket. "Cancel a couple of viewings and set up some other ones?"

"Sure," I say. "That would be great."

He leaves us in the bonus room and heads downstairs to make the calls in private, which is absolutely impossible in this acoustic nightmare. Every word travels up as clear as day, and it's obvious Beau has only arranged viewings in this specific and overpriced neighborhood and is scrambling to change course.

"I feel terrible," Graham mutters, pacing the width of the room. "You were right. We should have waited. Asking to view homes so soon after Misha's death is tactless."

"No," I assure him, "*you* were right. I think the reason Beau's showing us these places is because he needs the commission. We knew these houses probably weren't going to be our thing, but we're trying. We're…helping." Plus, I have a week off work for compassionate leave to help me "reunite" with my sister, and I'm seizing every opportunity I can to get away from her.

"I never thought finding a place would be so hard. Finding the right person was supposed to be the battle, and that was a breeze."

He catches my eye, and I blush, flattery and shame duking it out.

"We'll find a home," I tell him.

"What about Becca?"

"What about her?"

"What's she doing with her time?"

"Eating all my cereal, mostly. I think her leg hurts more than she lets on, and she's using bingeing Netflix as a cover for lying on the couch all day."

"So nothing's changed."

I smile. "Becca hasn't, but I have. She doesn't control our future. We do."

My smile fades as I glance out the window at the street to see a car idling at the curb, a now-familiar head of excellent hair peering out the driver's side window. Nikk.

I utter a silent prayer that he's just searching for Lilly and not a private place to confront me.

I'm still debating what to do when Beau leaps into the

room. "I've got three more places lined up," he announces proudly. "Ready?"

Beau drives, Graham's in the passenger seat, and I'm in the back, making it difficult to check to see if Nikk is following without making it obvious I'm looking for a stalker. I get out my phone and turn on the front-facing camera, holding it over my shoulder and aiming it out the back window, but a city bus blocks my view.

Nikk trails us to the next two houses, parking a few doors down so you'd only spot him if you were paranoid, which I am. The houses are decent, under budget, and boast exactly zero marble. One, however, is half an hour from the closest elementary school, while the other has a gravel pit for a backyard, which doesn't bode well for Felix. Beau's trying his best, but I can't get excited about them, though it's a toss-up if my lack of enthusiasm is due to the houses or the man following us.

"Door number three," Beau says, stopping at the curb in front of a green two-story Cape Cod on a corner lot. "Baker Street. It's been partially updated, so it's move-in ready but leaves lots of opportunity for you to put your stamp on it. Five minutes to the elementary school, twenty minutes to downtown. How are we feeling?"

Graham's eyebrows rise in pleasant surprise. So far, anyway, the house is decidedly not horrible, and when I turn in a circle as though taking in the family-friendly street, I don't see Nikk, which makes it even better.

"Let's take a look." We get out of the car and walk up to the door. A yellow rosebush is starting to bloom under the front window, its blossoms glowing golden in the afternoon sun. Through the open curtains, I spot a brick fireplace on one wall, and when we step inside, I see the renovation included an open-concept ground level with a small but nicely updated kitchen.

"Wow," Graham says, because he's never been good at a poker face.

Beau perks up. "Nice, right? Tastefully done, but no expense spared. New hardwood floors—the real stuff—and a new roof, too. Now, what's this?"

He crouches down to pick up a gold hoop earring from the floor, studying it before tucking it into his pocket. "Another buyer must have dropped it. This place is popular!"

Graham and I exchange a look that says Beau totally dropped and then "found" the earring to make this place seem more appealing, but the ruse was unnecessary. The three bedrooms and two bathrooms could use a fresh coat of paint but are otherwise fine, and I keep waiting for the other shoe to drop as each room makes me think more and more that this place could be my home. Our home. Graham's clutching my hand excitedly, and I know we're on the same page.

We enter the spacious primary bedroom, its windows overlooking the backyard. Beau talks about the walk-in closet, and Graham joins him to check it out as I take in the view. The yard is fenced in, which is perfect for a puppy, and a manageable size, since neither of us are good at yard work. I'm about to join them in the walk-in when Nikk Boulter unlatches the gate and strolls into the yard, hands tucked in his pockets. He peers around as though checking for witnesses before approaching the house and disappearing from sight. Graham and Beau have gone to check out the bathroom so I dart into the hall and hover at the top of the steps in time to hear the jiggle of a handle and a faint thud, as though Nikk's nudging the locked door with his shoulder.

Anxiously, I fidget with my bag, trying to figure out what to do. If he comes in, we're trapped up here. If he just wanted to talk, he'd have come in the front door. And if he reads the news, he may have taken inspiration from Misha's murder and thought this would be the perfect cover for his own crime and the easiest way to send a message to my sister.

My hands shake as I pull my phone from my purse, my thumb pressing the 9. There's another thud, this one louder, and another rattle of the door handle. The last thing I want is to involve the police, to have yet another showdown with Detective Greaves, another reason for him to ask me question after question, determined to catch me in my own web of lies.

But most of all, I don't want to die.

I press the 1.

"What are you doing?"

I nearly jump out of my skin when Beau appears at the bedroom door.

"I—" I begin. "There's someone downstairs—"

His brow furrows like he wants to tell me I'm imagining things, but we're interrupted by the unmistakable sound of wood groaning as it's pried apart.

"No," Beau says, his mouth setting in a determined line as he reaches into the inner pocket of his suit jacket. "Not this time."

Then he pulls out a small silver gun and dashes past me down the steps.

I squeak in shock and stumble back as Graham hurries out of the bedroom. "What's happening?" he asks, taking in my face and the phone in my hand, followed shortly by Beau's shouts from downstairs.

"Nikk—" I start, interrupted by the crack of a gun being fired. It's a single shot followed by a yelp and then more shouting as Beau charges back up to the front of the house. I hear a car start and tires squeal as it races away, and we tiptoe down the stairs to see Beau framed in the open door, pistol in hand, looking like a satisfied sheriff who's just run off the bad guy.

"What on earth was that?" Graham demands.

Beau replaces the gun in his jacket. "An intruder."

"You carry a gun?" That's my high-pitched voice.

"I'm licensed. Plus, after what happened to Misha..." He blinks rapidly and turns away before reaching into his pocket and pulling out a tissue, dislodging the earring from before. It slides across the floor, and for a minute, I just stare at it, the metal glinting in the sun, making something at the back of my brain start to tickle. Not a warning this time. A suggestion. I pick up the earring, the gold warm in my palm, and return it to Beau.

For a minute, the three of us just stand there awkwardly, not quite sure what to say or do.

"I promise this is a really good neighborhood," Beau offers eventually. "Ten minutes from the hospital."

CHAPTER 20

Becca walks into my bedroom the next afternoon and interrupts my nap. Planting her hands on her hips, she dramatically paces the short length of the room. "I've been thinking."

"Please don't."

"The person trying to frame me for the latest hit-and-run deaths... It's kind of weird that they've precipitated some pretty convenient advances in Kill Seeker technology."

"What?"

"Emilio's creepy little crime-hunter group is just a bunch of desperados looking for something to feel empowered by. And who benefits from their desperation?"

I shake my head. "You?"

"Emilio."

"His name is Emmett."

"Footloose is dead, I'm back, and Lilly's back. Freda disappeared in December—"

"Fiona."

"—and nothing crazy has happened since."

I sit up in bed. "Yesterday Nikk tried to murder me during a house tour, and our new real estate agent, Beau, shot at him, because you stabbed our previous agent to death."

Becca sighs. "You're missing the point."

"I hate it when you try to make a point."

"The Kill Seekers have nothing to seek, Carrie. A bunch of cold cases that professionals couldn't solve? A stupid note from a missing teenager? Have you actually looked at their Facebook page?"

"Briefly."

"Most of the comments are just people calling them losers because they're not doing anything."

"Aren't you describing all of social media?"

She snags a lipstick from my dresser and swipes it over her lips, admiring her reflection in the mirror. "They meet at the library twice a month for a creepy presentation from a guy with too much time on his hands."

"A lot of people fall into that category."

"So what if Emilio decided he needed to stand out? Drum up some publicity for his little gang?"

"Huh?"

"The hit-and-run deaths, Carrie! It's obviously him. No new murders to solve? Let's invent some. There. I've now solved one more mystery than Detective Graves."

"Greaves. And that's not—"

"Now, I'm no hypocrite. If someone wants to drive a little too fast once in a while, what's the harm?"

"All the murders."

"But if he wants to bring even more attention to Brampton? Now we have a problem."

"We don't have a problem because those hit-and-runs barely got any media coverage! No one but me even seems to care that they happened."

"Well, they're clearly about me, so now I care, too."

I roll my eyes. "If you stop killing people, all the attention in the world won't be an issue. So how about you and I take a permanent break from the mayhem and let things calm down on their own?"

"Or," Becca says, "we catch Elijah in the act, let Greaves play the hero, and then all the crimes are solved, and our worries are over."

"Until you strike again."

"First things first. Now, let's move."

"What? Where?"

She holds up her phone. "Who's got a job delivering pizzas in a car that's kept scrupulously clean?"

I sigh. "I think you're projecting."

"I don't know what that means, but let's go. Eli's just started his route."

The last thing I want to do is spend a Sunday afternoon trailing a pizza delivery boy to prevent my sister from killing him, but something I want even less is for the leader of the Brampton Kill Seekers to wind up dead, so I grab my keys and follow Becca to the front door. She pulls it open and stops so abruptly that I walk into her back.

"Huh," she says, pushing the door open wider so I can see the steak knife stabbed into the wood, a piece of paper pinned to the end. Written in a hasty scrawl are the words *I want what's mine.*

"Seriously?" she asks, yanking the knife out and crumpling the note. "Nikk's the lamest stalker ever."

For most people, a threat stabbed into their door might feel like a noteworthy event, but for someone who grew up with a serial killer, buried thirteen bodies, faced off with a second serial killer, and pushed a teenager off a cliff to cover her own ass, it's just a blip in my day.

"When he says *mine*, does he mean Lilly or the jewelry?"

"Doesn't matter. He's not getting either."

"Do you even *like* Lilly? Is that possible for you?"

Becca shrugs. "She helped me when I needed it. And when someone helps you, you help them. It's what sisters do, right?"

She sticks the knife in her purse and continues outside as I reluctantly follow, getting in my car and driving until we intercept Emmett on his delivery route and trail him slowly through the suburbs.

"What exactly are we hoping to find?" I ask as he jogs back to his car after completing another successful delivery.

"We'll know it when we see it."

We spend half an hour driving in circles, but things get slightly more interesting at the eighth house. Emmett parks, and we find a spot three car lengths back, ducking low in our seats as he climbs out, his hands empty. We're in one of Brampton's nicer areas, the homes about ten years old but much larger than average, and he walks up the drive of a two-story white colonial with red shutters and columns flanking the front door.

"This is it," Becca murmurs gleefully.

"How could this be 'it'? He's not even in the car. If he's the hit-and-run copycat, he wouldn't walk to his victim and invite them outside to stand in the road."

"You don't know that."

Knocking on the green front door, he stuffs his hands in his pockets as he waits. He wears the ever-present flannel shirt and knit cap, his hair poking out at the edges. To my surprise, the door opens, and Ravjinder greets him with a broad smile. To my even greater surprise, Emmett grins back, and they kiss.

"What the hell?" Becca demands, sitting up straighter.

I cringe. "Ew."

"They're in on it together."

"They are not. Ravjinder just has questionable taste in men."

"Death," Becca intones. "Disappearance. *Yearning*."

"Stop," I order, trying not to laugh.

We sink low in our seats as Ravjinder and Emmett

walk to his car, hands joined, unlinking their fingers only when it's physically impossible for them both to get in the car otherwise. They drive away, and again, we follow.

"Two killers," Becca murmurs. "Genius."

"They're not killers. They're kill seekers."

"It's the perfect disguise."

"It's far-fetched."

"We've been doing it for ten years."

I don't have a reply to that, so I make the turn onto Hartford Avenue and head in the direction of the community garden we recently vandalized. As we approach the barn, Emmett flips on his blinker and makes the turn into the lot. I drive past and stop a block away.

Becca chews her lip. "What if they figured out the clue?"

"How could they?"

"It was only a matter of time before somebody put it together." Becca doesn't know what *just in case* actually stood for or how I'd "put it together" and wound up at the garden. She'd just taken the shortcut to the end, as usual.

"Well, even if they did, we already have the key. They're too late."

"Yeah, but they're still looking."

"In the wrong direction. That's a good thing."

"Well, go make sure."

I turn to her. "Go back to the scene of the crime?"

"No one knows it's your crime, Carrie. Buy a plant if you feel bad."

"You should feel bad," I mutter, even as I take my keys and climb out of the car. I trek up the quiet street and enter the store when it's actually open, a handful of shoppers browsing the open-concept space and its farmhouse-chic style. Picnic benches serve as display tables, showcasing everything from small plants and garden tools to locally made preserves and arts and crafts. Garden implements spray-painted silver and gold decorate the walls.

Emmett and Ravjinder are nowhere to be seen.

I know the stairs to the lavender garden are on the back half of the structure, but as far as I can tell, the only way to get there is through a wooden door with a sign that reads EMPLOYEES ONLY. If Becca were here, she'd knock over something valuable to cause a distraction and slip through the door unnoticed. I, on the other hand, manage to appear so lost that I snag the attention of a store clerk. She wears a purple smock and a name tag that simply says VOLUNTEER.

"Can I help you?" she asks, approaching.

"Um…I'm interested in the community garden. I'd like to start my own plot."

Her smile is apologetic. "There's a wait list, I'm afraid. Would you like to add your name?"

I hesitate. No, I would not like to leave my name anywhere in the building I vandalized. "Maybe I'll just buy a few plants," I say instead. "And try my luck at home."

"Absolutely. What are you interested in?"

I peer around, trying to spot a label on any of the vague

green plants growing around me, but I can't see a single word. "Vegetables?"

Now her smile is sympathetic. "Of course."

The floor squeaks overhead, and I imagine Emmett and Ravjinder investigating the lavender-growing beds, trying to figure out if the vandals found what they were hunting for or left empty-handed.

The volunteer recommends that I start with tomatoes, cucumbers, and pole beans, which are apparently easy options for beginners and promise a large yield. My arms are filled with plants I still can't identify when Becca shows up. The few heads in the store turn at the sight of a gorgeous blond woman pausing dramatically in the doorway. Her head swivels until she spots me. Ignoring everyone who's watching, she strides over and stares at my soon-to-be purchases.

"What's this?"

"I'm taking up gardening."

"When I said buy a plant—"

"Oh my *goodness*!"

We're all spared the end of Becca's sentence by two voices crying out in unison from the back of the store. The volunteer, Becca, and I turn to see Emmett and Ravjinder gaping at us.

"You're Becca Lawrence!" Emmett exclaims with the same reverence one might use when spotting the face of Jesus in a piece of toast. He darts forward, Ravjinder hot on his heels. "And you're *alive*!"

Anyone who wasn't already watching Becca is definitely watching now, and as always, she loves the attention. "Why, yes I am," she declares grandly. When she and Lilly had made their miraculous returns from the dead at the police station, she'd begged them to keep the news quiet, claiming she needed privacy to recover. Greaves hadn't bought the story, but he's smart enough to deduce that she lives for the spotlight, and probably kept things quiet just to spite her.

Ravjinder meets my eye, and I shoot her a tiny smile, sorry my sister is alive and hers isn't and that mine killed hers. Then I spot her necklace. It's a broken-heart pendant with a small black gem in the upper swell, the kind that's meant to fit with a matching half. I'd seen it at the Kill Seekers meetings, but now it dawns on me that I'd seen it somewhere else, too. My heart begins to pound as the idea that had whispered at me yesterday starts to raise its voice, to make itself known.

"I'll take these plants," I say hastily to the volunteer, hurrying to the front counter and fishing my debit card from my wallet.

She looks confused by my sudden urgency but also pleased by the sale and quickly rings me up. Moments later, I have a tray of plants and hover impatiently next to Becca, who's recapping her encounter with Footloose for Emmett, who's recording the whole performance on his phone.

"It's a miracle," I agree, when Becca gets to the part about hiding in a drainpipe.

"And Lilly Fiennes is alive, too," Emmett muses. "So it looks like Brampton's safe after all."

"And all the hit-and-run deaths will stop forever," Becca says firmly.

Emmett frowns, missing the murderous intent behind the statement. "What?"

"What brings you two here?" I interrupt, hoping to stop him from saying something Becca will interpret as "incriminating." Her definition of "justifiable homicide" fluctuates depending on her mood.

Ravjinder lowers her voice and leans in conspiratorially. "We're refocusing our efforts on Fiona McBride's note."

My voice is too high-pitched when I say, "Oh?"

Emmett nods eagerly. "We're still not sure what *just in case* refers to, but the break-in at the McBride house and the destruction of the lavender garden have to be connected. Who else would torture such a sweet family?"

I study my hands like I'll never get the spots out while Becca snorts and covers it up with a cough.

"It's so nice you two are investigating," I say uncomfortably, edging back toward the door. "The community needs you."

"And you," Emmett says quickly. "Will you be at the next meeting?" Though I'm technically the one who spoke, it's Becca to whom he addresses his question. He thinks he's getting the Kill Seeker scoop of a lifetime, failing entirely to realize he might simply get killed.

"We'll see," Becca says with a wink. "Who knows what could happen?"

My hands are full of a box of unwanted plants, so I nod goodbye and hustle out of the store, Becca following leisurely behind now that her murder plans are temporarily out the window.

"What's the rush?" she asks as I dump the seedlings in the trunk. "Don't tell me you're actually interested in planting those things?"

"Something like that," I say.

CHAPTER 21

You're being weird again," Becca complains as I drive home at the speed limit, lost in thought.

"It's the law," I remind her. "It's not weird to be considerate of others."

She wrinkles her nose. "Not that. Something else. What are you thinking?"

I bite my lip, not sure if my slowly forming plan is ready to be shared but also not wanting to deal with her questions the rest of the afternoon. "I think we have to frame Nikk."

"What? How did we get on that topic?"

"Ravjinder wears a necklace—"

"Who?"

"The woman you just met at the store. You killed her sister. She wears a half-heart pendant necklace. The kind that has another half that fits with it perfectly."

"You want us to get matching necklaces?"

"God, no." I flip my blinker and take the exit for the highway. "I want to go to your murder closet to get the other piece."

Becca grumbles when I drive the posted speed on the highway but surprisingly doesn't argue with the plan itself. A plan that currently consists of little more than "frame Nikk."

We don't have disguises this time, so we settle for sunglasses when we reach Topline Safe Storage, a handful of people moving things in and out of the exterior units as we head inside and Becca signs in with a fake name. We keep our heads down as we pass a man with a dolly in the hall, winding our way through the rows of identical blue doors until we reach C969. Becca fishes the key from her pocket and lifts the door a few inches, using her phone to scan the interior before nodding and rolling it up halfway. We duck under and emerge in the same quiet, unremarkable unit as last time, the three tables and their dusty mementos waiting to be acknowledged.

"What's the point of keeping these things if you don't even visit?" I ask, heading to spot number five on the middle table, home to a now-tarnished silver half heart with a small diamond winking at the bottom.

"I remember them," Becca says with a shrug. "People keep photo albums, but only total losers actually look at them. The point of the album is that it's there if you need it, not to take sad walks down memory lane."

"You remember them?" I ask. "The people?"

She makes a face. "More like the…experience."

Kamaljit "Kami" Bains had gone missing after leaving home to run a late-night errand at the grocery store five years ago. She was twenty-two when she disappeared, a recent college graduate with a bright future in accounting. Now she's buried at the abandoned fairgrounds on the outskirts of town, and I'm holding her pilfered necklace in my hand.

"What was this *experience* like?" I hold out the pendant.

Becca chews her lip, eyes narrowing as she thinks. "It was dark. I had to stay late at work because someone misplaced one of the keys to the display units and we had to call a locksmith and a second security guard, and they both took forever. I was starving and tired, and it was almost midnight and the mall was closed, everything except the grocery store. I always parked down there so I could get dinner on my way out, so I went in to grab something, and there was this woman in line in front of me who was talking on her phone and taking forever to pay. Like, forever. And there was only one lane open because it was so late."

"That was Kami."

"I didn't ask her name. Anyway, finally I suggested she hurry up and pay, and she gave me the filthiest look, like I was the asshole. Then I swear she took even longer on purpose." She grits her teeth, like the rage of the moment is just as intense now as it was then. "I dropped my sandwich and left."

"Left the store," I amend. "And went to the parking lot to wait."

"I wasn't waiting, exactly. I was calming down and trying to think of which places were still open that I could get food. And then she walked out."

"And you hit her."

"She didn't even see me coming. There were maybe four other cars, and she just walked right in the middle of the road, didn't even stay on the sidewalk. It was like target practice. I hit the gas and got her from behind, and she just flew up in the air..." Becca's eyes have taken on a faraway look, like she's reliving a favorite memory.

"We buried her at the fairgrounds."

"You took so long to show up that I even ate the salad she bought." She grimaces. "It was terrible."

"Yes, it must have been a difficult night for you." I tuck the necklace into my pocket and head for the door, Becca following.

"So that's one piece of incriminating evidence," she says, locking up before we head back down the hall. "And I guess I still have that butterfly ring from Nina."

"Misha."

"And that's it? We frame Nikk for two deaths?"

I shake my head. "No. I know of one more. But you can't come."

—

When I pushed Fiona off a mountain, I did it to save myself. Even while helping Becca bury bodies, I'd been reluctantly aware of the loved ones who would forever mourn the loss of their husband, son, daughter, or friend. I'd even contemplated ways in which I might covertly reveal the location of a missing person so the family could have closure and the possibility of moving on with their lives. Not once had I thought of visiting their home, raiding their daughter's room, climbing a fence into their garden, and later destroying lovingly tended plants meant for charity. I'd never wanted to hurt them more than my sister already had.

But here I am.

After dropping a whiny Becca at home, I once again ring the bell to the McBride house. The afternoon sunshine has morphed into an overcast, drizzly spring evening, appropriate for the occasion. A cacophony of bird calls announces me, and moments later, Heather McBride opens the door with a small smile.

"Carrie," she says. "Nice to see you again."

"Sorry for the short notice."

She gestures me in. "I was surprised to hear from you, but also quite curious. You sounded anxious on the phone."

"I'm sorry for the mystery." I remove my coat and shoes and follow her down the hall to the kitchen. Her husband is nowhere to be seen, but there's another charcuterie plate set up on the marble island, and my mouth waters. I resist the urge to accept the snack, taking even more from this poor woman than I already have and intend to still. "It's a bit...sensitive."

Heather looks intrigued. "In what way?"

My stomach churns, but I plow on. "I don't know how closely you're following a local group called the Brampton Kill Seekers..."

She rolls her eyes. "They've contacted me for interviews a dozen times. A hundred, maybe."

"I went to a couple of their meetings and learned about a missing woman named Lilly Fiennes."

"Okay."

"Who's not missing."

Her brow furrows. "Okay."

"She's hiding. From her husband."

Heather sits down on one of the wooden stools and spears a cube of cheese. "Dangerous?"

I nod, relieved to be honest about this part of my visit. Find a safe place for Lilly...and steal a "memento" from Fiona. "Yes," I say. "I believe so. She doesn't have a lot of resources, no friends or family."

"And she needs a place to go."

"You were the first person I thought of. Your philanthropy..."

Heather studies the vase of flowers on the counter and reaches over to carefully roll a soft green leaf between her fingers. After a moment, she picks up her phone from the counter and hits a few keys.

"Who are you calling?"

"No one." She types and frowns at the screen.

I sit up tall and try to peer over the top of the phone, but I can't see what she's doing. My palms grow damp, and I wonder if she's calling the police. If she's somehow figured out my plan to steal from her yet again.

"Hmm," she says.

"What?"

"She's tiny." Heather shows me the screen. She's on the Kill Seekers website with photos of the missing women. Clicking on a picture takes you to an information page about each, and there are three shots of Lilly: the close-up I'd seen before, one of her on her wedding day, and another candid shot on a beach. In each she wears long sleeves and a smile.

"I can make some calls," Heather says. "It wouldn't be a problem."

"That would be great."

"And we probably have some clothes that would fit her. Fiona was…is…quite slender."

I shake my head to argue, though I can't believe my luck. "You don't have to do that. I was just hoping for a lead on a safe place she could go to get her bearings."

Heather waves me off. "It helps," she says. "To have something nice. It's that little something more that makes you feel human. Makes you believe there's more, no matter how many things are taken from you."

I force out a thank-you past the giant lump of shame in my throat, and Heather smiles and gets to her feet. "Now, let's go take a look—"

A million birds begin squawking, and we jump at the sound of the wretched doorbell. Heather laughs. "I'm so sorry. I'll never get used to that thing. It was my husband's idea. I will definitely *not* miss it."

"Miss it? Are you going somewhere?"

She pauses. "Home to Boston, maybe. Everyone says we should get out of here, start fresh. I don't...I don't know if it's time yet. I suppose I'm waiting for a sign. It's silly, I know. I—"

Another flock of birds attacks the house, and again we jump.

"Maybe that's the sign," Heather says with a tiny laugh.

"Are you expecting someone?"

"Nope." She laughs again and heads up front as I scan the counters for a knife block, prepared to defend myself against Nikk's murderous intentions.

"Detective Greaves!" Heather exclaims a moment later. "What brings you by? Do you have"—there's a pause, like she's gathering her courage—"news?"

I give up on the weapons hunt and instead blatantly eavesdrop. Greaves's voice is low and calm as he repeats the party line about how they're working on it and avoids the question. I scowl and step into the hall, since he and I both know his arrival is no coincidence. I haven't spotted him following me in a while, but I've felt him. Watching. Waiting.

"Ms. Lawrence," he says, failing to sound surprised. "I didn't realize you were here."

"And I didn't realize you were right behind me," I lie back.

His mouth twitches, and Heather looks between us, perplexed. "Carrie was just..."

"There's no rush," I say, resisting the urge to stomp my feet since I'll now have to plan a fourth visit to loot the home. "Please call me with any information."

"No need to leave on my account," Greaves says as I yank on my jacket.

"I insist."

"What brings you by, Detective?" Heather asks.

"The backyard. We'd spoken about me checking it out at night, and I happened to be in the area. I'm sorry to interrupt. I can come back another time."

"No," Heather says quickly, and I realize how lonely this poor woman is. Her absent husband, her dead daughter, and her giant house filled with a billion invisible birds. "Please come in. We have charcuterie. Carrie, you can stay, too, if you like."

"That's very generous," I say, crouching to tie my shoes. "Another time."

"Well, Detective, more for you, I suppose. I'll show you to the back."

They wave as I step out and stand on the doorstep, glaring furiously at the neighboring homes as though they somehow interrupted my plans. I don't know how I'm going to invent another reason to return, to face that poor woman and—

I freeze as I hear it: voices coming from the backyard. The rain has stopped, and fog clings to the dark ground, giving the area a cloaked, otherworldly feel. I dart around to the side of the home where a tall wooden gate leads to the back and press my ear to the wood, straining to hear Heather and Detective Greaves again. After a second, I do. They're outside, and the house is empty.

Patting my pockets as though I've forgotten my car keys, I hustle back to the door and let myself in, hurrying to the hall closet where the strawberry-patterned suitcase waits for an owner who will never return. Amazed and appalled at my own audacity, I unzip it and rummage through the meager contents. Fortunately, Fiona hadn't packed much, because she was never intending to get on the plane. Nerves blur my vision, but I force myself to focus, unzipping a small toiletry bag that includes a toothbrush, acne cream, and a gold hair clip. Bingo. I stuff the clip in my pocket, zip up the bags, and rush back outside. It's only twenty yards to my car, but I'm breathing hard like I just ran a marathon. Resting one hand on the window for balance, I dig in my pocket for the keys, my sweaty fingers failing to find a grip, the metal clattering to the ground. I crouch to collect them just in time to spot a pair of feet approaching quietly.

I yelp and whip around, arms raised defensively as I wait for Nikk to pounce, but it's Greaves staring back, hands tucked in his pockets, expression bland.

"You're still here," he observes.

I clutch my chest, feeling my heart thud against my breastbone. "What the fuck?"

"Just doing my job."

"That's reassuring."

"What are you doing here, Carrie?"

I scoop up the keys and jam one in the lock. "Helping a friend."

"Your sister?"

"No."

"Where's Fiona?"

"You tell me."

"What about Shanna?"

"Let me know when you find them."

"Do you think it's true?"

I sigh. "What's true?"

"That there's a new serial killer in Brampton."

New? No.

"I think there are a lot of panicked people and now a lot of panicked police officers trying to appease them, even if it means grasping at straws and stalking innocent women."

"Nikk Boulter came to see me."

"He came to see me, too."

"I heard. Do you know where his wife is?"

I shiver, the damp creeping under my jacket. "You know he beats her, right?"

"She's never pressed charges."

"Maybe being missing is safer."

He glances back at the McBride house, as though he's known that part of my reason for coming all along. "Maybe you're right. This time."

I open my door. "Good night."

Greaves lifts a hand and starts back toward the house. He must have invented an excuse to chase after me and left Heather waiting in the backyard for an intruder that won't be returning. I take a breath and brace myself against the car, my limbs weak from the ebbing adrenaline. I'm about to get in when an icy finger traces its way down the back of my neck, and I stiffen. I know that warning too well.

Whipping around, I see Greaves in the middle of the street, ten feet from the curb. Bearing down fast from the other direction is a car, its lights off. Maybe if I had more time to consider my actions, I'd make a different choice, but I don't. I just react.

"Look out!" I shout.

Greaves doesn't even hesitate, diving between two parked trucks as the car races over the spot he'd stood a split second before. It clips the edge of a truck before speeding away, its taillights never glowing red. For an endless minute, neither one of us moves, the growl of the engine fading, absorbed by the night, another secret kept.

Eventually, Greaves gets to his feet and wipes his hands on his jeans, unharmed. He stares down the road, though there's nothing to see, just as he's seen nothing for the past ten years. If anything, I appear more shaken than him. Finally, he turns to me, his expression its standard inscrutable mask as he gets out his phone and makes a call.

CHAPTER 22

I had to file another police report," I inform Becca the following morning. She'd played dead when I got home last night, and I hadn't bothered to muster up the energy to fight with her.

We're having toast with jam because Becca's eaten every box of cereal in existence, and she's making her displeasure known by grimacing with each bite.

"Did you tell them you're a terrible host?" she asks, flicking a crumb off the table.

"Greaves is already suspicious of me. All we have to do is lie low and give him nothing to look at."

"Easy for you to say. You look like you. I look like me." She winces and nibbles the corner of her toast like a mouse being tortured. "If he's smart, he'll think it's Nikk."

"He *is* smart. That's why he'll think it's you."

"Sure, Carrie. He's going to go on record saying that

one of Footloose's victims—who he did nothing to save—tried to run him over. The hit-and-run deaths have been happening since before my return."

"Your 'return' is irrelevant. The mere fact that you're alive is reason enough to suspect you."

"As always, you're missing the point."

"Have you just invented one?"

She tries to kick me under the table, but I move my leg so she hits the chair. "He thinks you're a lunatic killer of women," she reminds me. "And now he knows for sure you couldn't have been driving that car. So you're safe."

"Except for the part about Nikk trying to kill me."

She groans and gets up to pour a glass of juice. "You're always so negative."

There's a knock on the door, and Becca peers down the hall. "Who might that be?" she muses. "Detective Greaves, here to arrest you again? Nikk, here to threaten you again? Or Graham, here to make sure you're still here? Again?"

"I told you, we're going to see more houses."

The sound of keys jangling answers the question, and a second later, Graham enters, Felix scurrying down the hall ahead of him, a bulging-eyed ball of black and white with no destination beyond "forward."

"Hey," Graham says, smiling as I step into the hall. "Good morning."

"Good morning."

Becca steps out of the kitchen, wearing an old shirt

with a cartoon on the front and a pair of shorts, her hair in a ponytail. She looks the same as she did in high school, beautiful and plotting. The only new addition is the eight-inch scar on her left thigh.

"Hello, Graham."

"Becca," Graham says politely. "Welcome back."

"It's good to be home."

Graham is that guy who's too nice to say he hates someone, but if it's even possible for him to experience such a strong emotion, that's how he feels about Becca. It's one of the reasons I love him. He doesn't fall for her act, and he knows better than to let her know when she's gotten under his skin. He gets her, even if he doesn't know why.

"Not for long," he says, startling both me and Becca. His friendly smile never wavers. "I'm sure you know Carrie and I are looking for a place of our own."

"It's a difficult market."

"We're very determined."

I can't help but be impressed by my boyfriend, even if I'm going to have to talk Becca off a ledge later. He's laying down the law, and she doesn't know quite what to do when someone won't just let her steamroll over them.

"Anyway," I say brightly, "shall we go?"

Felix is weaving between Becca's feet like he's auditioning for a dog show, and she doesn't seem to notice him at all. Her gaze has taken on that far-off, glazed look, the one I know means she's visualizing something evil. It's one of her most common expressions.

"Come on, Felix." I crouch and pat the floor. The puppy pauses and stares at my tapping fingers, lunging for me a split second before Becca moves, stomping her foot on the spot he'd just been.

I scoop him up and grab my purse from the hall table, opening the door like she didn't just try to kill a puppy. "We'll see you later," I tell her, though she's barely listening.

I usher Graham out before Becca can grab a kitchen knife, and we're silent until we get in the car and pull away.

"So," he says, "probably not the best idea to leave Felix at your place while Becca's staying there, huh?"

I nod, feeling guilty for acknowledging the obvious, even though I'd feel way worse if Felix "disappeared."

"I was thinking," Graham continues.

"Oh yeah?"

"About…your history."

"What?"

"How Detective Greaves said you knew Shanna and Fiona."

My stomach clenches, though he's only pointing out the tip of the iceberg. I'd reluctantly told him more about my trip to the precinct and Greaves's theory about my involvement, though I'd laid it out as more of an "inquiry" than an "interrogation."

"Okay…"

"Well, Becca knew them, too, right? She worked with Shanna, and she was held captive with Fiona."

"Uh-huh…"

"And Becca's stolen car confirms it was used to kill Shanna, before she was dumped in the trunk, her body hidden somewhere. And Fiona's car was found at the base of Barr Lode Trail…"

My pulse jumps, and I feel dizzy, gripping the door for support. "Right."

"So that's two women and two cars and two disappearances. And I always kind of noticed that Becca traded in her car every year."

"She just likes new things." The words come out breathy and unconvincing.

"Does she like anything else?" Graham is watching me carefully, stopped at a red light.

"No," I whisper, because there are a few things she does that bring her joy, but I'm not about to name them.

"Exactly."

"Exactly what? Becca trading in her car is irrelevant. Her car was stolen in high school."

"What it if wasn't, though?"

"It was." My voice comes out too sharp, and I try to soften it. "She cried about it for a week. She'd begged my parents to buy it for her, and they'd made her promise to take care of it. The car was the only thing she cared about. She was devastated." Everything but "devastated" is true.

She'd sobbed hysterically when my parents had informed her that they simply couldn't afford to buy her another car, though I'd overheard them talking late at night about taking out a second mortgage so they could.

Graham purses his lips, like he's considering saying more, but settles on a shrug. "Okay."

"How did you even start thinking this?" I ask warily.

His second shrug is equally unconvincing. "I just did."

Apart from the lies I tell to cover up crimes, Graham and I have no secrets between us. At least, I didn't think we did. Which is why his behavior today seems so out of character. That, more than anything, makes an itchy uneasiness slip under my skin, one that doesn't abate when we stop in front of a white-brick bungalow where Beau waits outside, beaming.

Three hours later, we've seen four houses, and Beau has twice offered to adopt Felix. While none of the houses were quite as outlandish as the first one we'd toured together, none came close to feeling as right as the one in which Nikk had attempted to break in and murder us.

"Are you thinking what I'm thinking?" Graham asks quietly. Felix is asleep in his arms as we stand in the living room of a newly built home, half the size of my current one but with much more modern finishes and a furnace that doesn't sound like it's plotting your death.

"If you're thinking about the house on Baker Street, I'm thinking what you're thinking."

He grins. "I can't *stop* thinking about it."

"It was at the top of our budget, but it was perfect."

"What are we waiting for? Let's tell Beau."

I think of my current home. I think of Footloose in my closet, punching me. Fiona in my living room, extorting me. Greaves touring the main level, investigating me. I'd purchased that home thinking it was a great investment, a place where I'd make lasting memories. But I don't *want* the memories I've made there to last, and I know without a doubt that I'm ready to invest in my future. On Baker Street. With Graham and Felix.

"Beau?" I call.

He's been pretending to look at stuff on his phone on the front steps, and now he bounds back inside. "Thoughts?" he asks eagerly. "Questions? Special requests?"

"Baker Street," Graham says. "We'd like to make an offer."

Beau's bottomless enthusiasm has barely dwindled over the course of our unsuccessful house hunt, and I'd been expecting him to fist pump through the ceiling with excitement at the news. But instead, his face goes comically blank and then comically—and alarmingly—cringey.

"Oh," he says. "Um."

"What is it?"

"I know you guys enjoyed the tour of the home—until the gunfire—and I'd thought about bringing you back there today to see it under better circumstances, but when I called the listing agent, she said they'd priced it to sell, and they already have half a dozen offers. They're picking the best one at midnight tomorrow."

"What?" I ask. "What does that mean? There's still time?"

He picks at his collar. "Well, technically you have time. But I know you two have already expanded your budget, and you'd have to go over asking to have a shot at getting the home."

"How much over?" Graham asks. "It was already at the top."

"They priced it low to get multiple offers. It was probably worth forty thousand more than the listing price. And with half a dozen interested buyers, it'll go well over that."

As though he understands real estate, Felix lets out a tiny whine of despair.

"That sucks," I say, scratching his head.

Beau nods. "It's a tough market. But we saw some great places today…"

I glance around the tiny living room that melds into the tiny kitchen. Graham loves to cook, and that place wouldn't hold half his appliances, never mind anything I might want to bring. The yard is miniscule, and I can hear the noise from the six-lane road out front through the closed doors and windows. And this was the best of today's options.

"We'll think about it," Graham says, trying to mask his disappointment. "And get back to you."

"Sure." Beau is even less successful at hiding his disappointment. "I'll wait for your call."

We thank him and head back to our car, rolling down the windows and waving as Beau drives away.

"What do you think?" Graham asks as Felix gnaws on the gear shift.

"It's too small," I say. "And there's too much traffic."

"I mean about Baker Street."

"You mean forty thousand dollars just to get in the fight, and then however much more on top of that to actually win?"

He lifts a shoulder. "It's the best thing we've seen. And I'm tired of waiting. I want to move in with you. I want to move forward with you." Felix yips. "And you," Graham adds. "The question isn't how much. The question is, How bad do we want it?"

Bad, I don't say, thinking of the things I've done. *Very, very bad.*

"I want that, too," I tell him. "But things will be tight for a while, if we're going that far over budget."

"I'll work overtime. I'll donate blood. I'll host a car wash. I'll mow lawns."

I can't stop a smile from spreading across my face. "Are you serious about this?"

"Not the blood part—you know I'm squeamish. But everything else? Yes. One hundred percent. I'd do anything for you."

I blink away tears. "Okay. Same. I'm in."

Graham reaches over and takes my hand as Felix clambers into my lap and promptly passes out. "We're going to get this house," Graham says, thumb stroking across my knuckles. "And then we should celebrate."

"What are you thinking? Another dinner at Chez Luc? Oh, no wait. We can't afford that anymore. Gas station nachos?"

"What about a hike at Barr Lode Trail? We can take Felix and have a picnic at the top."

I can't hide my flinch. "Barr Lode—that place is dangerous. They closed it years ago."

"So it'll be extra private. For, y'know, us."

Never in the years we've been together has Graham suggested a hike or even acknowledged the existence of Barr Load Trail. And if not for my criminal history with the place, the words probably wouldn't make me tense and edgy. But they do.

"Breaking the rules doesn't sound like you," I hedge.

"You don't want to go?"

"I'm just surprised at the choice of activity."

He studies our joined hands. "One of the first dates I'd planned for us was a hike," he admits. "And then there was a torrential rainstorm, and then it was winter, and I guess it just slipped my mind. But I always thought it would be romantic. A nice place to, you know… make out."

His thumb is still tracing across my knuckles, and in the brief pause before he said "make out," it stopped on my fourth finger. My ring finger. I close my eyes. He's finally going to propose. Just one more hike.

"Barr Lode Trail," I say, opening my eyes. "We'll buy a house, we'll get a dog, and then we'll...make out." I don't mention the part about how first I have to frame Nikk for several murders in order to put the past behind me, once and for all, but one more secret won't hurt.

Graham leans over to kiss me. "I can't wait."

CHAPTER 23

That afternoon, Becca and I sit at the kitchen table, Misha's butterfly ring, Fiona's hair clip, and Kami's necklace between us next to a bucket of fried chicken.

"*Just in case*," Becca says. "Nikk has an expensive jewelry collection, and he keeps all the cases they come with in his secret man cave. It's the perfect spot to stash his mementos. We'll go tonight."

"Wait," I say, when she stands.

"What?"

I hesitate. I know I'm right, just like I know what I'm about to say is insanely risky. "We need one more."

She sits back down. "Who? Why? What?"

"Shanna. It's our chance to pin her death on Nikk, too. Greaves already has the murder weapon—we need to give him a suspect so he stops investigating us once and for all."

"What token do you want to use from Shanna? You want to grab her bones? They're probably not even there anymore."

I grimace. "No, I don't want to grab her bones."

She bites into a drumstick. "Well, I don't have anything. The car was the memento, Footloose stole the keys, and Greaves stole the car."

"Nothing else?"

"It was only my first—no, second—time. I hadn't developed a system yet."

I slump. "Okay, well, I'll think of something."

"How'd you get Fiona's hair clip if you didn't kill her?"

"Not everybody gets things by killing people," I say. Then I pause. "I went to her house to see her grieving mother and stole it while I was there."

Becca stares at me in shock, which seems a bit ridiculous since I've done much worse than steal a dead girl's barrette, mostly at her urging.

"Well done, Carrie," she says, getting to her feet. "You've inspired me. I know how to get something from Shanna."

"How?"

"Like you said. We'll ask her mom."

———

At the time of her disappearance, Shanna Lewis was twenty years old, working full-time at Robson Jewelry, and living at home while she saved money for veterinary school. At least, that's what her obituary said. Becca insists she was planning to move to Vegas to work at a brothel, where her skills would be best put to use.

A quick search online reveals that her parents still live in the same town house in which Shanna grew up, and they leave the porch light on 24/7 in the hope that she might find her way back.

The Lewis home looks like it hasn't been updated since Shanna's death, the end unit on a block of identical blue homes with peeling white window frames. The porch light is indeed on, shining on hanging baskets that overflow with flowers.

"Ugh," Becca says as we walk up the driveway. "I really hated her."

"Try not to let that show."

"You know who'd be good in this moment?"

"Don't say Diana Speedwell."

"Diana Speedwell."

We'd spent the last two hours bickering about how best to approach this seedy plan, with Becca adamant that she'd dress up as Diana Speedwell and go door-to-door passing out flyers for her missing dog. The "missing" was supposed to prompt Fran or Hank Lewis to invite her in, at which point she would somehow find something of Shanna's and somehow steal it. The only good part of the plan was that I played no role. The bad parts were Becca's acting skills and the inevitable failure.

Eventually, we'd settled on arriving as ourselves, sharing Becca's safe recovery from Footloose's attack but explaining that her lingering trauma had brought back memories of Shanna's disappearance and heartache. She's been unable to open up to me because I haven't been through such pain, and the only people she feels will understand her are the Lewises.

Okay, it's not a great plan, but at least she's not Diana Speedwell.

I'm reaching out to ring the bell when Becca lets out a tiny gasp. I pause and glance over, jaw dropping when I see that she's sliced open the back of her hand with a steak knife.

"What the hell?" I jump away in case she has plans for me.

She tosses the knife into a bush and pulls out a large bandage from her back pocket, fastening it over the wound. Finally, she looks at me, her eyes shiny. "That hurt," she whispers, blinking hard so the tears spill over and she does indeed resemble a woman dealing with serious psychological issues.

"I guess that means we're ready."

I ring the bell. We hear it chime inside, just an ordinary bell ringing, no flock of birds collecting the homeowners. After a moment, there's a thump and the turn of a lock before the door opens to reveal a stooped woman with dyed red hair and a purple tracksuit. I'd seen Shanna's parents once before, when they'd come to our school to speak with the principal to ask him to keep an eye on me since I was the prime suspect in the mystery of who'd slashed Shanna's car tires at the winter dance. (Answer: Becca, once again "helping me" after Shanna took my crush to the dance.) It was almost thirteen years ago but Fran Lewis had looked thirty years younger than she does today, glaring at us as she clutches the doorknob to hold herself upright. A man in a button-down shirt and threadbare tie materializes behind her. Shanna's dad, frail and suspicious as he peers out.

"Who're you?" Fran asks.

Becca's suddenly sobbing too much to speak, leaving the task to me, though she'd written the script.

"Um," I say uselessly, suddenly picturing the broken families of all her other victims in a similar state, wasting away as grief and questions gnaw at them day after day, with no end or answers in sight.

"What's happening?" Hank demands. "Who's this?"

"I'm Carrie Lawrence," I say, immediately realizing my mistake. Becca actually *killed* Shanna, but I'm the one who'd allegedly threatened their daughter, and right away their eyes spark to life with resentment as they recognize my name.

"Get out," Fran says, though we're not inside.

"P-please," Becca whimpers, bracing herself against the house like she might collapse. "I have nowhere else to go."

Now Fran and Hank look alarmed.

"I'm sorry," I say quickly. "This was a bad idea. My sister is...weak."

Fran does a quick blink and focuses in on Becca, her eyes narrowing to slits despite my sister's fragile state.

"You," she says, sounding like a witch about to cast a spell. "You hurt my daughter."

Becca stops sobbing long enough to say, "What?"

Hank steps forward to take charge, though he's far less intimidating than his wife. "We spoke with Detective Graves," he says, and I don't correct him. "He told us he found your car. He told us you might come here. We know what you did."

Becca clutches her chest. "No, I...I had nothing to do with it. My car was stolen. I was nearly killed by Footloose. You can help me..."

"Get out!" Fran roars with sudden vehemence, though again, we're not inside. "I always knew it was you! You and your psycho sister!" She shouts this at Becca, implying that *I'm* the psycho.

"Okay," I say, hastily backing away. "We'll go. This was a bad idea, Becca. I'll take you to a hospital. Maybe the doctors can help."

"Nothing can help!" Becca wails. "I need to speak to them!"

I lead her back to the car. Somehow it appears she thinks our plan might still work, though Fran and Hank look half a second away from fetching pitchforks and chasing us into the street. A handful of neighbors have poked their heads out of doors, and I feel paranoid eyes on my back as I guide Becca away. She's still playing her part, forcing me to bear half her weight as I stagger down the driveway, nearly crumpling under the burden.

"That's enough," I hiss as we reach the car and I yank open her door. "You're overdoing it."

"My suffering just won't end!" she shrieks as I slam the door and round the front. She buries her face in her hands as I get in the driver's seat and jam the keys in the ignition, pulling away from the curb so fast my tires squeal. We go two blocks, and Becca's still covering her face, but now she's stifling laughter, not fake sobs.

"Seriously," I say. "You're the worst."

"They really hated you," she says through guffaws. "Like, a lot."

"For everything you did."

"It's not my fault you're easy to hate. Diana Speedwell would have done much better."

"Well, that was our shot. How else are we going to frame Nikk for Shanna's disappearance?"

"Framing people is a lot of work," Becca complains. "Let's just invite him on a hike and let nature take its course. It's worked before."

Pushing people off cliffs has become the Lawrence family go-to in times of trouble.

"If I thought he'd agree, I'd say go for it," I tell her. "Unfortunately, I don't think he's that dumb. We have to stick with the original plan to frame him."

"Fine," Becca mutters. "I'd probably have to run him over before the hike, anyway, and he's heavy. I'm not sure you're strong enough to help me get him up the trail."

"How?"

"Because you never work out—"

I interrupt. "How'd you get Missy up the mountain? I didn't help you that time."

"She walked up herself. I invited her."

"Just like that? You weren't even friends."

"We were both on the cheer squad, and the coach said our animosity was ruining the group dynamic, so we had to set aside our differences. Obviously, it wasn't easy, because Missy was a raging bitch, but one day she complimented my butt and asked what workout I did, so I told her I went hiking a lot. She asked to come along, and I said yes, and it just…happened."

"You never went hiking," I point out, because the murder was most definitely premeditated.

"Whatever. With her gone, I scored top spot on the pyramid, and the cheer team picture got a full-color spread in the yearbook."

I hit the brakes as the light turns yellow. "That's it."

"It was yellow, Carrie! Why are we stopping?"

"The yearbook," I say. "You and Shanna graduated together. Her picture's in it, right?"

"I guess. Who would even care?"

I grip the wheel. "Nikk Boulter."

—

Becca spends two minutes admiring her unsurprisingly gorgeous yearbook shot and mocking mine before deftly slicing out Shanna's photo with a paring knife. We meticulously clean the picture, Misha's ring, Fiona's hairclip, and Kami's necklace so our fingerprints are nowhere to be found, and then Becca produces a black velvet box that used to be home to a diamond tennis bracelet—one of Nikk's apology gifts to his wife and one of the items Lilly and Becca stole back—and we stash the items inside. Even as my plan starts to take physical shape, I'm seeing all the various flaws in it and doubting everything.

"It's not going to work." I stare at the closed box of incriminating evidence.

"Why not?"

"Because his fingerprints aren't on any of those things. They've obviously been cleaned."

"Nikk's a neat freak. He vacuums, like, three times a day and has a bottle of bleach in his car 'just in case.' It'll fit right in with the rest of his things."

Apart from "frame Nikk," I hadn't really thought this through. Last year, I'd been drugged and taken to the home of a serial killer, so willingly going again to the house of a man who wants to harm me feels like the wrong choice. But with the end in sight, it also feels like we're already so far into this mess that the only way out is through.

"Can we call the grocery store and find out when his next shift is?" I ask. "Then we'll go when he's at work." Even as I speak, Becca's typing on her phone.

"We can go now," she announces.

I immediately start to sweat. I've never been that person who got a burst of energy when the finish line came into sight. Adrenaline is not my friend. It's making me weak and jittery, a thousand deadly what-ifs speeding through my mind.

Becca shows me her phone. She's on the Kill Seekers website where they've added a special banner announcing an emergency meeting with Nikk as tonight's guest of honor. She stands and uses a plastic bag to scoop up the jewelry case. "It's meant to be. I'll drive."

"No way. The last thing we need is a speeding ticket confirming we were in Nikk's neighborhood."

"Well, I'm not giving you the keys, so I guess you can walk."

"It's my car."

"We're not taking your car. We can't risk having someone spot the license plate."

"Then what car are we taking?"

Becca pulls keys out of her pocket. "Nikk's. It's the one Lilly and I took to the B and B."

"And the police never found it?"

She shrugs. "I swapped the plates."

"You—"

"Stop stalling," she orders. "We're going."

Fifteen minutes later, we're in Lincoln, one town over and one much more affluent than Brampton. The houses are new and set back from the road, allowing for expansive, well-groomed lawns. The Boulter home is a light-colored, three-story colonial with a cobble-stone driveway and four-car garage. At the moment, the windows are dark and Nikk's car—his other one—is nowhere to be seen.

"He parks in the driveway," Becca explains, stopping a few houses down and parallel parking between two SUVs. "The garage is his home gym."

I glance around nervously, but the street is empty. "Is that where we should hide the case?" I ask. "If he spends a lot of time there?"

"Nope. Definitely the man cave."

"The four-car garage home gym isn't it?"

Becca shakes her head and climbs out, and I hurry to follow her. We're both wearing black jackets, the hoods pulled over our hair. There are three houses between us and Nikk's place, and I hold my breath the entire way, waiting for someone to sound the alarm. But it stays quiet, the air warm and stifling.

"In the back," Becca whispers as we approach. There's no fence to hop, so we slip into the shadows and around the side to where a large yard waits, replete with an in-ground pool and fancy barbeque setup. The people next door appear to be adding an extension to the back of their already enormous home, the yard a construction site with mounds of dirt everywhere. At least they're unlikely to step outside and spot us breaking in.

Becca points at a second-floor window on the right side of the house. "That's the man cave. He keeps the only key in his wallet. Lilly said she's never been inside."

"That's terrifying."

"That's why it's the perfect place for him to keep his mementos."

I can't argue with her logic, even though I have no idea how she expects us to make the twelve-foot climb up the side of a house.

"Ladder," she says, reading my mind.

"That's a great idea. Do you have one?"

Even in the dark, I can feel her glare. "Unlike you, I don't take credit for ideas I can't actually make happen. There's one next door." She nods at the construction zone and then back up at the opposite side of the house. "My guest room was right there. I saw the ladder a hundred times, and if my leg hadn't snapped in two, I'd have been in the man cave a long time ago."

"Okay," I say. "Let's get this over with."

For a minute, we both just stand there.

"Go get the ladder," Becca orders. "You know I have a sore leg."

I grumble about the convenient emergence of her injury but trek across the yards and eventually spot the ladder lying on its side in a pile of dirt. It's made of lightweight metal, so I easily cart it back to Nikk's house, where the extension rungs promptly come loose, dragging across the patio stones and letting out a deafening squeal.

"Jesus!" Becca exclaims. "Shut up!"

For another minute, we just stand there, this time waiting for a barking dog or inquisitive neighbor or SWAT team, but again, nothing happens. I guess not everyone has reason to be paranoid every day.

Shooting me another glare, Becca arranges the ladder against the side of the house and climbs up, her leg miraculously fine. Something protrudes from her back pocket, and when she reaches the window, she pulls out a screwdriver and uses it to force the window open with ease.

"We're in," she calls, dropping the screwdriver and nearly hitting me in the face. Sliding the glass up, she wriggles through and disappears into the house.

I exhale anxiously, my hands sweating through my gloves, before following. It's only twelve feet, but I swear the wind grows stronger as I climb, and the flimsy metal sways with it, threatening to topple me off. I brace one hand against the siding and peer around. The construction site is quiet, and a full moon hangs low over the trees, watching everything. I feel self-conscious and paranoid as I pull myself through the open window, landing in a plank-like position before scrambling to my feet.

Becca uses the flashlight on her phone to inspect the spacious room, the walls covered with typical sports memorabilia—framed jerseys and posters, a collection of baseballs in clear boxes, and a signed basketball. A set of matching brown club chairs face each other across a low wood table, and a well-loaded bar cart waits nearby. A wall-mounted shelf holds a collection of heavy leather-bound books that have likely never been opened. For all its secrecy, it just looks like a fancy man cave, not Nikk's evil center of operations.

Using my own phone to light the way, I head for the large walk-in closet and step inside. It's home to Nikk's expensive wardrobe and organized by what appears to be season and color. Boxes of shoes line one wall, photos of their contents fastened to the front. The center of the closet is dominated by an island with a glass lid that displays his collection of men's watches and jewelry.

Becca looks on as I try one of the drawers. It slides open to reveal an assortment of ties. The next drawer is home to approximately fifty leather belts. The third is a selection of black velvet boxes, the same kind she has in her hand.

My phone, on silent for this act of trespassing, vibrates in my coat pocket, making me jump like I've been shocked.

"What is it?" Becca demands.

I falter, patting my hip. "My, um...my phone."

"Seriously?" She stares in disbelief as I pull it out and Graham's smiling face beams up at us.

I'd been ignoring his texts for the past hour, but he has to be calling about the house on Baker Street. If I don't answer, he'll keep calling and then drive to my place, worried about Nikk or any of the other criminals roaming the streets of our nation's crime capital.

"I have to take it," I whisper. "It'll just be a second."

Becca looks like she wants to strangle me but instead busies herself shifting the boxes in the jewelry drawer so she can slot in ours inconspicuously.

"Hey," I say, stepping out of the closet to answer the call. "Sorry, I had my phone on silent."

"We're one of the top two offers," Graham says in response. He sounds giddy. "Beau thinks it's ours if we go up another five."

"Five thousand?"

"I know it's a lot more than we planned, but if it's our dream house and a fresh start…"

I glance around Nikk's fancy man cave. I might have to take a page out of Becca's book and steal some of his diamonds to help pay for this dream.

"Okay," I say into the phone as Becca exits the closet, eyebrow arched expectantly. "Do it."

"You're sure?"

"Positive."

I can almost see Graham dancing around his living room in excitement. "Let me call Beau. I'll put you on three-way."

"No," I say quickly.

"What?"

"I, um…I promised Becca some quality time tonight, since she knows our living situation is coming to an end. You know what she's like if she doesn't get my undivided attention."

She flips me the bird.

"Yeah," Graham says. "I do. Okay. I'll give Beau the go-ahead and text you soon with good news."

"Thanks," I say. "Fingers crossed." We hang up, and I turn my phone off all the way. "He thinks we're going to get the house," I tell Becca.

"Fantastic, Carrie. That's incredible. I framed Nikk. Now, let's go."

A loud squeak comes from the hall outside, a sound I know too well from my stairs at home. Before the warning can properly register, the door bangs open, and Nikk looms in the doorway, large and furious.

"You bitch!" he roars, swinging a fist at the closest person, which happens to be me. I jump back, and he clips my shoulder, sending me staggering against the club chair and toppling over the coffee table. He stalks toward me, his intention focused and deadly.

"Get away from her!" Becca shouts, throwing a leather book at his head. It bounces off his arm, and he whirls on her as I scramble to my knees, shoulder throbbing.

She swings at him with a bottle of liquor from the bar cart, but he dodges the blow and grabs her wrist, twisting her arm so hard she drops the bottle and cries out. I whip around desperately, but despite the abundance of things in the room, exactly none resemble a weapon. I see Becca clawing at Nikk's face, but he snatches her hand in his fist and squeezes hard enough that she whimpers, even as she lands a solid blow to his crotch with her knee.

They're blocking the bar cart, preventing me from grabbing another bottle, so I snag a second heavy book and dart forward, whacking Nikk in the ear. He's still got Becca's hands ensnared in his angry grip, so the blow lands but appears not to affect him at all. His rage is zeroed in on my sister as he hooks his foot behind her calf and knocks her off balance, following her to the floor and kneeling above her. I swing again with the book but this time he's ready, releasing one of her hands and belting me in the face. The punch splits my lip, the taste of blood filling my mouth. A flashback of the time Footloose did the same thing turns my vision black, the shock and horror of that exchange making me numb. I blink and see Nikk with his hands on Becca's neck, bearing down with all his might. She's got her teeth gritted, blood smeared on her cheek, and she's scratching at his face, her legs kicking futilely.

"Run," she manages, her voice strangled. "Carrie. Run."

They're in front of the door, leaving the window my only exit, and I look frantically between the two before meeting my sister's eyes one last time. She flicks her gaze to the window, giving me permission, and I scramble back and out the window, half falling down the ladder. My hands scrape against metal as my feet bump over the rungs, never quite finding purchase until I smack into the patio, my knees wailing at the impact.

I stumble back around to the front of the house, my footsteps staggered and uneven, my head spinning. The street is still dark and quiet, the neighbors blissfully unaware of the violence next door. Down the block, the getaway car waits, the keys still in the ignition, calling me.

I've spent most of my life wishing Becca were gone, dead or alive, just anywhere other than in my life, and this is my chance. If I keep going, Nikk will kill her, and I can tell the police she went to see him and never came home, and have they checked his personal jewelry collection? But though Becca's a horrible sociopath, she's also my sister, and I know her final word to me can't be *run*. I can't live knowing she died like a hero.

The front garden beds are composed of rosebushes and mulch, and I root around uselessly for a brick or stone or something, knowing I don't have time for this as thorns scratch my arms, underscoring the point. I give up on the search and try the door. Nikk didn't lock it behind him when he came in, so I slip inside. The carpeted steps muffle the sound of my sneakers as I run upstairs, trying to make myself as quiet as I can, even as panic and adrenaline take the place of common sense.

The man cave is to the left, its door open, the sounds of grunting and gasping guiding me to the room. Nikk and Becca are in profile, silver moonlight gilding their features, like murderous statues. He kneels over her, his hands around her neck, one knee across her thighs, pinning her down like he's had lots of practice at this very thing. She's the most dangerous person I've ever known but she's losing this fight, her fingers scraping at his wrists, pitiful, exhausted grabs that he easily ignores.

I charge into the room straight at them, rearing back with my right leg and swinging forward, kicking Nikk's head like a soccer ball. There's a loud *crack* as I make contact, and his neck twists sharply. For a split second, I expect to see his head fly across the room and right out the window, but it doesn't. Instead, he immediately collapses onto the floor, either unconscious or completely dead, I'm not sure.

Becca wheezes noisily as she tries to draw in breath through a crushed windpipe, her chest rising and falling, fighting to pull air into her lungs. She turns to me, and I drop to my knees at her side, fumbling uselessly, trying to figure out what to do.

"Get it…" she rasps.

I blink. "What?"

She lifts a shaky hand in the direction of the closet where she'd stashed the case. "Get it," she repeats. "Finger…"

Maybe it's a sign that I've been partaking in this type of shady behavior for too long, but I immediately know what Becca means and hurry to the walk-in closet to retrieve the box of murder mementos. When I return, Becca has pulled herself to a sitting position. She takes one of Nikk's hands while I take the other, and we carefully press the tips of his fingers into the mementos and the velvet box. I shoot worried glances at his head the whole time, convinced he's going to wake up and murder us both, but the side of his face is already a mottled purple, and his eye is horrendously swollen. Still, I see his chest rise and fall, so at the very least, he's not dead yet.

"What about him?" I whisper when we've placed the last incriminating fingerprint.

Becca looks pensive, which is almost more terrifying than when she looks murderous, and then she slowly reaches up and undoes her ponytail. She passes me the black elastic, a couple of blond hairs still attached.

"Add it," she says, nodding at the box in my hand.

The elastic joins the other sad souvenirs, and I replace the box in the drawer before creeping back into the room, half expecting to see Nikk with a knife in his throat. Instead, I find Becca standing at the door, waiting for me.

"Let's go." Her voice is hoarse.

"We're just going to leave him?"

"It's not like he's going to tell anybody. If he tells on me, I'll tell on him." Becca's idea of criminal quid pro quo is something I'm all too familiar with.

I follow her down the stairs and out to Nikk's second car, where Becca reluctantly agrees to let me drive us home. My adrenaline is beginning to ebb, my limbs growing heavy and weak, but my mind is clear. We did it. The plan is complete.

No alarms sound as we drive away, and at a red light, I

risk taking a peek at my phone, finding two missed calls from Graham and one celebratory text.

We got the house!

It's accompanied by five balloon emojis and one dog emoji, and despite everything, I can't help but smile. Nikk is framed, Becca and I both survived, and my life is slowly, finally, moving in the right direction. It's the wrong way to feel, but I'm...elated.

"See?" Becca says smugly, misinterpreting things as usual.

"See what?"

"It's fun, isn't it?"

"Being attacked? Not really."

"Living," she says. "Living our best lives forever."

"That's not what just happened. That was a near disaster."

"You're too negative, Carrie."

I don't bother answering.

"Fine," she says. "Why are you smiling, if not because you just beat the crap out of Nikk?"

I roll my lips and consider remaining silent so she can't burst my bubble, but she's going to find out anyway, so I say, "Graham and I just bought a house."

For once, she's the one who's quiet.

CHAPTER 24

Just stay here," I tell Becca, the way you'd tell your dog to sit. "Don't go out; don't do anything."

"But I'm bored."

"No, you're not. This is what you love to do."

She'd slept until ten and is now watching cartoons and eating too much cereal.

"Fine," she mutters. "I'll try. Have fun on your 'hike.'"

"I don't know what the air quotes are for. It's an actual hike."

"Dressed like that?"

"It's just a new shirt." I'd bought it last night in anticipation of today's date. It's just a black tee with tiny pink hearts, exercise and proposal appropriate.

"You're different."

"So you keep saying." Graham's bringing the water and champagne, and I'm responsible for the lunch: baguette,

Brie, and prosciutto. I carefully pack everything in a bag with an ice pack, catching sight of my left hand: unadorned, but not for much longer.

"More different," Becca emphasizes. "Weirder." She's got a frozen banana pressed against her bruised throat.

"You're one to talk."

"What's happening today?"

"I told you. We're going for a hike. I think Graham's going to propose. We've been talking about it."

"You don't seem very excited to marry that loser."

"He's not a loser. And I'll be excited when he asks. First I have to climb a mountain."

Becca laughs. "First time in ten years."

"It'll be fine."

"I bet the ring's tiny. Definitely a fake diamond. He'll probably call it a temporary ring until he can afford something better, then 'forget' to ever upgrade it."

"I don't care about the ring."

A car honks outside. Graham. Right on time.

"Well, bring me home some takeout. Sushi. No, fried chicken. No, both." She pauses. "I'll text you."

"Can't wait."

"Don't do anything I wouldn't do!" she calls as I grab my backpack and head outside.

It's a beautiful Saturday in late May, the sun shining, the sky blue, the clouds faint wisps in the sky. Graham's parked at the curb, waving at me through the passenger window. We kiss hello as I get in, and he beams.

"You look beautiful."

"Thanks. You too." I flush. "I mean, you look good. You know what I mean."

He winks. "I do."

In fact, he looks very good. I'd chosen a nice shirt that was still hike appropriate, but Graham's wearing a black button-down shirt like what he'd wear to work. He grew up going camping and fishing, so he has to know that's not the best hiking attire.

"You're dressed up," I remark.

He fiddles with his collar. "It's just an old one. I have a T-shirt underneath. I'll take it off if I get hot."

We pull away from the curb, and I check the back seat. "Where's Felix? I thought he was coming."

"Nah. He's in an adventurous phase, meaning he likes to jump off any surface he's on. The last thing I want is for him to take a running leap off the edge of a mountain."

My palms grow immediately clammy. "Better safe than sorry."

"Everything okay?"

"Great," I say. "Just nervous about the climb. I haven't exactly been sticking to my fitness regime."

Graham grins. "And you've never looked better. How's Becca taking the news about the house?"

"About how you'd expect. But she'll be fine. It's not like she didn't live alone before."

"That's odd, don't you think?"

The mountain looms up ahead, doubling in size as we

grow near. It's part of a tree-covered range that disappears into the horizon, small by world standards but grand for us. The peaks loom up dark and jagged, stabbing into the blue sky. Barr Lode Trail was closed years ago after a number of hikers fell to their deaths. I'd hiked up twice after its closure, each time hiking down with one less person than with which I'd ascended.

I force myself to focus on the conversation. "What's odd?"

"That she's always lived alone."

"I've always lived alone."

"Yeah, but you're not *alone* alone. You're not a loner."

"Well, she's hard to get along with if you don't keep your cereal cupboard well stocked." I laugh, but Graham doesn't join me.

"Why wouldn't she have contacted you?" he asks.

"What? When?"

"When she was 'missing.' Why allow you to believe she was dead? You grieved for her."

"I'm supposed to."

"That's because you're a good person. Why wouldn't she pick up the phone?"

Because she enjoyed the idea of my emotional suffering, I don't say. She wanted me to be relieved she was gone *and* devastated she was gone, confused by the dueling emotions. *Then* she wanted me to be both devastated and relieved again when she stalked me in a barn and revealed herself to have risen from the dead.

"I don't know," I say. "That's not her style. Why are you asking this?"

He shrugs. "I was just thinking about it."

"You've been asking about her a lot," I press. "More... negatively than before."

"I've always felt this way. I just never said it."

"Why?"

"Because I didn't want her to interfere with our relationship," he says testily. "Because it was only when she was gone that it actually felt like we had a chance to really be together, and now that she's back, it's... annoying."

I'm quiet for a second. "It's super annoying."

Graham's laugh is relieved. "You didn't tell her she could live with us, did you?"

"God, no. I even lied about the address."

"Where's she going to go?"

I shrug. "Not our problem."

He grins and reaches over to snag my left hand, rubbing his thumb across my knuckles. "This day really is perfect."

I stare down at our linked fingers, at the promise there, the potential. I shake off the uneasiness of his questions. We're going to be married. We can't have secrets. Well, not many.

Ten minutes later, we turn into the parking lot at the base of Barr Lode Trail. It's a beautiful morning but the empty lot feels ominous, deep grooves etched into the dirt, overgrown weeds poking through. A NO

TRESPASSING sign hangs from a single nail, waving at us like a half-hearted warning.

Graham finds a spot in the shade, and we get out, strapping on our backpacks and looking at each other expectantly. "Shall we?" he asks.

We start up the trail, the morning sun immediately obscured by the thick tree cover. Despite having been designated off-limits more than a decade ago, the trail is still easily visible, the ground soft and spongy beneath our feet, the smell of pine and earth filling the air. Yellow patches of sunlight speckle the trail like they're leading the way, and it's quiet. It's so, so quiet. The way it had been the night I'd hiked down alone after pushing Fiona off the cliff.

"I checked the map," Graham says over his shoulder. He's a few feet ahead, his back straight and steps high, like an eager Boy Scout. He's kind of adorable. "There are three lookouts. I think we can reach them all, if you're up for it."

"Why not?" I've never been to a proper lookout, just an unmarked path through the woods that leads to the cliff edge.

He grins back at me and reaches to take my hand, squeezing my fingers. "When was the last time you were hiking?"

"A long time ago. Before it was closed."

"Was Becca with you?"

I blink. "What? On the hike?"

"Yeah."

"No. She doesn't exactly enjoy the outdoors." At least, not in the way people who enjoy the outdoors enjoy the outdoors.

We walk another few minutes in silence, the sounds of our feet crunching over stray branches and pine needles interspersed with the occasional call of an unseen bird and the responding chatter of a squirrel.

It takes forty-five minutes to reach the first lookout point, a green sign tacked to a tree, steering hikers onto a well-worn path off the main trail. The trees thin, and the ground gives way to a swath of gray rock, its edges softened by years of footsteps. The sky, hidden from view, reveals itself abruptly, offering an uninterrupted vista of the gentle curve of the sprawling range.

We set down our bags, and I immediately take a seat while Graham goes to the edge. Sweat beads at his temples and on the back of his neck. I watch him for a moment, so proud, so honest. So clearly planning to propose with his button-up shirt and champagne and Brie. Honest and predictable. Safe.

I unzip his pack, much heavier than mine because he's carrying the drinks, and root around until I feel something slick and cold. I pull out a half-thawed bottle of water. "Want a drink? You look hot."

"I'm okay for now."

"Why don't you take off your second shirt?"

He smiles sheepishly. "Bugs."

I hadn't noticed many bugs on the way up, the late spring weather not yet giving way to swarms of midges and mosquitoes. I smile back and drink the water as I peer covertly into Graham's bag for a telltale ring box, but all I can see is the top of a champagne bottle, the glass wrapped in a nest of newspaper.

"Hey," Graham says, catching me peeling back a corner to try to spot the brand label. "That's for when we reach the top, you lush."

"I just want to make sure you bought the best one."

"For you? What else?"

I laugh, but the sound abruptly cuts off as I spot something on the corner of the newspaper. It's the front page, the *Brampton Chronicle* header glowing bright blue. But next to it, in the top right, is an ad. Red and white, no bigger than a Post-it. BRAMPTON STORAGE SOLUTIONS, FOR YOUR SUPER STORAGE NEEDS! The first initial of each word is printed in yellow. B.S.S.

Brampton Storage Solutions. The facility where Becca had stashed the car she'd used to kill Shanna.

Where Greaves had found it.

Where Graham had written the initials on a business card, circling them in red pen, like X marks the spot.

I turn slowly to peer over my shoulder, the wall of trees dark and judgmental. *You're crazy*, they say. *You're right.*

"What are you looking for?" Graham asks.

I hadn't realized I'd stopped breathing, that the world had stopped spinning, until his words start the world turning again on its axis, a light breeze lifting sweaty hair from my neck, forcing my eyes to meet his.

"I thought I heard something," I lie. My heart pounds so hard I think he must be able to hear it. He must know.

But he's frowning into the woods like his concern might urge the truth to come out. "Like what?"

"I don't know."

"It's probably nothing. Ready to keep going?"

I'm not, of course. I'm ready to run back down the mountain and out of the woods, back home to my sister, to tell her what I've learned, to ask her what it means that Graham had the initials of one of her murder storage units on the back of Greaves's business card. But practicality and a decade of cover-ups mean I know better than to show my hand. I still don't know what I know, after all. And I don't know what Graham knows.

I smile and follow him back to the main trail. I peer around but we're still alone, the forest silent and watchful.

"Detective Greaves called me," Graham says, as though he's been reading my mind, trying to figure out the connection.

I stumble over a root. "What?"

"Two nights ago. He was, um…asking about Becca."

"Why?"

"I guess he's curious about her sudden return, too."

"Is that why you were asking about her in the car?"

"Yeah. Maybe." His cheeks are flushed, a combination of exertion and embarrassment. And something else.

The day I'd seen the boring movie with Graham, Greaves had been there. He'd followed us out, next to the box with the newspaper announcing the second hit-and-run victim, a story I hadn't heard reported anywhere else. When I got home and searched online, I learned of the first victim on the *Brampton Chronicle* website. I'd seen the last article at work, in the paper in the lunchroom. Troy said Greaves had dropped by the office earlier to pay me a visit. And plant a seed.

"You should tell me when he calls," I say, trying to keep the accusing note out of my voice. "You know he's been harassing me."

"He also asked if you'd ever mentioned someone named Missy Vanscheer."

I trip over a tree root and fall down, banging my knee. I stay on all fours a second longer than necessary, the mention of Missy's name making my eyes wide. Becca's car had Shanna's DNA in it, not Missy's. Missy just…ran away. Everybody knows that.

"Who?" I accept Graham's hand as he helps me to my feet.

"He said her name was Missy Vanscheer. She went to school with you."

I wipe my pine needle–flecked hands on my jeans and press them into my thighs, trying to hide the shaking. "It's been a long time since I thought about her. She was on the cheer team with Becca."

"So you knew her?"

"Knew of her. The cheerleaders were way cooler than me. I think she got pregnant and ran away."

"She was Becca's friend?"

Hardly.

"Becca was popular. She got along with everyone."

"And Missy just took off?"

"That's how I remember it."

"What did Becca say?"

I give him an odd look. "What did Greaves ask you?"

"Just if the name had ever come up. I guess they were reviewing cold cases, and Missy's file was in there. One of the evidence boxes had her journal and her last entry said she was going hiking."

It takes everything not to let my eyes bug out in shock. "What?"

"That's what he said." His expression is so earnest, so sincere, that I want to believe it's a coincidence. The business card, the storage unit, the mountain. The questions. But I've been through too much to believe in coincidence. I shouldn't have believed at all.

"Why would he call you about it?"

"Because he can't call Becca to ask? Because Shanna Lewis also went to school with you guys and also disappeared? And Becca's car was found with her DNA smeared on the front?" Graham looks anxious, his voice coming out sharp. Whatever he sees on my face softens his tone. "And your coworker…died. Maybe he's just trying to tie up loose ends so he can stop following you."

I swipe the back of my hand across my sweaty forehead. "Let's just keep going. This is ruining the day."

"It's strange, though," Graham says quickly, like he doesn't really want to but can't stop himself. "That the last note from Missy said she was going hiking and Fiona's car was found at the base of a mountain."

"Do you want to go back?" I ask. "Is that what this is about? You're trying to scare me? Because I thought today was about something else."

My eyes prick with tears, and my breath is coming fast, anxiety making me jittery.

He takes my hand. "No, it is. It is about that. That's all it's really about. Just you and me and…That's it."

We're mostly silent until we get to the sign for the next lookout, another forty minutes away. My new shirt clings to my chest with sweat, and Graham's not faring much better. The trail has gotten at least a million times steeper, and it's getting more and more difficult to find footholds. When we reach the second lookout, it's a relief. The small, flat expanse of stone offers a cool breeze and respite for my screaming thighs.

I drop onto the rock and grab a drink from Graham's bag. "Want some water?"

He comes over and accepts a bottle, taking it back to the edge as he drinks. The breeze picks up, ruffling his hair.

"This could be far enough," I say. "It's a good hike. A perfect view." I'd made a similar offer to Fiona. Given her lots of opportunities to turn back, change her mind. Change everything.

Graham sounds disappointed. "Really? It's only another thirty minutes to the top."

I arch a brow.

"Forty-five if we're slow," he amends. "According to the internet."

I pull out my phone. "Let me confirm."

He shrugs and politely turns away, like he thinks I'm stalling in order to catch my breath. Not that I just remembered something. I mumble a grateful prayer when I see two bars on my phone and quickly navigate to the *Brampton Chronicle* website. I search for hit-and-run deaths but find nothing. Car crashes—nine last week—but no hit-and-runs. I scroll through the past month of covers but don't see the one Greaves must have planted at the theater. Closing my eyes, I try to picture that moment, the cover of the paper, the name. Maybe it hadn't been the *Chronicle*. Maybe it was something else. We have two smaller local papers, but searches on both sites generate the same nonresults. I know that when people jump off bridges or in front of subways, the press doesn't report on it, not wanting to give someone else the same bad idea. But not alerting the public to a reckless driver who'd already claimed three lives feels, well, reckless.

I know I read about three deaths. I'd even made a list of reasons Becca was dead so I could believe she wasn't behind them. I'd read the articles on the *Chronicle* website, and I'd seen the third story in the newspaper at work, the accident happening in my neighborhood, though Mr. Myer hadn't known about it, and he makes it a point to know everything. And now, the stories are gone, like they never happened. Like I was the only one who was meant to see them.

A bead of sweat slithers down my spine, making me shiver though I'm flushed and feverish. I'd been so pre-occupied with Fiona's clue that I'd ignored these details, things that didn't make sense, that felt wrong but I hadn't wanted to acknowledge.

Bindi Carmichael, I remember suddenly. The second hit-and-run victim. I search again, and after a minute, I find the Facebook page I'd seen before. Her smiling face, her six posts. Two of avocado toast, one close-up of a rose, and three generic sunsets. All posted in the same week. Nothing before, and obviously nothing after.

Panic blurs my vision as I copy Bindi's profile photo and do a reverse image search, the way I'd seen done on television. It takes nearly a minute for three pages of results to link the image to a stock photo site. Same for the toast and the rose. I squint and shake my head, as though that might make things better. But it doesn't.

Bindi Carmichael isn't real.

None of it was real.

Something aches in my chest where my heart is sup-posed to be. It's the disappointment when you wake up from a great dream and realize you're in your bed, alone, with just the dark and its secrets for company.

"Ready to keep going?" Graham asks, crouching next to me to tuck his empty bottle back in his pack.

"Okay," I say. "If that's what you want."

The trail is eerily quiet as we climb, the weather and terrain shifting as we ascend, the temperature dropping noticeably, the trees thinning on our left, where the cliff lies. Someone strung up a thick rope between trunks in the steep parts, and I grip it with both hands, the coarse strands scratching my palms as I pull myself along, gravity and common sense urging me back down the trail, all the way home to my sister, where it's safe.

When I make it to the top of the incline, my palms sting, and sweat trickles down my temple. There are still two more steep pitches until we reach the top, and not a single person in sight between here and the end. At this altitude, every step is a lookout point, just ten to fifteen feet between the trail and the edge of the mountain, the green bowl of the valley a dense mystery lurking thousands of feet below.

"The car thing's still weird," Graham says, tugging his collar away from his neck, the skin slick with sweat.

"What are you talking about?" I ask the question because I'm supposed to, not because I need to.

"How Becca's car was used to kill Shanna and Becca trades in her car every year."

"I already told you. She likes new things."

"Where does she trade them?"

I duck, narrowly avoiding a stray branch to the eye. "I don't know. I don't go with her."

"You never asked? All these years?"

"You've seen my car. It's old. I never needed to ask."

"Did you ever ask her about anything else?"

"Like what?"

Another branch, this one half-broken, dangles in the path, and Graham lifts it for me to pass under.

"About Missy. Shanna. Angelica. Fiona."

I exhale. "I didn't realize there was anything to ask."

"The rumors say she was talking about leaving town."

"So?"

"But she needed money first. And she knew where to get some."

"Her parents?"

"Nikk Boulter said Becca stole from the jewelry store and sold him diamonds for cash."

I freeze. "What?"

"He came to my office one day, and he—"

"He went to your *office*?"

"—wanted to warn me."

"About what?"

"About Becca. It was after we met at the Kill Seekers meeting. After his wife disappeared again—"

"He beats his wife," I interrupt angrily, raising my voice, though not for Graham. "And she didn't disappear; she escaped. There's a difference."

"And the diamonds?"

"I imagine the store would have noticed if diamonds were missing, Graham. He knew Becca from the store and gave her a place to stay after Footloose. She learned he was beating his wife, and she helped her leave him. Becca *helped*. That's the woman she made disappear. A battered one."

"Well, he's really—"

"Are you honestly this naive?" I snap. "Some guy tells you a deranged story about my sister, and you just believe him? Did you check his story? Did you ask questions?"

Graham looks flustered. "I'm checking now. I'm asking you."

"Did Greaves really tell you about Missy?"

"What? Of course he did."

"Because Nikk knew her, too."

It's his turn to trip. We're still ten feet from the edge, but it's so close. He catches his balance before he goes down but looks startled by the revelation.

"He did?"

"Yeah. Becca told me, and after one of the Kill Seekers meetings, I had coffee with Nikk, and he said he knew her. Shanna too. He went to private school in Lincoln, but they were all in the same grade, went to the same parties." Most of this is untrue, but it'll be hard to disprove after all these years.

"You think Becca had a thing for him?"

Somehow we've managed to reach the peak. My lies

are coming in half pants as I gulp in breaths, my hands shaking as I set down my bag and pull out the last bottle of water. The lookout area is about twenty feet wide, sheer rock on two sides, the others patchy trees that eventually give way to forest. The wind is stronger, the breeze cooling my overheated skin, and from where we stand, it feels like we're the only two people on the planet.

"I don't know," I say, because Graham still seems to be waiting for an answer to his question. "Becca was pretty. I guess if she wanted Nikk, she could have dated him."

"He said he only likes brunettes."

"He only likes people he can manipulate."

If Graham catches the insult, he ignores it. "How come you never had any pets growing up?"

I sigh. "Because my father's allergic."

"She didn't even acknowledge Felix."

"So? She's not a dog person."

"And she doesn't appear at all traumatized by her run-in with Footloose."

"She has a limp."

"But no memories of the attack?"

I shrug. "My memories are patchy."

"It's too convenient, Carrie. I know you love your sister, but I don't think you're seeing the whole picture. The real picture." He glances past me when he says the words, as though the "picture" lurks in the forest. Which, I suppose, some of it does.

"What's the whole picture, Graham?"

"She displays all the characteristics of a psychopath."

I act astonished. "What? That's—"

But the floodgates are open and Graham's on a roll. "She doesn't feel emotion. Guilt, empathy. She hurts you constantly and never feels bad, never stops. Never apologizes. She's manipulative and narcissistic. The only person she has any connection to is you, and that's just because you're the person she likes to hurt most."

I stare at him in shock. Not because any of what he's saying is new information, but because hearing someone else say out loud what I've known for too long is a strange and novel experience.

"It was you," I say finally.

He blinks. "What?"

"Footloose told me."

Graham flushes. "Told you what?"

"That he sent you something. A key."

The flush deepens, confirming my suspicions. Fitting another piece in a very warped puzzle, one I realized too late had too many new players.

"Footloose sent you the key to the storage unit with Shanna's car. I didn't know what he was talking about. But you left a business card at my place one night," I lie, "and it had a bunch of initials on the back. One of them was different. B.S.S. Brampton Storage Solutions."

Graham's shaking his head. "I...I didn't know what it opened, Carrie. Or who sent it. But it came with a note that said, *You don't know your girlfriend.* And I...I knew you were hiding something. And I wanted to understand. I researched all the places I could think of that might use that type of key and just...visited them all."

I'd figured this out an hour ago, but hearing Graham admit it is like watching the ground between us cleave and slide apart, pushing us farther and farther away from ourselves.

"You think I had something to do with Shanna's disappearance?"

"No, of course not. I didn't know what the car had to do with anything when I found it. But there was a smell..." He looks lost. "I told the police. Whatever it was, it wasn't good."

"When was this?"

"I got the key in the mail in early December, and I found the locker in February. I told the police right away. I didn't know it belonged to Becca, and I'd never heard anything about Shanna before then."

"Why did you really bring me on this hike? To ask all these questions about my sister?"

"Because she killed them!" he shouts. "Why can't you see that? The police think you did it, or you knew about it, but I told them you didn't. I told them I'd prove it."

Graham the honest. Graham the dependable. Graham the good guy.

"Is that why you brought me here? You were never going to propose?"

His hands are shaking as he fumbles with his pack.

"Of course I was. I wanted to ask you at Christmas, but then I got that note…"

"And you believed it?"

He's not wrong, but we're all playing our parts now.

Graham dumps empty water bottles and champagne on the ground, a box of chocolates, a jar of marmalade that promptly rolls away. It rattles across the stone, straight to the edge of the cliff, and drops out of sight like so many other lost causes.

"Here," he says, pulling a small red box from the bottom of the bag. "I've had this for months. It's for you. It's all been for you, Carrie. I swear."

He extends the box, but I don't touch it.

"Why here?" I ask again. "Why this mountain?"

"Because of Fiona's car."

"She just left it here, Graham."

His eyes are sad. "She didn't, Carrie. Becca brought her here and killed her, just like she did to Missy. They might not have found the body, but she left a clue."

"That clue is just a waste of time—"

"Not Fiona's clue. Missy's."

I take a step back, this move entirely genuine. "What?"

"Her journal, she said—"

"She was going hiking."

"She said she was going with 'Bitchface.'"

"And that means Becca?"

Graham sighs. "Greaves showed me the note. It had five capital letters. The *B*, the *E* …"

I picture the word in my mind, a teenager's flowery scrawl, the last words she'd ever write: *BitChfACE.*

"When they found Becca's car and the DNA, they dug back through the records, and Greaves saw Shanna had worked with Becca. Then he began looking for other cases, and he learned about Missy. He reviewed the file and found the journal entry. He said they don't have any bodies, but Fiona disappearing and her car at the base of the mountain and Missy going hiking…It all makes sense."

"It doesn't." I shake my head helplessly. "None of it does."

"I'm sorry, Carrie. I just wanted us to have our lives…"

"How?" I swipe at tears I don't even have to fake because he confirmed everything I thought I knew, and every confirmation was another tear in my heart, in the fabric of the life we were building.

"They said I had to help them."

"Is that what you're doing now? You brought me up here, let me believe you were going to propose, and thought you would lie to me some more?"

"I've never lied—"

"Why are you wearing that stupid shirt?" I interrupt. The wind whips past, drying the tears on my cheeks.

Graham looks down, fingers going automatically to the buttons. "It's just…"

"They're listening, aren't they? They're here?"

His gaze flits over my shoulder to the tree line. Slowly,

he nods and undoes the buttons. The white T-shirt beneath does nothing to hide the wire strapped to his chest.

"Did you ever want to have a life with me?" I whisper. "The house? The dog? Any of it?"

"Of course I did. I do. I do. I want that more than anything. But first we have to help them get Becca—"

I shake my head as Greaves steps out of the trees, a cluster of officers in dark clothes following. They start toward us, the game over. The pieces played. They're not in the right place, but they're all on the table.

"All this time," I say, fresh tears dripping off my chin. "You've been lying to me. None of it was real."

Graham's fingers tremble as he opens the ring box, the beautiful princess-cut diamond glittering in the sunlight. "It was all real. I swear."

It's hard to look at him, his own cheeks wet. It's hard to lie to him, and it's hard to understand that he's lied to me, too. That he did it for the right reasons and I didn't. That we both wanted a life together, but I was burying secrets while he helped dig them up.

The whole world is spread out before us, the future at our fingertips, and it's slipping away on the breeze, and there's nothing I can do to hold on to it, no magic secret, no diamond ring that will save us. No house, no dog, no wedding. Graham wants a truth he can never have. A life that's no longer on offer. A Carrie that doesn't exist.

Greaves walks past me and stops a short distance away, placing himself between me and the edge of the mountain, as though I might try to jump. His expression is neutral, eyes steady on mine. I let him see that he's broken me, that he's torn it all apart, hunted through the shattered pieces of my life and my history, and there's nothing to find.

And that's true, as much as he'll ever know. Because while Becca's the one who likes to dress up, invent characters, and tell stories, I'm the one who's been playing a part for ten years, and today is the performance of a lifetime.

CHAPTER 25

That total fuckhead!" Becca fumes when I come home that afternoon, red-faced and in tears, blurting out my sad story between hiccups. "I always knew he was the worst!"

I sob pathetically, flopping onto the couch she'd just vacated and covering my face with a pillow. Even once I'd realized today wasn't going to end with a proposal, even when I realized Greaves had been using Graham to get to me, I hadn't expected Graham to believe him quite so much. Hadn't expected him to admit it. Hadn't really, honestly thought it was possible that the kindest, best man I'd ever known had been lying to me almost as much as I'd been lying to him.

"Don't worry, Carrie." Becca sits on the edge of the couch and pats my arm. Her fingers are cold and stiff like a mannequin hand, and she probably feels just as much empathy. "We'll kill him."

I lift the pillow. "What? Who?"

"Graham. Why? Who were you thinking?"

"No one! No one else dies. No one else does anything bad. Do you know how close today was? How much could have fallen apart?"

Her brow furrows. "But nothing did."

"My life did."

"Graham wasn't your life, Carrie. He's so boring I can't even remember what he looks like, but I'm sure you could possibly do better. I'll help you."

I cover my head with the pillow again. "For the love of God, no more help."

The couch shifts as she stands, and the floorboards creak as she paces the length of the room, thinking out loud. "So Footloose found the key to my first storage unit, stole the key to the second unit with the car, and sent it to Graham with a note saying he couldn't trust you, and then Graham, having nothing better to do, spent months trying to figure out what the key opened and found the unit. The car smelled bad, so he reported it to the police. They tested for DNA, and because stupid missing Shanna was in the database, they found a match. Your DNA was in the trunk as well, and you're in the system because you gave them a sample after Angelica's death, so they ID'd you, too."

I peek out from under the pillow to see that she's now

gazing dramatically out the window. "Greaves becomes convinced you're a lunatic killer of women and recruits Graham to help incriminate you. To speed things along, he gets the paper to post fake stories about three hit-and-run deaths, thinking you'll panic and mess up. Then Graham, out of the goodness of his heart, goes along with the plan in order to *exonerate* you"—even with my head covered, I know she's rolling her eyes—"and when I come back from the dead, he decides to pin it all on me instead."

"You did it all."

She ignores that. "He tells Greaves he's always had his doubts about me, and Greaves looks into my past. He finds out about Missy, digs up her file, and reads her journal, in which she called me a bitchface and spelled out my name."

I remove the pillow. "They know everything. They just can't prove it."

"That's the key, Carrie. Proof. And you know where the proof is?"

"In the first storage unit?"

"Well, some. Not for long. Now that Graham's on the case."

I rasp out a painful laugh.

"It's in Nikk's man cave," she points out when it becomes obvious I'm not going to come up with the answer.

"Oh yeah."

"So now that you've done your part and convinced them they were looking at the wrong person, it's up to me to nudge them in the right direction."

"Don't nudge Greaves with your car unless I have a solid alibi." I don't actually want to kill a police officer—or anyone else—but the man's spent six months trying to ruin my life, so I'm not going to argue too strongly against it.

Becca pats my arm again, and I get goose bumps. "See? Your sense of humor has returned. You're already over Graham."

New tears well up, and I don't know if the worst part is that she actually believes that because she can't feel human emotion or because it's so patently, eternally untrue.

"I'm not over anything. All of this insanity has been to get my life back. A house, a dog, a husband. And now…I have nothing."

"It's the twenty-first century, Carrie. You don't need a husband. And you already have a house. Stop being so negative."

"I was just the target of a sting operation! I was going on a hike expecting my dream proposal, and now I'm home and single."

"You have me."

That only makes it worse.

"And we can get a dog, if you insist."

I sit up in alarm. "No."

"You just said—"

"Becca." I look at her as sternly as I can through bleary eyes. "You living here is temporary. You know that. We can't live together as two spinster sisters."

"Who called me a spinster?"

I sigh. "You know what I mean."

"Then which is it? You don't want me to nudge the police in Nikk's direction, but it's not safe for you to stay here alone while he's out there. His jaw won't be broken forever."

"It's broken?"

"He posted a picture on his Instagram. I liked it." She winks, and impossibly, I laugh. "If you really want your 'life back'"—inexplicably, she uses air quotes—"then we have to deal with Nikk. I'll tell the police he attacked me. Nikk's not the only one who takes glamorous selfies of their injuries." She touches her throat where the ring of bruises dots her neck like a yellowing pearl necklace.

"Just because today's sting operation failed doesn't mean it's over," I remind her. "I thought it was over last December, but Greaves was just biding his time. If he doesn't believe me, a non–serial killer, he's definitely not going to believe you."

Becca pouts like she's about to argue but then snaps her fingers. "Fine. I know who he'll listen to."

———

Several days later, we're sitting in an interrogation room at the Brampton police station. Detective Roy Forrester, the man in the brown suit from our last visit, sits opposite Becca and Lilly, who clutch tissues in their fists as they recount their terrible run-ins with violent, and possibly even *murderous*, Nikk Boulter. I sit off to the side—for "moral support," as Becca called it, though really she insisted I be here to rub it in Greaves's face as part of my emotional healing—and Greaves himself stands at the far end of the room, glaring stonily at me while Becca and Lilly talk. I hadn't been privy to their conversations about what they'd say today, so my reactions to the revelations are as genuine as they can be, considering the circumstances. Forrester seems to be buying what they're selling, though Greaves still looks like he'd rather take his chances squaring off in the parking lot against my sister and her car.

"I'd been afraid for so long," Lilly is saying, plucking apart the tissue in her hand and watching the pieces flutter to the table. "And when the opportunity came to escape…I took it." She shoots a tiny glance at Becca, making her perhaps the only person in history to make eye contact with my sister and not immediately look away in a panic.

The police already know the story of Lilly's first escape, and now they're hearing about her second time hiding away with the help of Heather McBride, who'd gotten her a place at a shelter so she can rebuild her life. It's a slow process, but I think she feels like she has an opportunity she hasn't had for a long time. And she's grabbing it with both hands.

"I thought Nikk was my friend," Becca adds. "I knew him from the jewelry store, where he was always buying something for Lilly. I thought it was a gift. I didn't know it was an apology."

Lilly sniffles. A single perfect tear trickles down her cheek.

"When I went to stay with them," Becca continues, "I saw how he treated her and realized I'd misunderstood. But I was naive. I thought if she just got away, he'd stop, and she would be okay. Everything would be okay. But I was wrong."

She sniffles, too, and swipes at her cheek, copying Lilly, but there are no tears there. She can't muster up actual emotion. She can only try her best to imitate it. Greaves has taken a break from eyeballing me to stare at Becca, unimpressed.

"He's been coming to the house," she goes on. "Stalking my sister, hunting me. He left a threatening note on her door and followed her when she went to view homes. The real estate agent had to chase him off."

Greaves and Forrester exchange a look. That much they know is true. Beau, who has a much better reputation around here than yours truly, gave the statement.

Becca lets out a shaky breath. "I thought I could talk to him. I don't know why. I just...I wanted to make it stop. He was so fixated on getting Lilly back, but he was also fixated on the jewelry she'd taken. He wouldn't stop talking about it. He was…obsessed."

"He's filed a report," Forrester says, which we already knew. "Saying it was stolen."

"It's mine," Lilly interjects. "I…earned it. The things I took were in our bedroom. The pieces he's really protective of are in his room."

"He has a second bedroom?"

"A man cave. With a lock on the door. He keeps his personal stuff in there. I don't know why he thinks that's okay. We're supposed to be married. We're not supposed to have secrets. But…"

Her tears fall freely now with cinematic perfection. She looks at Becca for support, and Becca squeezes her fingers.

My sister takes over. "When I was staying there, some of my things would disappear. Just small things. An earring, a hair clip, a pair of underwear. I thought I'd just misplaced them, but I checked everywhere."

"Me too," Lilly adds. "Everywhere but…"

"The man cave," Forrester supplies.

Becca wipes away another imaginary tear. "When I went to talk to Nikk, he acted so nice. So apologetic."

Lilly's nodding like she knows all too well how this story goes.

"But as soon as the door closed, he changed. He grabbed me. By my hair, then my neck. He threw me on the floor and tried to strangle me." She touches her fingers to her throat, the lingering bruises an ugly yellow green, a new memento of a different crime. The police have already photographed them.

"I passed out, and when I woke up, I was in a room I hadn't seen before. The door was open, and I could see the upstairs hallway. It was the man cave. My head was hurting, and I realized Nikk was pulling out my hair elastic. Some of my hair, too. I played dead, and he went into the closet, and I heard him open something. A drawer. Like he was…saving the elastic. The way he'd taken my other things. To remember me." She breaks off and buries her face in her hands, presumably to contain her emotions but most likely to hide her laughter.

"What happened then?" Forrester prompts.

She lifts her head, her eyes unfocused, like she's lost in the memory and not trying her best not to giggle. "I ran. I don't know how, because I could barely breathe and my legs were weak, but I knew it was my only chance. I crawled out of the room and ran down the stairs, and I was outside before Nikk followed. He didn't come into the street because he didn't want his neighbors to see, so I got away."

"You didn't report this?" Greaves pipes up. He's got his arms folded across his broad chest, his normally neutral expression betraying just a hint of irritation. I know how he feels. Becca has that effect on people.

She sniffs. "I was terrified. He…When he was

strangling me, he said, 'You're just another one they won't find.'"

Lilly gasps. "He said that to you, too?"

"He said it to you?"

"All the time. Every…every time."

Greaves steps forward. "Who are the others?"

Forrester shoots him a warning look, and he stops but doesn't back up.

"I don't know," Lilly whispers. "I was too afraid to ask. But he said he'd been doing this a long time to girls who…turned him down. I should have said something. I know I…I know I should have done more. But there was no proof. Just his word against mine. And people always believed him."

"Why did you decide to come in now?" Forrester asks.

Becca and Lilly exchange another look, but this time it's Becca seeking encouragement. Or pretending to.

"This was left on my pillow," she whispers, reaching into her pocket and pulling something out. Her hand is closed in a fist around the object, arm shaking as she slowly uncurls her fingers. I have to squint from where I'm sitting, the fluorescent lights glinting off the metal. And then, in spite of myself, I gasp. It's a silver pin in the shape of a cheerleader with two tiny red initials. MV. Missy Vanscheer.

"That was in my house?" I demand.

Becca nods, blinking as she stares down at it. "I didn't want to scare you."

"He was inside the house, and you didn't tell me?"

I'm pulling off the performance because I didn't know what the hell Becca would be saying today—she said it would lend "authenticity" to my reactions—but also because I know Nikk didn't leave that pin on her pillow. The last time I saw it, it had prime placement in her storage unit, her first-ever murder memento. If she's turning it in, she knows we're desperate, and she's pulling out the big guns.

"What's that?" Forrester asks. Becca puts the pin on the table and he uses a pen to draw it closer to himself.

I glance at Greaves, and a muscle tics in his cheek.

"It belonged to Missy Vanscheer," I whisper. "She wore it every day. Everyone on the cheer team had one. She went missing in high school. We…we thought she ran away with her boyfriend."

"I knew her," Becca adds. "She was one of my"—her voice breaks—"my best friends. We even went hiking together before she disappeared. She said she'd met this guy…" She shakes her head miserably. "I should have guessed."

"Guessed what?" Forrester asks. He and Greaves must have decided he would be the good cop today because he's doing a great job feigning interest in Becca's story while Greaves looks like he wants to explode.

"Nikk," Becca mumbles. "We all knew him. He was kind of possessive, but he was rich and handsome. And…I don't know. I was a teenager. I wasn't thinking about murder. But I guess he was."

CHAPTER 26

The Brampton Kill Seekers attend the funeral for Misha Collins en masse. Her family opted to hold the ceremony outside in a large park, the grounds awash in colorful spring flowers. Rainbows were her favorite thing, they remind us repeatedly in the small card that bears a picture of Misha's smiling face and the name and website of her favorite charity. She lived her best life forever.

The event is set up like a wedding with rows of chairs on the soft grass, the sun bright overhead. There's no coffin since it would have been a closed casket anyway, so up front is just a large projector screen onto which an endless slideshow of Misha's favorite quotes, photos, and social media posts plays in a way that would make Emmett proud. Across the aisle, he and Ravjinder appear riveted by the display.

Ravjinder spots me and shoots me a tiny smile, which I return. Following Becca and Lilly's interview, the police had obtained a search warrant for Nikk's home and found our carefully planted box of mementos, including the elastic with strands of Becca's hair and Kami Bains's half-heart necklace. The Bains family has no body, but I'd like to believe they have some closure. Even if that comes in the form of yet another serial killer who called Brampton home and who's currently being held without bail.

I don't turn around, but I can feel Greaves's stare drilling into the back of my skull. He was here when Becca and I arrived, me in the same black dress I'd worn to Angelica's funeral last November, Becca in something pricey she'd ordered after pawning another piece of pilfered jewelry.

Lilly's not here. She's using the opportunity to move away and put time and space between her and Nikk, and attending the funeral for one of the victims of her husband's murderous rampage hardly seems like a good idea for someone in her weakened mental state. I'm still not sure how much of what she said in the interview she believed to be true, but she played her part in a way that clearly made Becca proud—she said I have the range of a plank of wood, but Lilly could melt even Greaves's icy heart—and convinced Detective Forrester to follow up with the claims about Nikk's man cave. Greaves doesn't feel quite the same way, but there's not a lot he can do about it.

The crowd is large, lots of gawkers coming to the funeral of a murdered woman they never knew, but the buzz about a second Brampton serial killer is making the rounds, and people are curious. Emmett texted me yesterday to ask if I was coming. They can't believe they invited Nikk to their meetings and failed to notice he was insane.

Next to me, Becca yawns. She wears a floppy black hat to protect herself from the sun and a pair of over-sized sunglasses for the dramatic effect. There's no wig today, but she looks every bit like the mysterious Diana Speedwell and not the woman responsible for today's funeral. Sometimes I'm not even sure she remembers she murdered Misha.

"I'm hot," she complains out the side of her mouth, her lowered voice the only concession to the somber occasion. "Are there refreshments? Snacks? Where?"

"There's a reception after," I reply, tapping the address on the back of the card. "Friends and family only."

"Perfect. I'm famished."

As though she'd overheard, the minister takes her place at the front of the scene and gets things started with a few kind words. Misha's father speaks next, though it's hard to hear through the tears and Becca's grumbling about being hungry. We all suffer through Misha's niece singing "The Rose," and not nearly soon enough, it's over.

Becca gets to her feet, the first one in the crowd to stand. "Beautiful ceremony," she says to the woman behind her, who appears flummoxed by the sudden movement. "Meet you there," she adds to me, stomping on my foot as she steps over, and ignoring my yelp of pain as she makes a beeline for the parking lot.

People slowly begin to disperse, and though I know I shouldn't, I slip my phone out of my bag and stare at the screen. I'd had it on silent, but as it's done all week, it vibrated once every thirty minutes. Graham has had the good sense to stay away from my home—and more specifically, my sister—but he's left seventy-one voice messages and sent 203 texts and six emails. I deleted them all.

Today's text says, *I miss you. Please talk to me.*

I delete it, too.

"Fancy seeing you here," Greaves says from Becca's seat. I jolt and drop my phone on the grass. Greaves picks it up and hands it back. "You need a ride home?"

He'd offered me a ride home after the hike debacle, too, but I'd called a cab.

"No."

He's silent for a moment, studying a quote from Vivian Greene on the projector up front. *Life is not about waiting for a storm to pass but learning to dance in the rain.*

"Nikk Boulter never knew Misha Collins," he says.

"That's what he said about all the women he killed."

"And he says you broke his jaw."

I laugh. "Sure."

Greaves doesn't laugh. "I'd like to find the bodies. Give the families some closure."

I glance over to where Ravjinder and Emmett speak to a couple of other Kill Seekers. I've thought about it, for sure. Revealing a couple of locations. Kami Bains, Fiona McBride. Let those families heal, move on. Kami's at the old fairgrounds, Fiona the base of a mountain, with company. But Becca had always threatened that exposing her hobby would expose me because she'd tucked something of mine in alongside each of the bodies. Maybe that's true, and maybe it's not. At this point, it's irrelevant. I may not have killed them, but I helped dig the graves and hide the bodies and I kept the secret. I'm not innocent, and I haven't been for a long time.

"He hasn't shown you?" I ask.

"He can't help me find what he didn't hide."

"What if you offered him a deal if he told you where they were?"

"That's a fine idea."

The sun is out in full force, and sweat trickles down my spine. I get to my feet. "Goodbye, Detective."

"I know it wasn't you."

I remain standing, staring at the screen up ahead. Misha's smiling face gazes back. *Try to be a rainbow in someone's cloud.*

That's great advice, Maya Angelou. If only it were that simple.

"Good," I say.

"How long has she been doing it?"

"I don't know what you're talking about."

"I can help you."

My mouth twitches, but I don't smile. I've wanted help for as long as I can remember, but that's the thing about sociopaths, about Becca. You're afraid to ask for help. Not just because of what might happen to you, but because of what will happen to everyone you care about.

"You can't," I assure him.

"Nikk Boulter might go to prison for crimes he didn't commit."

"What about the ones he did?"

"What about the person who did it?" Greaves counters. "If she's still out there, it'll keep happening. Can you live with that?"

"*You* failed, Detective. You failed to protect the people of this town. You failed to protect Misha Collins, Fiona McBride, me, my sister, and a hundred others. Can I live with that? I guess I have to, don't I? I don't have a choice."

"You do. Right now. Tell me about your sister."

"She's a fighter. She survived a serial killer. She helped a battered woman escape her abusive husband. She's never had so much as a parking ticket."

Greaves stares at me for a moment. "You can call me anytime, Carrie. Despite what you may have been made to believe, you're not alone in this."

He gets up and walks away, out the opposite end of the aisle. I watch him go, a broad, dark figure in a crowd of other dark shapes, a mass of sad strangers, confused and

thrilled by the drama. The group has thinned, a few strag-
glers murmuring near the projector, a couple of people
sobbing in the front row. Beau is there, weeping heavily
into a handkerchief. Our eyes meet, and he gives me a
small, sad nod, due, I'm sure, in equal parts to Misha's
passing and Graham and I backing out of the purchase of
our long-sought-after dream home. Someone else already
bought it. I drove past twice to stare at the SOLD sign,
further proof my dream was dead. I look away.

The seats on the other side of the aisle are empty. The
Kill Seekers have already left, joining Becca for the free
food and drink, probably recruiting her for their next
meeting, which she'll gleefully attend, playing her part
for another unwitting audience.

Becca took the car, so I walk out in the opposite direction, away from Greaves and the people heading to their
vehicles. I had to come to the funeral, but I can't stomach
the thought of mingling and keeping up the charade
when everything inside me and everything I thought
waited for me in the future feels like broken glass rattling
in my stomach. There's a smaller parking lot on the
north side of the field, and when I reach it, I see Heather
McBride loading plants into the trunk of her SUV.

"Carrie," she says, when she spots me. "Hi."

"I didn't see you at the funeral."

She shakes her head. "I didn't attend. I just supplied
some of the flowers. These are extras."

"They're beautiful."

"Least I could do. Here." She retrieves a small lavender plant in a cup and extends it to me. "Keep it in a warm spot in your house. It'll smell nice."

"I don't have a green thumb," I protest, even as she keeps her arm extended and I have to accept the gift. The seedlings I bought at the community garden are currently rotting in the trash can in my backyard, their future as dim as mine.

Heather winks. "Here's a secret: You don't need one. Food, water, shelter, love. The recipe for life. Flowers just dress it up."

"Well, thank you. And not just for the plant. For everything you've done for Lilly, too."

"Of course." She tries to smile but it only deepens the grooves around her mouth and the circles under her eyes. Her daughter's reckless behavior is responsible for some of those, but so am I. And every day that she continues to live in that huge, old house with those invisible birds for company, they'll continue to deepen. We all have our demons. Some are missing daughters, some are not-so-missing sisters.

"A few weeks ago, you mentioned moving," I say, nodding at the stack of packing boxes in the trunk. "Have you decided to go?"

"What? Oh, Boston?" She forces a laugh. "My husband really wants to. I guess I'm just going through the motions, making him think it might really happen."

"But you're still waiting for a sign."

She tilts her head, as though she's embarrassed. "Maybe."

Waiting is dangerous, I know. Like Greaves said, the person who killed Misha and more than a dozen others is still out there. Can I live with that? Can I continue to live while she continues to kill? What am I waiting for? A sign? Another slaughtered real estate agent, another late-night phone call to "move furniture"? What will it take?

But all I say to Heather is, "When you're ready, you'll know."

"Thank you, Carrie."

I can't speak around the lump in my throat, so I give her a tiny wave and cup the plant in my hands as I start toward home. I don't make it far before I get that strange feeling on the back of my neck again. It slides down my spine, wraps itself around my waist like a vise, and squeezes. I'm on the sidewalk, six lanes of traffic racing past, and I feel like I'm about to collapse.

I've spent the past week with Becca keeping a constant vigil over me, her creepy, unwelcome version of caring, and I've had to put on a brave face, my bravest one yet, and pretend I didn't really care that my life had fallen apart. That the breakup with Graham was totally fine, that Greaves's ability to infiltrate my life while I was blissfully, stupidly unaware didn't bother me at all.

And while it had to be the world's worst performance of anything, ever, Becca remains chronically incapable of recognizing or appreciating genuine human emotion, so she had to rely on my stoic words and lack of tears. And she bought it. She had to. Because if she didn't, she'd have been at Graham's house with a car or a carving knife or any other murderous implement, making him pay for his betrayal and existing in general.

More than everything I've done, every horrible decision, every secret, every lie, every body in an unmarked grave—and some now marked—the thing I can't live with, the thing I can't stuff inside a box and tuck away and ignore forever, is hurting Graham even more. Betraying him further. He betrayed me, sure, but his heart was in the right place, even if he doesn't quite have all the facts and would feel very differently if he did.

"Carrie," Graham says.

I wipe tears off my face and tell myself I'm hearing things and need to get it together before I get home. Becca will only content herself with free food and beverages for so long; she doesn't have much of a tolerance for weepy people, or any people, and she'll be on her way back soon. She can't see me like this. She's still looking for a reason to kill someone.

"Carrie," I hear again.

I duck my head and walk faster, like I can escape my conscience.

"Carrie."

I stop abruptly, teetering on my black high heels like my mind can't decide to stay or go, if I should risk a look over my shoulder in case Graham's voice is real and not just a desperate figment of my imagination. I waft like a stalk of grass in the breeze until the sound of tentatively approaching footsteps cements me in the moment, and I do turn and I do look, and there's Graham, maybe five feet away in a suit and tie, watching me nervously. He's got Felix on his leash, tail wagging ferociously, pink tongue flopping out.

I guess Graham *does* know how to play dirty.

"Hi," he says.

The last time I saw him was at the top of the mountain, when the sting failed, when he failed, when he held the diamond ring in his hand and I walked away and hiked back down the trail, a tedious, painful trek that left me with blisters and heartbreak.

Things were always going to end that way, if I'd been honest with myself. All my relationships have to end because you can't have a happily ever after with a serial killer in your life, and that's what I have. It's what I've always had. A serial killer sister and so many dark secrets it would take years to bring them all to light, and before I'd gotten to the second, third, fourth confession, Graham would run screaming in the opposite direction, and Greaves would take his place.

He'd run if he were lucky. But in reality, Becca would be waiting nearby, and he wouldn't get far. Because that's my life. I can't have nice things. I might have deserved them once but not anymore. I've made my choices. I kept my mouth shut and carried my end of the murder carpet and dug graves and pushed people off mountains and let my real estate agent get slaughtered. That's who I am. Not the woman Graham thinks he knows.

"I'm sorry," he blurts out. "For everything. I...I...I don't know how else to say it. I'm so, so sorry. I didn't think I had a choice, and I convinced myself it would help you, and...it didn't. I'm sorry, Carrie. Please forgive me."

Because this is who Graham is. Heart on his sleeve, lying because he has to and believes it's the right thing, the only thing. If he'd gotten lucky, maybe it would have worked out. Maybe I'd have confessed, and Becca would be sitting in prison right now, filing her nails and plotting revenge. But I'd be in the cell next to her, and that's the part he'd never understand. Never accept. There must be some mistake. Carrie wouldn't do that. But Carrie would, Graham. Carrie's done a lot of bad things.

"It's fine," I say. Already I can feel the tear tracks drying on my cheeks, the skin stiff. It's like a mask I slip on, a role that I play. But after too long in character, it becomes impossible to distinguish where you end and the pretend begins. After too long, it's all you.

"It's not fine. I...I hurt you." Graham has no masks. His pain is stamped all over his handsome face, for everyone to see.

"Yeah." I stare past his shoulder because I can't bear the eye contact. "You did."

"Please look at me."

I know I shouldn't. I know I should keep walking and tell him to leave me alone, and he'll continue to gently prod until he takes the hint—the life-saving advice—and slinks away, but I'm a selfish person. I always have been. I meet his eyes.

His face crumbles, and I know I've made a huge mistake. My heart disintegrates in my chest, reforming itself only to immediately break apart all over again.

"I'll do anything," Graham says, "to make it up to you. To prove that I'm sorry and I love you, and I trust you, and—" He's fumbling for something in his pocket, and if seeing the tears in his eyes was bad, seeing that ring again is going to be the end of me.

"It's too late," I say.

"I talked to your sister."

I freeze. I don't know if it's because I'm shocked he did it or because he survived it.

"You what? When?"

"Just now. When she was sprinting to the parking lot. I—we—stopped her." Felix yips, like he's confirming the story.

Well, that explains how he survived. Becca doesn't kill with an audience. But it doesn't mean she won't try later.

"I explained everything," he continues. "I told her how sorry I was, how much I love you. How I don't believe anything Detective Greaves was saying, anything I said.

He's grasping at straws, Carrie, trying to make people feel better. But if he had proof, he'd have shown it by now, and he doesn't. I'm sorry I fell for it."

I'm reeling. "What did...what did Becca say?"

"She said she accepted my apology. She was very gracious."

We just attended the funeral of a woman she murdered, and *she* was accepting apologies. Graciously.

I think I might faint.

"I know it's too late for Baker Street," Graham adds. "But maybe we can make one of the others work. They weren't perfect, but what is?"

I want to laugh. "Nothing," I admit. "And they were all terrible."

Felix barks his agreement.

"So we compromise," Graham says, "and we wait until the right house comes along. And until then...you wear this."

I blink and see the ring in his hand, the same one from the mountaintop, from the jewelry store window. The one I'd wanted for so long. It winks in the sunlight, and Felix barks again, and I look between the three and wonder if maybe this is the only sign I need.

CHAPTER 27

"Oh my God. I hate dogs," Becca grumbles for the tenth time the next night. "Remind me again why we're doing this?"

"I've reminded you, like, seven hundred times," I reply.

The beam of my headlamp catches a stray branch a split second before my forehead. I snag and lift it for Becca to pass under. Clutched in her arms, Felix writhes around to lick her chin, further confirming he lacks the survival instincts to be my pet. I carried him for the first half hour, until the terrain got too treacherous and I kept falling and he refused to walk on his leash, so Becca became the only option.

"I'm climbing through a ravine at midnight," she counters. "Remind me again."

"Because Heather McBride needs a sign."

"And you think dropping a dog in her backyard and

running away is a clearer sign than, say, a phone call saying, 'Hey, Heather, you should move to Boston. Your dead daughter would want that for you'?"

"Felix is a Boston terrier, and she wants to move to Boston. It's a very clear sign. She's looking for a reason to move home, and I'm giving her one."

"It's not clear at all."

"Is too."

"You know what this sounds like?"

"Insanity. You've said."

"An apology," Becca counters. "But for what, I wonder?"

I'm never going to confess to my serial killer sister that I murdered Fiona, so I ignore the not-so-rhetorical question and focus on not gasping for breath. Eventually, we reach the top of the steep embankment. The tall fence that borders the McBride property comes into view, the house looming dark behind it.

"Think of Felix as a thank-you present," I suggest, wiping sweat from my temple. "For everything Heather did for Lilly."

Becca rolls her eyes but doesn't argue. We both know that's the only reason she agreed to come along tonight and hasn't already strangled Felix, who's doing his very best to kiss her to death.

I retrieve the footstool from my backpack and set it up on the ground, but when I reach for Felix, Becca waves me away, steps on the stool, and unceremoniously drops the dog over the fence. There's a tiny yelp—one from Felix and one from me—but when I peer through the gap in the wood slats, my headlamp highlights a confused but otherwise unharmed dog.

"You could have hurt him," I mutter.

"Thank God he's okay." Becca holds out the harness and leash, and I stuff them into my bag with the stool. We stick close to the fences as we walk a few houses away, eventually finding an opening that lets us squeeze through to the dark street where we'd left my car earlier.

"You haven't told me the other part of the plan," Becca says when we've driven a few blocks. I slow for a red light and try to work through the script I'd been planning since yesterday, when Graham and I reunited. I accepted his proposal but asked him to keep the ring until I broke the news to Becca, who would have been just as likely to kill me and make the ring her newest memento as congratulate me. It's also why I got Felix to safety before updating her.

"I'm going to move in with Graham," I say as the light turns green.

"What?" She whips around in her seat to glare at me. "When?"

"Soon."

"How soon?"

How soon do I start the next chapter of my life? How much longer do I put it off, worrying about what my sister might do? How long until I start living on my own terms?

"Next weekend," I answer. "I need some time to pack."

"You said you weren't buying the house."

"We're not. I'm moving into his apartment. When we find the right place, we'll be ready. That house was too expensive, anyway."

"That's why you didn't keep the dog. It wasn't a stupid sign."

There were a lot of reasons we couldn't keep Felix, and Graham accepted them all. No pets in his building. My sister might kill it out of rage. Heather McBride needed it more.

"The dog *was* a sign."

"Graham tried to get us both arrested last week," she snaps. "*That's* a sign."

"He said you accepted his apology."

"That's what I *said*. It's not what I meant. There were people around."

"Well, I want you to mean it. He thought he was doing the right thing. I accept his apology, and you need to do the same."

"Oh, well, if that's what *you* want. By all means, Carrie. I live to serve."

"And in exchange," I begin just as she says, "He's going to do it again."

"He's not," I counter. "And in exchange for accepting

his apology and not trying to murder him—or anyone else—you can have my house."

"You know I can't promise that."

"You definitely can."

Becca mulls it over as we pull into my driveway. I cut the engine, and we sit in silence.

"This whole house?" she says finally.

"Yes."

"I don't want your ugly furniture."

"You can have a bonfire."

"You're serious about this?"

"I'm serious about moving on with my life. Don't hurt Graham."

She stares at me, nostrils flaring as she drags in a breath. "I'll kill him if he hurts you."

"He won't."

"Then we have a deal. Give me my keys."

I know she already has a set because she keeps stealing and copying mine, no matter how many times I tell her to stop, but I go through the motions of pulling the keys from the ignition and passing them over. Becca hops out of the car and flounces up to the door, letting herself into her new house. I'd explained to Graham that I'd have to keep making the mortgage payments on this place while she got a job and got back on her feet, and he agreed to cover the cost of his apartment until we found a new home of our own. Then we'll get married, and we'll get a dog, and we'll live happily ever after.

CHAPTER 28

One month later

I visit Misha's grave on a day where there are no other guests, no onlookers, no one with a camera or a hidden agenda. I don't have to pretend; my grief and my guilt are all too real as I add the bouquet I'd brought to the small mountain of flowers and gifts from people who'll never know the truth about the night she died. I blink back tears and look around, imagining the ghosts of the people whose bodies I'd hidden watching this show, wondering when it will be their turn, when they'll be acknowledged, when their families will get answers.

"You're the last one," I whisper. It's a pathetic offering, but it's the best I can do.

A light breeze lifts the hair from my neck, but today there are no icy fingers, no warm prickling of awareness.

Becca is at my house—her house—doing whatever Becca does in her free time.

The Brampton Kill Seekers have gotten quite a lot of publicity for their handy chart of unsolved disappearances, and while I'm no longer attending meetings, I still check their website from time to time to see if they're making progress. Like Detective Greaves, they're not. They may know something nefarious lurks in the shadows of Brampton, something blond and blue-eyed works behind a counter at a high-end jewelry store, something curly-haired and meek designs stationery for a living, but they don't know the truth, and they never will.

Greaves can gnash his teeth and plot and plan, but he had his shot, and he missed. He's got twenty years' experience with the Brampton PD, but I have a lifetime with Becca, and my survival instincts are well honed.

According to her Facebook page, Heather McBride has moved to Boston. Her account is still populated with posts about Fiona's disappearance and a reward for any information on her daughter's whereabouts, but now it's also peppered with photos of her new dog, Basil, who seems to keep her happy as she starts a community garden in the city. She posted that she'd been waiting for a sign to move on, to give her permission to move to Boston, and she finally got one in the form of a *Boston* terrier. Suck it, Becca.

Nikk Boulter continues to profess his innocence, but people are desperate for answers and for closure, and the sordid details of his life and crimes are too juicy to ignore. Combined with Lilly filing for divorce and someone leaking photos of her with a black eye, the world is convinced that Nikk Boulter is enemy number one.

Graham and I still hear from Beau from time to time. He texts us new house listings, and maybe one day we'll head out to view them, but for now, we're happy where we are. Graham's apartment is small, but it's home. There's no creepy furnace grumbling to life at inconvenient moments, no memories of a serial killer lurking in my bedroom closet, no sign of the one currently residing in my former bedroom. It's not the new life I was picturing, but I have all the things that matter.

I leave the cemetery and walk back to my car to make the drive to my—to Becca's—house. She has a new car and new curtains and has painted the front door yellow. She even joined Mr. Myer for tea one afternoon. He told me she seemed lovely. She said he was an idiot. Her perfect neighbor.

Once home, I knock on the door. There's no answer, but Becca invited me for dinner and her car's in the drive, so I turn the knob and the door swings open. The house feels strange, though it's only been a month since I moved out and she moved in. She hasn't burned my furniture because "I still need somewhere to sit," but the house I'd called home already feels like a distant, foggy piece of the past.

"Becca?" I step inside. Something's cooking, and the smell makes my stomach growl.

I take off my boots and walk down the hall to the kitchen where a slow cooker sits on the counter next to an open bottle of wine and two pots simmering on the stove. The back door is open, and through it, I see Becca on her hands and knees in the grass. A shovel is propped against the fence, and I can't stop the heartrending terror that comes with seeing my sister next to a hole in the ground, the immediate impulse to look around for a dead body. But there's nothing more than a bunch of seedlings and garden implements waiting nearby as my sister slowly drops the plants into the earth, pats down the dirt, and gently waters them.

"What are you doing?" I ask, stepping out onto the porch. I seldom came out here because the back door is so difficult to open, but Becca's got a small table and two chairs set up, like a normal person who won't let a stubborn door stop her from living her best life.

She doesn't look up. "Planting tomatoes," she replies. "And some other stuff."

The garden plot is about ten feet by five feet, and she's already cut out the grass and tossed it aside, tilled the soil, and yanked out a few large rocks. She even has little wooden stakes to identify the vegetables she's growing: tomatoes, cucumbers, and pole beans.

In the very center of the plot is a much larger hole than the others, about the size of a shoebox. I move closer and

peer inside, but it's empty. Frowning, I study the gardening paraphernalia until I spot the item that doesn't belong:
a wooden box with distinctive slatted sides and etchings,
and the conspicuous absence of any type of opening.

"What's this?" I tap it with my toe.

"A puzzle box. Like the one Footloose had, but bigger.
Better."

I pick it up, and Becca doesn't try to stop me. Carefully,
I give it a shake and hear the clatter of several small items
jostling inside.

"What's in it?"

She doesn't answer.

"More keys?"

She pounds a little metal trellis into the dirt with
her fist before fastening a droopy seedling to it with
plastic rings.

"Becca?"

Her task finished, she finally glances up at me. "I had
to cancel the storage unit," she says. "It wasn't safe. If they
found one, they could find a second one."

"These are your mementos."

"What's left of them." She's still nursing a grudge
that we had to use Missy's pin and Kami's necklace to
frame Nikk.

"You think burying a wooden box is the best way to
keep them safe?"

"I'm going to put it in a plastic bag and bury it deeply."

"And when you need to add to it?"

Her mouth quirks. "I promised you I wouldn't."

We both know her promises hold little weight, but I don't waste time pointing it out. Instead, I watch as she pulls a garbage bag from her pile, takes the box, wraps it tightly, and drops it in the hole. With a deft hand that can only come from years of practice, she swiftly fills the space around it and tamps down the soil.

"Now it looks weird," I say. "It's just plants on each end and a suspicious space in the middle."

"Not so, Sister." She retreats to the small shed at the back of the yard, disappears inside, and returns with a hammer and the FOR SALE sign that had briefly been staked in my front lawn. Beau's smiling face beams back at me, the wooden post now strangely nailed to his forehead. As though she senses my next question, Becca turns the sign to show that she'd flipped over the board and painted the words BECCA'S DREAM GARDEN on the back.

The irony of Becca's dream garden holding the answers to a dozen families' nightmares is not something she would ever appreciate, so I keep the observation to myself.

Pleased with her creativity, she hums as she hammers the stake into the ground behind the puzzle box. Pulling a packet of wildflower seeds from her pocket, she sprinkles them around the base of the post.

"Ta-da," she says, wiping her hands on her shorts. "All done."

She waits expectantly, and because I came here for dinner and not an argument, I say, "It looks great."

"I know. I hope you're hungry. I made short ribs."

"Starving."

"I'll wash up, and then we'll eat out here."

She heads inside, and I remain where I am, staring at her garden, at the vegetables she planted with such unexpected, painstaking care. She'll probably forget about them by tomorrow. They'll wither and die, and the grass will grow back, and it will be as if this burial, like so many others, never happened.

After a minute, I go inside and find the red wine on the counter. Pouring us each a glass, I take them back to the porch and sit down. Eventually, I hear Becca return and plate up the food, bringing out two dishes of steaming short ribs and parsnip puree.

"That looks amazing," I say, because it does.

"Thanks. I think having a nice home really suits me. I like making it my own. It's much better than when you lived here."

I ignore the insult and take a bite. It's delicious. It's the only dish Becca knows how to make that's not cereal, but as usual, when she puts her mind to something, she excels.

"Let's toast." Becca picks up her glass and glances at my engagement ring, but as she's done for the past month, she doesn't acknowledge it. "To new beginnings."

I touch my glass to hers. "To new beginnings."

She sips her wine and starts to eat. I do the same, my gaze fixed on the garden over her shoulder, the happy, benign display. For ten years, I've carried murder carpets through forests, dug graves, and kept secrets. I've lied, stolen, and killed. All for this. A new beginning. The ring on my finger and the normalcy it promises. And though I've been wearing it for a month, it's only now, in this moment, that I finally start to believe I can be free.

I don't know if it's truly possible for Becca to have a new beginning. If the box she buried really holds the last memento she'll collect, the last life she'll take. But Misha will be the last person who dies without justice, the last secret I'll keep. For a decade, I've wondered how to stop Becca, how to get the upper hand. But it was impossible. I couldn't go to the police without implicating myself, and I'm too selfish to make that trade. But now I have something in my back pocket, too. I don't need to use it now. I just need to know that I can. That it's possible.

BECCA'S DREAM GARDEN.

I needed a sign.

ACKNOWLEDGMENTS

It was only after I'd written the acknowledgments for my first book, *Look What You Made Me Do*, that I learned about all the other people working behind the scenes to ensure we produced a wonderful, readable story. I haven't met them yet this time, either, but now I know better and offer my profuse advance thanks to all the proofreaders to come, to everyone who'll painstakingly contemplate my random word choices and terrible timeline failures so my readers don't have to.

Thank you, of course, to Alex Logan, a fantastic editor who somehow manages to read in record time, use a red pen on every page, and help me tell the best story possible. I have learned to change the things you cannot accept and accept that I cannot use commas correctly. But at least you can!

Thank you to copyeditor Kristin Nappier, whose painstaking attention to detail is unparalleled and much appreciated.

Thank you to my agent, Jill Marr, who made the life-long dream of selling one book a reality and took it a step further by helping me sell a second.

And enormous thanks to everyone who bought and read the last book and now this one! You're amazing. It was beyond touching to receive messages and photos from family, friends, coworkers, and readers who had read my book or spotted it out in the wild, showing their support in phenomenal, unexpected ways. I had no idea this story was ever going to exist, but your enthusiasm made the hard work of every word so rewarding. Thank you!

ABOUT THE AUTHOR

Elaine Murphy is a Canadian author who has lived on both coasts and several places in between. Among other things, she has volunteered in Zambia, taught English in China, and jumped off a bridge and out of an airplane. She has a diploma in writing for film and television but has never worked in either field. Recently, she took an interest in the dark side and began plotting suspense and thrillers. She enjoys putting ordinary people in extraordinarily difficult situations and seeing what they do about it. She lives in Vancouver, Canada.